DECEPTION

Dan Lawton

Also by Dan Lawton

Operation Salazar

For more information, contact:
info@danlawtonfiction.com
or visit:
www.danlawtonfiction.com

Cover designed by Samuel G. Wilson
http://designskills.samwilson-online.com

ISBN: 978-0-9964076-0-1

Originally Published First Edition: June 2015
Third Edition: April 2016

This book is for Sheldon Thayer, who passed before its publication.

And for Amaya Lawton – Always follow your dreams.

CHAPTER ONE

GEORGE

I'm going to turn myself in today. It's been eight days since I left Kansas and I'm already tired of looking over my shoulder. I rest on the edge of the dock and let my feet dangle over the water one final time. The bright sun reflects off Lake Erie beneath my toes, and I take a moment to reflect on what it is that I have done.

I'm an accomplice to murder, a co-conspirator to a multi-million dollar heist, and I'll likely be charged with some other lower class felonies that the prosecutor will throw on top for good measure. I'm facing a long time in prison, not county jail, but prison; the big house. I don't expect that I'll ever see the sunshine as a free man again.

In the eight days since my leaving Kansas, I have spent every penny I had to my disposal, which wasn't much, and my pockets are completely empty besides a few clusters of lint. With nothing left to distract me from doing what I'm going to do, I push myself to my feet and casually stroll over the wet wooden planks that hover above the water, all the while wondering to myself how I ever got to this place. How did someone like me, an admitted loner who avoids confrontation at all costs, wind up getting involved in something like this? I was pulled in by the love of a woman who I thought loved me back, and all I'm left with is a broken heart and a future behind bars. I regret ever walking into the library eight weeks ago or picking up that ringing phone later on.

I wish I never even met her.

The Luna Pier Police Department is just a few blocks from where I am, and I ponder whether I should wait until after the lunch hour so I don't inconvenience the local deputies on duty, but I don't think I can wait that long. I just want this to be over with. They'll be silently thanking me for the national exposure they'll get for finding such an elusive fugitive. They'll take all the credit and I'll let them bask in their glory.

The small town of Luna Pier, Michigan is boring and quiet with very little criminal activity besides some minor drug use by the un-stimulated youth, I assume, so they could use some excitement around here. When the news spreads of my hiding out in their town, the gossip will run rampant amongst the residents. The little old ladies at the nail salons and hairdressers will come up with ex-tensive criminal enterprise conspiracies, but they'll be all wrong. They have no idea about the circumstances that brought me here, and they probably never will. I picked the town randomly and would be perfectly content to have zero interaction with the locals, but that won't stop them from locking their doors at night and wondering why them. Curfews will be put in place and fathers will require their daughter's home before dark, and they won't rest until the trial is over and I'm locked away for good. It'll be a long journey for everyone involved, that's for sure. Not until then will Luna Pier go back to its ordinary, underwhelming existence.

With my hands buried deep within my hollow pockets, I take one final gaze at the family of minnows that burrow in the sand be-low the water. The fishing pole and tackle box that I left on the beach sit alone, waiting for their next lucky amateur fisherman to scoop them up. The planks of the dock creak slightly as I approach the ramp, each step bringing me closer to my dreary, inevitable fu-ture.

I look up briefly and notice a shadowy figure that appears to be waiting at the end of the pier. I wonder if they're waiting for me. It must be the police, here to escort me away to my impending reality. Honestly, I'm surprised it took them this long to track me down, and the timing is actually quite convenient as it'll save me the trip on foot over to the station. Although the walk through the cloudless sky might be enjoyable, I'll have plenty of time to walk while I'm pacing around the perimeter of the prison in Topeka in my orange numbered jumpsuit.

I don't see any police lights or hear any sirens in the back-ground, so they must not want to make a scene. I put my head down and walk the rest of the way with full intentions of cooperating fully. I take a deep breath as I approach the figure and prepare myself for what is about to happen.

This is it.

My life as I know it will never be the same again.

CHAPTER TWO

BILLY

All I can think about is my dead brother. I've had to restart counting the money three times now due to my lack of ability to focus. I was hard on him, I realize, but it's only because I cared about him. I still do. He was nothing like our father and me, which is maybe why I lost my patience with him too quickly at times, but I really do miss him already. It was horrific how he died, and I feel bad about that, but it was partly his own doing. I've come to the realization that if he was more careful, like me, none of this would have ever happened and we'd already be on our way to Mexico; all three of us. But now, it's just me and the girl left.

I try to clear my mind and count again. The bills are in stacks of one thousand, ten hundreds wrapped together. Each of the stacks are scattered in front of me and are piled high on the table. I count out stacks of tens and place them in separate piles to the side. I toss each pile into the bag individually, counting aloud in ten-thousands. This takes some time, but I'm able to shut my mind down long enough to count all of the stacks.

Ten million even.

I zip the bag and toss it over my shoulder, then stand from my seat and start toward the door. I can still hear her crying in the next room. "Enough of that," I say to her as I make my way into the room that is adjacent to the one I was just in. "What's done is done, time to move on."

"Oh, shut up! You just don't get it," she says, becoming more upset with each word that stutters from her mouth. Her eyes are swollen from the steady stream of tears, and her face is bruised. She hasn't stopped crying since he left two hours ago. "He didn't deserve that, he's a good man."

"Get over it. We had to do what we had to do."

"We?" she snaps. "It was all your idea!"

"Maybe so, but you're the one who did all the real damage to the guy. You're the one who broke his heart, not me."

"What choice did I have?"

"I don't think he'll see it that way." I grin at her. She puts her face in her hands and weeps some more. I roll my eyes and look out into the empty corridor. I give her a moment before continuing, "We have a long drive ahead of us, let's go."

I leave the room and start down the hallway, expecting her to follow. When I realize that she's not, I turn around and head back to the room. She's standing in front of the chair with her arms hanging to her side when I return. The tears have suddenly stopped.

"I'm not going," she says as she wipes her nose on her torn sleeve. "And I want my portion now."

Her stubbornness frustrates me, and I really don't have the energy for this shit anymore. "You either come with me or you get nothing. It's as simple as that."

"That wasn't part of the deal. One million for me and my family, and the rest for you. That's what you said."

"Well, when I make the rules, I'll say what's part of the deal and what's not, you got it?"

She says nothing. She slides her hands behind her back and reaches for something in the waist of her jeans. She makes her way toward me and stops when she's just a few feet away. She pulls her arms forward and points them at my forehead. Her arms are shaking, but I can't tell what she's holding. I take a couple of steps back until it becomes clear.

It's a gun.

I pat myself around my chest and waist, feeling for mine. It's gone. "How the hell did you get that?"

She leans in and blows me a kiss. Bitch. She must have grabbed it when she stuck her tongue down my throat before.

"You underestimated me, Billy," she says.

Visions of The Mirage, the boat I already named but haven't yet bought, run through my mind as I stare into the barrel of my own gun. I see myself coasting through the Gulf of Mexico with my bag of hard-earned cash and an expensive bottle of red wine. I can almost taste the bitterness of the perfectly aged grapes now. It won't be long before it's a reality.

"Do you even know how to use that thing?" I say, mocking her.

"I always knew you were dumber than you looked," she says, chuckling to herself. "Just like your brother."

I clench my jaw and can feel my heart starting to pump more rapidly. "Leave him out of this. You know nothing about him."

"I know that you think you're better than he was. I know that you think because of who you used to be that you could control him."

The adrenaline is building within me and I'm thinking about making a move for the gun. If she keeps moving her lips I might blow her brains out.

She continues, "I know you made him do all your dirty work while you reaped the benefits. You're nothing more than a coward."

My fingers twitch. I want to jump her and take the gun, but I do all I can to hold myself back. She'll mess up soon enough. She's just trying to get a reaction out of me, and I'm not going to give in to her little game. I force myself to settle. "I should have just killed you when I had the chance."

She chuckles to herself again before cocking the gun. Craziness has taken over for the sorrow that was once in her eyes. The bullet pings as it slides into the chamber of the gun and it makes my skin crawl. For the first time, I think I might be starting to fear her.

"Like I told you, I knew you were stupid," she says. She presses the barrel of the gun into my forehead. Her hands are trembling.

"You won't do it. You don't have the stomach for it," I say, staring at her, almost daring her.

Tears fill up her eyes again. A single one slides down her cheek and I think I can see my reflection in it as it moves down her face. She clenches her hands tightly around the handle of the gun and closes her eyes. Her face scrunches up as if to protect herself from a looming explosion.

My heart is racing, but I'm calling her bluff. Sweat beads on the back of my neck. She's thinking irrationally and won't be able to go through with it. I know this girl, and I know she doesn't have the willpower to do something like this. If there is one thing that I can say for sure about her, it's that she won't do it. She won't pull the trigger.

CHAPTER THREE

GEORGE

Eight weeks earlier.

It's a summer afternoon and I'm in the public library in town looking through the shelves for a good read. I settle on a crime thriller from a debut author. As usual, I open the book and start scanning the first chapter.

"Excuse me," says a soft woman's voice from behind me. I turn slightly and look over my shoulder.

"Hi, can I help you?" I say.

"Hi, I'm sorry to bother you, but..."

I don't hear a word she says after that. Standing before me is the most beautiful woman I have ever seen. Her face is long and proportionate, her eyes soft and welcoming, and her features are seemingly perfectly symmetrical. She licks her lips without realizing it and I can't help but stare. Her brunette hair is pulled to one side, and she twirls it as she speaks.

"Hello?" she says.

"What?" I say, jumbled.

"Are you okay?"

"Huh?"

"I asked if you know where the non-fiction section is."

"What did I say?"

"Nothing."

I take a moment to gather myself before responding. Her beauty has me rattled. "I'm sorry. Yeah, the non-fiction is right over there." I point to the sign hanging from the ceiling across the library.

She blushes. "I know...I'm sorry, I don't usually do this."

I didn't realize how tense she was until now. She's no better at this than I am. "Do what?"

"I don't know, I'm sorry."

"Please stop apologizing."

She lets out a long sigh and some tension within her is released. "I just really wanted to talk to you. I saw the sign." She seems relieved for saying so, and it flatters me. Women are sometimes hesitant to approach men, and women like her especially don't approach men like me.

"You wanted to talk to me?"

"Yeah, I see you here all the time, and I just really wanted to talk to you."

"Really? I've never seen you here before. I think I would have noticed someone like you."

"Well, not all the time, just sometimes. Okay, not sometimes, just today." She throws her face into her hands and shakes her head in embarrassment. After holding the position for a moment, she slides her hands up over her face and whips her hair back. "Can we start over?"

"Hi," I say, smiling, restarting the whole thing.

"Hi, I saw you over here and I just wanted to come and say hello." She extends her hand to me and smiles. I take it.

"Well, hello then. My name is George."

"Does George have a last name?"

"Sanders, George Sanders."

"Hi, George Sanders. My name is Alicia Diaz. It's nice to finally meet you."

"The pleasure is all mine."

MEETING NEW PEOPLE HAS always been a bit awkward for me. The truth is, I lack confidence, especially around women. I never know precisely what to say or do, so I generally avoid it. Although the awkward beginning, conversation comes very easily between Alicia and me. It feels natural, almost like it was meant to be. We spend most of the afternoon in the library, talking and laughing, and more than likely disturbing a few folks. The afternoon quickly turns into the evening, and we move the conversation to a coffee shop across the street.

"What brings you to Kansas anyway? That's a long way from Southern California," I say.

"I came to visit my cousin for the weekend. I don't get to see her much," Alicia says.

"You came all this way to see your cousin? She must be pretty special."

"She is."

"Well, I'm glad you did. Or I never would have met you."

"Me too." She blushes.

Admittedly, I'm impressed with my charisma today. It's almost like I know what I'm doing. I glance at the clock hanging over the counter. "This place is going to be closing in a few minutes, are you just about ready to go?"

Alicia finishes the last bite of her light pastry and stands up without speaking, then we leave. The evening is brisk and the moon is almost full. It smells as if it might rain. I lead Alicia to my car, and she slides in the passenger's side.

"So what do we do now?" I ask. "Should I take you back to your cousin's?"

"No, she's working."

"Working? You came all this way to see her, and she's working?"

"She's a doctor. She was on call."

"Oh, that makes sense I guess. What do you want to do then?"

"Where are you going?"

"I don't know. Home I guess. Do you want to come over for a while?"

She nods her head and leans back in her seat, lying against the headrest. She turns to face me and shrugs. "Okay."

THE RIDE HOME IS short. We sit in the quiet mostly while Alicia takes in the views of a new place. Plus, I have run out of things to talk about. Again, that whole social awkwardness thing. I pull into the driveway and stop the car. She looks at the house with approval as we step out.

"Nice house. Cute," she says.

"Thanks. It's just me, so it works." It's nothing big, a raised ranch with about an acre of land. I bought it a few years ago shortly after I got my first job after college. "Come on inside, I'll show you around."

I give Alicia the grand tour. We walk into the living room as we enter, there are two bedrooms and one bathroom down the hall to the left, and an eat-in kitchen is to the right with stairs leading to the lower level. The kitchen opens up and conjoins with the living room to give an open concept feel. It makes the place feel bigger than it actually is.

"This is a nice place George, I like it."

"Thanks."

She folds her arms and goes on another mini tour, nodding her head to show her approval. I stand awkwardly, not sure what to do next.

"Do you mind if I use the bathroom?" she asks. "I'll just be a minute."

I nod. She finds the bathroom in the hallway and closes the door without looking at me. At the end of the hall is my room, so I go there to put my keys and wallet on the nightstand. I pull my belt through the loops and remove my shirt, tossing it in the laundry basket.

"George?" Alicia's voice comes from the doorway behind me, and I jump.

I turn to look at her. "You scared me."

She stands in the doorway with her arms above her head, her entire body leaning on the doorframe. Her clothes are gone, except for her underwear, pink and laced. Her smooth, cocoa skin shines in the light. The push-up shoves her perfectly shaped breasts into the air, and although I try not to, I can't help but stare. I eye her from head to toe and can already feel the blood rushing to my unit.

"Hi, George."

"Hey." My mouth is suddenly dry and the word sticks to the roof of it.

She turns her back to me but keeps her head turned around and her eyes locked on mine. She reaches behind her and unclips her bra. She turns back to face me, cupping herself to avoid exposure. She takes a few steps toward me and drops one hand, then the second. She lets the brassiere fall to the floor, just in front of my feet.

"Kiss me," she whispers between her moist lips.

I look at her straight-faced and can't believe this is actually happening. It's been a while, so I hope I don't disappoint. Without further hesitation, I pull her toward me and do what I'm told before she changes her mind.

LATER THAT NIGHT, AS her naked body rubs against mine under the sheets, I lean on my side to face her. I prop my head up on my hand as my elbow digs into the mattress. I gaze at her, and she looks back at me.

"What are you thinking?" she asks softly.

"I want to know more about you. Tell me something most people don't know," I say.

"Like what?"

"Oh, I don't know. What are your dreams? What do you hope to accomplish in your life?"

She looks at the ceiling and thinks for a moment, then back at me. "I don't know, George. I've never really thought about it." I make a face, and she senses my dissatisfaction, so she continues, "To be free I guess."

Her response is strange, and I look at her awkwardly. She almost looks regretful for saying that. "What do you mean? You are free."

She brushes it off. "Nothing. I didn't mean anything by it. I just wanted to give you an answer."

I nod my head in understanding, although I don't really follow what she's trying to say, if anything at all.

"What about you?" she says, quickly moving on. "What's your happily ever after?"

I have never heard anyone say it this way before and it takes me a little off guard. I think I'm starting to really like this girl. "Just to live a simple life, you know? I want to move to Michigan and buy a boat and fish in the Great Lakes. Lake Erie. That's all I've ever really wanted to do."

Alicia ponders this for a moment. "What's stopping you?"

"Obligations. Work, a mortgage. Life gets in the way sometimes. Maybe someday."

She accepts the answer and moves closer to me. I can feel her smooth legs spoon into mine. She grabs my arm and wraps it around her body, then closes her eyes. I look down at her and take in the moment. Things like this don't happen to me very often, so I refuse to let it go to waste. I'm going to enjoy this. I met this girl not even twelve hours ago, yet I feel like I've known her my whole life. I don't believe in love at first sight, but if there is such a thing, this might be it.

"Who are you, Alicia Diaz," I whisper in her ear as I lean toward her, "and where have you been all my life?"

CHAPTER FOUR

BILLY

Seven weeks earlier.

It's 9:00 A.M. and I've already been at the station for an hour. My uniform is wrinkled but clean, and I wait impatiently for the Sheriff to arrive. He's only been on the job for a few months since he took over for my father. He's an outsider, a rookie who moved his family into the city from a small town just across the Missouri line. There was a silent uproar in the station when they hired from the outside, but there was no one internally that was ready for the job. I certainly wasn't an option.

After my father died, I became a changed man. I used to be a police officer because I loved it and because I really felt as if I was doing positive things for the community. Or maybe it was because I had no other options. Since then, it has become personal. There is a local gang in Topeka that is well-known in the law enforcement community and extremely violent, and they've been ruling this city for years. They're known as the Zved's. My father had made it his personal mission to take them down and spent the last five years of his life in trying to do so. He picked many of them off one by one, but they were always able to replace one with the next, each one more elusive than the one before. There was one guy, in particular, the mastermind of the whole operation, who always got away. He's the one who took out my father.

It was a cold night last December when it all went down. My father got a lead on the whereabouts of Adrian. Adrian Stephenson, I'll never forget his name for as long as I live. He's known as Snake on the streets, a nickname that developed over time as he avoided jail and got away with a string of contract hits. Slithered away I guess the nickname stemmed from, which is creative I suppose, but I'll never forget his real name: Adrian.

My father went by himself to the call. As the Sheriff, it was unusual that he went out on a call at all, never mind by himself. He felt something was going to happen that night, I suppose, and he was right. From what was gathered from the coroner's report and the crime scene, it was assumed to be one big setup. Adrian and his guys were tired of being tracked by the Sheriff, my father, so they called in a bogus tip and ambushed him. According to an anonymous witness after the fact, it was Adrian's right-hand man who pulled the trigger and not Adrian himself, but Adrian gave the order and stood there and watched while it happened.

My father died from multiple gunshot wounds to the chest and head. The medical examiner thinks he was dead before he even hit the ground. Since then, my father's mission has become my mission. This is no longer about justice for the city of Topeka, this is about personal revenge for me and my father.

I DIDN'T SEE THE Sheriff come in, but he's in his office now, so I head in that direction.

"Hey, Jack," I say as I knock on his door.

He looks up from his breakfast sandwich and invites me in. Jack Hearns is in his forties and still has a full head of thick black hair. He's tall and thick, and his chest hair routinely bursts out from the top of his uniform. Pictures of his wife and two daughters cover the walls in his office. I can tell from how happy his girls look in all of their pictures that he's a good father. He's a good Sheriff too, firm but reasonable, and he's always willing to listen to what you have to say. He reminds me a lot of my own father.

Except for when it comes to one particular subject.

"Come on in, Bill. Take a seat," Jack says.

I sit in one of the two chairs that are across from his desk.

"How are you doing this morning?"

"I got a tip, Jack. Another one is going down this weekend."

Mid-bite, Jack drops his sandwich on the napkin on his desk and snaps his eyes at me. He has a look of uneasiness on his face. "Bill, we can't keep doing this."

"I know, I know, but I think this one is for real. Just hear me out. I received a tip from a legit source late last night, someone from the inside."

Jack shakes his head. "Listen, I know you really want this, but you can't force it. I'm sorry about your dad, but-"

"Please don't talk about my dad, you didn't know him."

Jack raises his hands as if to calm me. "You're right, I didn't know him. But I knew of him. And I know that he wanted these guys to go down too, just like you do."

"Jack-"

"Let me finish. But you've come to me with five different supposed legitimate tips this month alone and nothing has happened yet."

"What about that double murder on Cranston Street last week? They could have had something to do with it."

"A, we're still investigating, so we don't even know if it was a homicide at all yet. B, it appears as if there was a sexual assault involved too, which really doesn't fit the profile of the Zved's."

I sigh and lean back in my chair.

Jack continues, "Bill, I've been thinking. Maybe you should take some time off, give you a few weeks to clear your head."

"No, I need to work, I need to keep myself occupied."

"It's not a request. Take three weeks, with pay, and get out of Topeka for a while. You didn't spend much time grieving. That's not normal."

"But this is my life, Jack."

"And it'll be here when you return."

I stand up from the chair and start toward the door, not wanting to argue with the man.

"Don't worry Bill, I'll tell everyone around the office that you're on vacation. See you back here in three weeks.

I nod and leave his office without saying anything. I can feel his eyes follow me as I gather a few personal items from my cubicle and head toward the front door of the station. I stop and glance at the framed headshot of my father that still hangs on the wall near reception before leaving, as I always do. A small granite plaque hangs below it. It reads:

In Loving Memory of Sheriff William H. Lewis Sr. He gave 25 years to the city of Topeka and lost his life fighting for what he believed in. He will be missed by all in our hearts and in our memories, always.

CHAPTER FIVE

GEORGE

Nearly six weeks have gone by and I haven't heard from or seen Alicia since that one night we spent together. I've spent many hours wondering what happened to her after she left here and what caused her to leave so suddenly. I can't help but think it was something I did to drive her away, although I don't know what that is. Maybe I was too aggressive with her. Maybe she just wanted a fling, a one-night stand sort of thing. I wanted more and maybe that was too much for her. I think about her every day still and wonder what could have been.

One thing I haven't been able to figure out, though, is the meaning of what she left behind. The fact that she acknowledged me and the connection we had makes me less certain that I actually did something wrong. Sometimes I wonder if something bad has happened to her.

I open my nightstand and pull out the note she left behind. The note was on my nightstand when I woke up the next morning, and she was nowhere to be found. I read it every now and again, hoping I'll find some sort of subliminal message embedded from deep within the text. I haven't yet. I read the note silently to myself:

Thank you for a great day, George Sanders.
XOXO

Alicia

That's it. I never even got her phone number. The heartache returns each time I read it, but I can't help myself. There is something special about that girl and she is going to be difficult to get over. I try to put her out of my mind and move on sometimes, but I swear I can still smell her perfume on the pillows on my bed. I think I would do just about anything to see her again.

I toss the note back into the nightstand and close the drawer. I sigh before making my way down the hallway and starting the shower. Maybe I should just fly to California and track her down myself. California's not that big, right?

IT'S JULY ALREADY AND the morning is humid and sticky. I sit at the table, eating breakfast while reading the newspaper as I prepare for another day of working for The Man. I have to leave in fifteen minutes, but my enthusiasm is at an all-time low this morning. I dreamt about her last night, so I'm feeling a little down today. I'd much rather sit around and mope.

As I scan through the daily business news, I can hear my phone ringing in the other room. It's quite unusual for someone to be calling me this early in the morning, so I make my way down the hallway and into my room to where my phone is being charged to check it out. It's an unregistered number. I shake my head in disgust and assume it's probably another telemarketer. I let it ring. Almost immediately, it rings again. It's another unregistered number, probably the same one as before. I pick it up this time.

"Hello."

"Is this George Sanders?" says an unfamiliar male voice on the other end.

"Yeah, who's this?"

"Do you know an Alicia Diaz?"

"Who is this?"

"Do you know an Alicia Diaz?"

"Who the hell is this?"

"Do you know an Alicia Diaz?"

"Tell me who this is."

"If you know an Alicia Diaz, meet me at Josie's Bar and Pub in thirty minutes."

"What the hell is going on? How did you get this number?"

"I'll be waiting."

Click.

16

"Hello? Hello?" I pull the phone away from my ear and look at it, then I return it to its original position. "Hello?"

The male voice on the other end is gone.

I spend the next few minutes pacing back and forth, thinking. What should I do? Is she in trouble? Do I even care? Do I want to get involved? I try to tell myself to think rationally about the situation, but my decision is obvious. My entire body is overwhelmed with the rush of emotion. I grab my keys, run out the door, and slide into my Honda Civic. I speed out of the driveway and head toward the interstate. I hit speed dial two. Bob, the manager of the bank that I work in, answers after the first ring.

"Hello," Bob says.

"Hi, Bob?"

"Yeah."

"Hi, Bob, it's George. I won't be in today."

"What do you mean? We have that meeting with the Joneses."

"I'm know, I'm really sorry. Ask them to reschedule, something has come up."

He notices my frantic tone. "Jeez, George, is everything alright?"

"I'm fine. I'll talk to you later, though, okay?"

"George, but-"

I hang up, cutting him off. I toss the phone on the seat next to me and loosen my tie. I merge my way onto the interstate in the direction of Josie's Bar and Pub, a local hot spot.

I arrive at the bar twenty-eight minutes later. The parking lot is almost empty besides a couple of cars at the far end, which likely belong to the employees. I hurry up the sidewalk to the front door, ignoring the closed sign in the window. My shoulder jams as I yank on the locked door handle.

What the hell?

I shade my eyes as I try to peek inside, but I see nothing. I try the door on the left, then the double doors at the same time, but neither will budge. "Hello?" I yell out to no one as I knock on the glass. I glance at my watch: It's been thirty-one minutes since the call. The sign on the door says the bar doesn't open for another hour. I turn to the parking lot, scan, and still see no one. With nothing left to do, I make my way back to the Civic.

As I approach it, a loud hum of squealing tires catches my attention to my right. A large white van rolls into the parking lot at a high rate of speed, nearly flipping on its side. The driver speeds toward me and slams the brakes to the pavement, spinning the van 270 degrees. The two back doors stare me in the face as the van comes to a stop. One of the doors swing open and a shadowy figure points his arm toward me. The arm reaches forward, grabs my collar, and pulls me into the van. The door slams and the driver peels off, out the same way he came in.

It all takes less than five seconds.

CHAPTER SIX

BILLY

The ride home feels like the drive of shame, as if I did something dirty. It's 9:45 A.M. and the streets are nearly empty. I'm able to cruise well above the speed limit in my patrol car and arrive home within fifteen minutes. It usually takes me twenty-five. I'm still a bit irked by the way Jack dismissed me the way that he did, but I try to tell myself it's not personal. But if he's not going to do something to help me either, I'll have to take matters into my own hands.

I unlock the front door and walk into the living room. My brother, Frank, is napping on the leather sofa. The TV is on in the background, as usual, and I don't recognize the midday programming. I intentionally slam the door to wake him. Frank's husky frame startles at the sound and he nearly falls onto the floor. He notices me standing in the doorway.

"What you doin' home already?" he says as he tries to pretend like he wasn't sleeping.

"I'll be home for the next few weeks, so get used to it. And get your feet off the table."

He does. "Did you get fired?"

"No."

"What happened then?"

I just stare at him, not wanting to get into it. "Vacation."

He nods, conceding the conversation. Frank moved in with me immediately after our father died. Our father was his caretaker, and he did an admirable job of it. Our mother died of cancer when we were young, so it was just the three of us up until a few months ago. Now all we have is each other.

"Did you take your meds?" I say to Frank.

He closes his eyes and thinks for a moment, his tongue protruding through his teeth. "Yeah. I think so."

"Are you sure?"

He thinks some more. "Yeah, I remember now, I did."

I nod and walk down the hallway to my bedroom. I place the box of personal items from my desk on the floor and start to remove my uniform. I place everything neatly on the bed before putting them on hangers. Frank walks in as I'm changing my underwear.

"Hey, Billy, I forgot to tell you something," he says.

I cover myself instinctually, then I drop my arms to the side to prove a point as I face Frank. He covers his eyes with his hands.

"Can I get dressed first?" Frank nods and walks backward until he's out of the room. I finish getting dressed and find him back in the living room. "What is it?"

"This came for you yesterday." He timidly hands me a sealed envelope addressed from the city.

I stare at him in disgust, as this isn't the first time he has forgotten to give me something that was dropped off at the house while I was out. I rip the envelope from his hand, tear it open, and read the notice: It's the final notification that my property tax bill is due today. I have the three other notices hanging on the fridge, but I keep forgetting to pay it. Maybe I should have listened to my broker when he suggested that I set up an escrow so it gets paid automatically with my mortgage. I guess I'll have to go pay it in person so it's paid on time.

I look to Frank. "Do you want to go for a ride?"

IT TAKES ME ABOUT twenty-three minutes to drive back into the center of town. I take my personal van, which is just an old painters van that I bought for a couple thousand bucks earlier this year. I had bought it with the intention of having something inconspicuous that I could use to track Snake without him knowing it was me. He hasn't seen me yet, as far as I know, so it seems the investment is paying off. The van has two front seats and a wide open back with a leather bench on either side. I've been tossing a bunch of trash back there for reasons I'm not quite sure of. It's unlike me to do that, but something about the condition of it makes me feel like it's better to be a mess.

City Hall is just a block from the police station. I park the van on the street and put a few dimes in the meter. Frank and I walk side-by-side up the stairwell and enter the brick building through the double doors in the front. The place is jammed as usual, so we stand in line in front of the glass that separates the public from the clerks.

There is a new girl behind the desk. I say girl, but she's really a woman. She's all woman. Her skin is tanned and her dark hair is held up in a bun. She's not black, but she definitely doesn't look like the people that live around here; she's far more beautiful than any of the locals. There is something exotic about her, and it attracts me to her instantly.

As I study her, my eyes find her chest that is bursting out of her blouse, and I can't help but stare and fantasize. She seems to notice, because she looks down and buttons the top button just moments later. She flicks her eyes up at me and offers a weak smile. I smile back and lower my eyes, embarrassed that I've been caught. The line eventually thins out and Frank and I approach the window.

"Good afternoon. What can I do for you today?" says the beauty from behind the glass. She smiles after, showing me her pearly whites. I slide the envelope from the city under the glass without saying anything. She opens it and reads. "William Lewis...that name sounds familiar."

"I'm a police officer here in town," I say.

She pauses. "That's what it is. You must be Junior. William Lewis Junior, right? I heard what happened to your dad. I'm so very sorry for that."

"Yeah, thanks. We're getting through it."

She looks down at the envelope again, then back up at me. "Payment method?"

"Excuse me?"

"How did you want to pay for this?"

"Oh, right. Personal check." I remove the checkbook from my back pocket and finish filling out the check using one of the pens with the flower on it from the cup on the clerk's desk. I slide the check under the glass. "You must be new around here."

"Yes, I am."

"Thought so."

"How'd you know? Is it that obvious?" She almost blushes.

"I've just never seen you around before, that's all. I know just about everyone who works for the city, or I know of them at least. You know, me being a cop and all."

She nods in understanding. "Right." She enters some information into her computer, marking me as paid I would imagine, then she slides the envelope back to me under the glass. "Do you want a receipt?"

I shake my head.

"Well, it was nice to meet you, William. Maybe I'll see you around sometime."

"Billy, you can call me Billy."

"Okay, Billy. Nice to meet you." She offers me the same weak smile as before.

"You too." I turn to leave, but stop myself before fully turning around. "I didn't get your name."

"Oh, sorry." She points to the wooden plaque that has her name inscribed on it that sits on the edge of her desk. "I'm Alicia Diaz."

"Nice to meet you, Alicia." I turn to leave again, but I can't get myself to walk away just yet. The middle-aged woman with her two young children behind me in the line mumbles something under her breath as I turn back to Alicia again. "You know, since you're new around here, maybe you'd like someone to show you around. I do know the area pretty well, you know, me being a police officer and all. So I was thinking maybe I could show you around sometime."

She ponders the offer.

"It never hurts to make friends with the police, especially in a new place," I continue, trying to seal the deal.

She laughs softly to herself, amused. She studies Frank and me, who I almost forgot was even here, and she considers the offer further.

"Sure, why not? That sounds nice," she says.

I smile at her. "Yeah? Okay, great. That's great."

"I've got nothing to do tonight. I get out at five. Are you free?"

"Tonight? Tonight is good."

"Good. I hear the pub a couple blocks from here is pretty good. Want to meet me there?"

"That sounds perfect."

She smiles at me through the glass again, so I return the pleasantry. My heart flutters.

Maybe Jack was right; maybe three weeks off is just what I need.

CHAPTER SEVEN

GEORGE

I'm covered in sweat and I have a dreadful headache. I try to lift my hands to rub my temples, but they're restrained. I try to pull my legs forward, but they're stuck too. I can't see anything but blackness. I start to panic. I try to jump in place, but the strain is too much on my torso.

"Help!" my scream echoes. "Somebody please help me!" My pleas go unanswered, and I begin to cry. In the distance, I can hear faint footsteps approaching. As they get closer, my heart begins to pound. The footsteps are heavy and sound like they're coming from a pair of boots. The steps are right on top of me now, but then all of a sudden, they stop.

Complete silence.

I wait and listen with anxiety. "Hello?" I try.

No answer.

"Somebody help me!"

A loud pop of the electrical system fills the room. Instantly, bright fluorescent lights illuminate overhead, and I instinctually close my eyes until I can adjust to the glow. In only a few moments, I'm able to open my eyes and focus on my surroundings. I immediately look down. My wrists are tied to the arms of a wooden chair, my ankles to the legs. The chair is bolted to the floor.

I'm in a large industrial room, empty it appears, except for me. It might be a warehouse. The walls are made of gray cement, the floors the same. There is a drop ceiling high above my head with cracked pipes and broken wires hanging lower than they should. There are numerous spots of water damage all around. Cobwebs fill the crevices. At first, I hardly even notice the two-way mirror that's on the wall directly in front of me. Behind me, I hear a door open, then close again. The thud of heavy boots approach me. Two hands rest on my shoulders, and I tense up.

A man behind me breaks the silence, "Georgie, how you doin'?"

I'm too terrified to respond.

"I'll forgive you for not being in a chatty mood. Although it is rude! Naw, I just kiddin'." The man laughs to himself and massages my shoulders. "Relax Georgie, I ain't gunna hurt you."

The door opens again and a new man's voice appears, "Leave him alone."

"Aww, come on. We was just talkin', right Georgie?"

"Goodbye, Frank. Go wait in the van."

The first man lets go of my shoulders. The door closes and I can feel the second man approach me from behind. He comes around to the front of the chair and looks at me. Our eyes meet as I look back at him. He's not a large man, rather small in stature actually, but he bleeds confidence. He's vibrant with power, like he's done this before, whatever this is. Although I didn't see the other guy, this one's clearly the brains of the operation. Just his presence alone tells me that.

The man continues, "I'm sorry about all of this, George." He points, referring to the chair. "You were out pretty good when we got here, and I didn't want you to fall and hurt yourself." He offers a friendly smile. "You understand that, right?"

"What's going on here?" I ask.

"I'm sorry, George, I'm being rude. You can call me Billy. My partner is Frank."

"Partner? Partner in what?"

"Partner in what?" Billy smiles as he repeats the phrase. "Partner in all of this." He spreads out his arms and looks around the room as if he's proud of himself.

I nod in understanding, although I don't. "What do you want with me?"

"You've got a lot of questions." Billy walks past me and out of sight.

My thigh almost spasms from the tension and I can't help but wonder what's about to happen to me. He returns seconds later with a chair and sits in front of me.

"We need your help."

I pause a beat before responding, not sure what to make of it. "With what?"

"We need you to help us get some money. Ten million big ones to be exact."

"Um, what?" I speed up, "Listen, I don't know who you think I am, but I'm not who you think I am. I'm just a banker, I can't just get you, I don't just have..." I pause and have a realization. "Woah, wait a minute! I can't just-"

Billy raises his hand to stop me. "Slow down, take a breath. I'm not asking you to take money from the bank."

"Oh. You're not?"

"Of course not. That would be too obvious. Much too obvious."

I exhale. "Okay, what then?"

"George, are you familiar with the Zved's?"

"Who?"

"I didn't think so. The Zved's are a gang here in Topeka."

"What kind of gang?"

"A hit gang," Billy pauses and waits for a reaction. I give him nothing. "They're hit men. They kill people for money."

My throat falls into my stomach, and I gulp. "What about them?"

"You're going to take ten million bucks from them."

My eyes widen with fear. "I could get killed!"

"Maybe," he says, coldly staring at me.

"What if I say no?"

"What if you say no?" Billy laughs. "No is not an option. Or it won't be that you might get killed, you will get killed. I can promise you that."

"And what makes you think I won't just keep the money for myself? Assuming I do actually make it out alive."

Billy gets out of the chair and begins to pace in front of the two-way mirror. His mood changes, and he becomes gentle and less intimidating. "You're a family man, wouldn't you say?"

"I guess."

Billy nods. "I thought so."

"I mean I'd like to be, but my parents died in a tornado a couple years ago. I'm an only child. I don't really have any family."

"Is that so?"

Billy continues to pace as if in deep thought. He moves to the far corner of the empty room and flips a light switch. The once dark two-way mirror in front of me lights up, and a room behind the glass is visible, although I can't quite see inside from my seated position. Billy makes his way back toward me and pulls a switchblade knife from his pocket. He snaps the blade out and shows it to me. He bends down and exposes a gun that's attached to his calf.

"Don't do anything stupid," he says, then he puts his pants back over his leg, covering the gun. Using the knife, he carefully saws the ropes from my wrists and ankles, freeing me.

I'm a little woozy as I try to stand up too quickly from the chair, and I'm forced to sit. I grab my head.

"Oh yeah, sorry about that," Billy says, pointing to my head. "I had to make sure you'd be out for a while." He makes his hand into the shape of a gun and re-enacts hitting me in the head with it.

He helps me from the chair and leads me to the two-way mirror on the wall. A woman, tied in the same position that I was, rests in a similar chair with her head leaning forward as if sleeping. Billy taps on the glass with his knuckle. Startled, the girl looks up. She flings her head back, ridding the dark hair from covering her face.

My heart falls to the floor. It's her.

"Alicia?"

Almost instantly, I drop to the floor and reach for Billy's gun. He slides out of my reach, then returns and kicks the back of my head so my face hits the floor. Blood pours out of my nose and onto the cement. Billy grabs me by the collar and pulls me to my feet. He leads me out of the room and into the hallway.

"I told you not to try anything stupid," Billy says, the gun now pointed at my head. He stares at me with fury, but slowly calms himself down. He pulls a handkerchief from his pocket with his other hand and hands it to me. The gun is still pointed at my head. "Here."

I look at him, confused, with blood dripping on my collar, and take the handkerchief.

"Now walk." He leads me a few steps down the hall to another door. He opens it and pushes me inside then slams it behind me.

This room is just like the one I was just in, just smaller. A lot smaller. It may have been a closet at one time. I find a light hanging from the ceiling and I pull the cord, lighting up the room. The handkerchief soaks up the blood as I apply pressure to my nose to stop the bleeding. A few moments later, before I'm even able to comprehend what's going on, the door reopens and someone else is pushed inside. I jump back at first to protect myself, but I soon relax once I see who it is.

It's Alicia.

"Two minutes," Billy says, then he slams the door again.

Alicia picks herself up from the floor and wipes the tears from her face. She looks horrible. Her makeup is running down her face and onto her neck. Her blouse is torn and her pants are filthy. She looks at me with fright.

"George?"

"Alicia?" She embraces me and sobs. "What happened to you?"

"I'm sorry. I'm so sorry!" Between the sobs, she talks a thousand miles an hour. "I never meant to...I wanted to...oh, George, I'm so sorry!"

I try to calm her down, and eventually, she does. "What happened?" I ask. "Are you okay? I got this call asking if I knew you, and I was told to go to a pub, then there was this van, and these two guys, and now they want me to steal ten million bucks. What's going on?"

Alicia is suddenly cool. "George, listen to me, please. There isn't much time to explain. I need you to do what they say, okay?"

"But-"

"No! Please, whatever they want. If you get what they want, they'll let us go."

"How do you know that? How do you know they just won't kill us both no matter what? How long have you been here?"

Footsteps are approaching from the hallway.

"Listen to me. Please," Alicia insists. "I know these guys, okay? Trust me. If you get what they want, they'll let us go. I promise, okay? I'm depending on you. Both of us are depending on you."

I have no choice but to agree, even though I don't comprehend a word she's saying. The door swings open, and Billy grabs Alicia's arm.

"But, Alicia-"

Billy pulls Alicia into the hallway and slams the door. I can hear her yelling as he drags her away.

"George, I'm pregnant!"

CHAPTER EIGHT

BILLY

I'm nervous. Maybe that's too strong a word, maybe anxious is more appropriate. I've been on dates, lots of them, but this girl is special. She doesn't think it's a date, but it is. It's also a business meeting, but she doesn't know that yet either. From the second I saw her I could tell she has something that most other women do not. I can't pinpoint it quite yet, but I will figure it out before long. I think she has what I'm looking for. I think she has what I need.

I'm torn between wearing a tie or not. I don't want to be too aggressive and intimidate her or push her away somehow, but I want to show her that I mean business too. My tie rack spins automatically, so I grab a couple as it rotates from its stationary spot in the closet. The black looks sharp under the blazer, and the purple fits well with the dark khakis, so it's a toss-up. With one in each hand, I rotate them back and forth to my collar as I look at my reflection in the mirror. A combination of both would be perfect, maybe a solid black with purple pinstripes, but that I don't have. That helps make my decision. I wait for the open slots to swivel around on the tie rack, then I hang both ties back in place. I'll go without tonight.

I can hear the TV blaring as I make my way down the hallway and into the open living area. The house is compact, but it was perfect for when it was just me. Space has become tight since Frank moved in, but I really didn't have a choice in the matter. I couldn't have just left him somewhere on his own. I don't think the state would have even allowed it. Frank pulls his feet off the table just as I enter the room.

"Get your feet off the table," I say.

"My feet aren't on the table."

"I saw you."

He looks away, just as a guilty dog would.

"I'm going out. Will you be okay by yourself? There are some leftovers in the fridge, you can eat that for dinner."

Frank nods and I storm out the front door before he can say anything. I don't need his distraction right now.

IT'S 5:02 P.M. AND I'm waiting outside Josie's Bar and Pub just down the block from City Hall. The parking lot is filling up quickly as happy hour has officially begun, but I don't see Alicia yet. I didn't ask what kind of vehicle she's driving, and I guess I probably should have. As I glance down the busy sidewalk, someone catches my attention.

I watch her as she struts confidently down the sidewalk and toward the pub. She's a lot taller than I expected. A form-fitting coffee-colored dress hugs her hips as she glides along in her matching heels. The dress is a shade lighter than her skin, and it's a stunning combination.

What I wouldn't do to get with her.

I get out of the van, stand beside it, and wait. Alicia waves to me as she approaches.

"Hey, Billy," she says as she makes her way toward me.

"Did you walk all the way here?"

"Yeah, I walked."

"No car?"

"No, not yet. It's on the to-do list." She's a little embarrassed.

"You should have told me, I would have picked you up."

"That's okay, I don't mind."

There is a brief silence as we stand around, unsure what's appropriate to say next.

"Shall we?" I say, motioning to the door.

"Lets, I'm starving."

Inside, the pub is jammed. The bar is nearly full and the bartenders are already running around like crazy. We wait a few minutes in the lobby before being escorted to an empty table with two wire chairs. Other similar arrangements surround us.

"Thanks for bringing me here," Alicia says as we wait for the young waitress to bring us our drinks. "I've heard this is the spot around here."

"It is a pretty common place for lots of the locals. Thanks for joining me."

"It's hard to say no to a police officer." She smiles at me, teasing.

"Yeah, well, I'll take it. It's not every day someone like you agrees to come out with me."

She blushes.

I continue, "I'm just glad that I can help you get comfortable in a new place. Where are you from anyway?"

"Florida. I moved into town a few weeks ago."

"Why Kansas?"

"It's a long story."

I glance at my watch. "I'm in no rush." I lean back in the chair, and it presses uncomfortably into my lower back.

"Okay. Where to start?"

The waitress swings by the table and leaves a dark beer for me and a light beer for Alicia, both tall. The hops tickle the back of my nose as I sip mine.

"I'm actually from Cuba," Alicia continues. "I moved to Florida some years back to go to FSU. I've had a few jobs since college, and I've been in the states on a work visa."

"You're not a citizen yet?"

"No, not yet. You're not going to arrest me are you?" She pokes her tongue out slightly, and I smile at her. "I probably won't even bother at this point."

"What do you mean? Why not?"

Uneasiness takes over her face and she looks a little bit uncomfortable. She sighs before proceeding, "I've got some...family issues back in Cuba. My mother has been sick for a while, so I'm thinking about going back to help out."

"What about your father?"

"He's around and he tries to help, but he works so much to pay for the medical bills, so it's tough."

I nod, offering my sympathy.

"He's been ready to retire for a couple of years now, but they just don't have the money."

"That's tough. What does he do for work?"

"It's kind of ironic actually, he works for the Cuban government. The Department of Justice."

She has my attention, but I try to hide my excitement. That might work out perfectly. "Were you able to get into the states okay? The relationship between the United States and the Cuban governments' isn't exactly...robust. I'm sorry if I'm being too blunt, I don't mean to interrogate you. I'm just curious."

She shrugs. "It's okay. My dad took care of the paperwork for me at the time. He handles visas and deportation and stuff at work, so he must have figured it out."

I nod, satisfied with the answer.

She continues, "So I might go back to help out with my mother. I just need to save up some more money first."

"Wow, that's really nice, putting someone else's needs before your own. It's really selfless of you. I'm not sure I could do that." I play with the rim of the glass and try to change the subject before it gets sappy and awkward. "What about the new job, though? You said you haven't been in town very long."

"Yeah, I know. I feel bad. It wasn't the plan, but things have gotten worse with mom's health in the past couple of weeks, right after I moved here basically."

"How did you end up in Kansas then? We never did get there. Florida, FSU, then what?" I take another sip of my beer.

"I did some work with the city of Tallahassee right after school for a while, then I saw this job opening here. It was a better job that paid more, so I applied and they flew me in for an interview, and here we are."

"Speaking of that, what are you doing for the city? I wasn't even aware there was an opening."

"I'm the City Clerk."

"What happened to Helga?"

"Who?"

"Helga. She was the City Clerk for as long as I can remember."

"Oh, I don't know. Retired maybe."

I grunt. "Good for her. She was a nice lady, always liked her. I guess I've been out of the loop lately. I've been a bit preoccupied."

"Why's that?"

I motion to her full glass and chuckle. "You may want to drink that up. You might need it."

She grabs the glass from the table and leans back in her chair. "I'm listening."

I tell her my story. I tell her everything about what's going on at work, the Zved's, Frank, and what happened to my father. I tell her too much information probably, but it's nice to have someone to talk to. Plus, I'm here for a reason, so I need to gauge her reaction to see if she's going to work. She eats most of her plate by the time I finish talking, but she listens politely. When finished, I exhale and guzzle the rest of my beer. Just talking about it has gotten my blood boiling.

Alicia takes the opportunity to chime in. "That's quite a story," she says.

I slam the empty glass on the table harder than I expected, and the clunk of the glass surprises me. It's time to talk business. "So I know we just met and all, and this may seem a bit sudden and out of nowhere, but I'm thinking we may be able to help each other out...if you're interested."

She contemplates while intently studying me, and I can tell I have her attention. She leans forward in her chair and rests her elbows on the table. "What did you have in mind?"

"What would you say if I told you I may be able to help you with your money troubles?"

CHAPTER NINE

GEORGE

I stand alone in the closet while my mind runs rampant with more questions than answers. She's pregnant? Did she look pregnant? That would make her six weeks along, could I even tell at this point? I didn't notice anything, but I wasn't looking either. Why would she tell me that if it wasn't true? Is it mine? It has to be mine, right?

Billy will be back soon, so I try to pull myself together. I take a deep breath and think. Okay, so what now? Option one is doing what these guys say and hope I don't die. Hope we don't die. Option two is refuse to help them and definitely die. I don't really have much of a choice, do I?

In the hall, I hear footsteps. Billy's coming. Moments later, the door opens and he enters.

"So," Billy begins, "what will it be?"

"You win."

Billy nods his head in agreement. "I thought you'd see it my way."

"Say I do get the money somehow, then what? What's in it for me?"

"You walk away. You and the girl. You can have your whole little family. I get my money, and you go home happy. Everybody wins."

"How do I know I can trust you?"

"You don't have a choice. There is no other alternative for you."

He's right.

"Fine. I'm in."

Without saying anything, Billy turns and walks out the door. He pops his head back in a moment later and looks to me. "Are you coming?"

I reach for and pull the string hanging from the ceiling, killing the light, then follow Billy into the hall.

I SIT ON THE cracked, faded, black leather bench in the rear of Billy's van, my hands tied together in my lap with a shaggy rope. It's the same van that grabbed me earlier, that much I remember. Billy drives in silence mostly, whistling a tune periodically. The other guy, Frank, sits across from me, obliviously picking his nose like no one is around.

The floor of the van is covered with shit. Not shit like feces, but shit like junk: Gum wrappers, cigarette butts, empty beer cans, and an old sneaker. The rear windows are tinted on the outside and covered with a sheet on the inside. No one can see in and no one can see out. I didn't notice before, but it's musty. It kind of reminds me of an old attic, or a wet dog. I can't pinpoint it exactly. A black bag rests between Frank's legs under the bench he's sitting on. Suddenly, and seemingly randomly, the van slows down and comes to a stop. We couldn't have gone much more than a few miles from the warehouse. The engine is killed.

"We're here," Billy says, now turned to Frank and me. "Get your finger out of your nose."

Frank looks surprised he was caught, and he quickly removes his index finger from his left nostril. He wipes his finger on the seat. Billy gives him a look, and Frank shrugs. Billy turns back and faces the front, then opens his door and hops down.

Moments later, the back doors swing open and Billy is silhouetted in the afternoon sun. I shield my eyes with my tied hands. Frank stands, approaches me, and motions for me to get up. He grabs the rope on my wrists and we leap out the back doors together.

The scene is unfamiliar to me, a place I've never been. I don't spend much time exploring new places, but I've lived in Kansas my whole life and this place looks foreign. To my right, a chain-link fence with high voltage warning signs encloses a large structure. It's huge, probably as wide as a tree trunk at the base and as tall as a skyscraper, although it does narrow out a bit at the top. I suspect it's a cell tower.

"What are we doing here?" I ask to anyone who will listen.

Billy looks around with his head pointed in the sky. Frank stands next to me.

"A lovely day, isn't it?" Billy says as he breathes in heavily through his nose, still looking up. He fetches a cigarette from the pack in his pocket and lights it with a Zippo. He flips the cover open and closed, the aluminum clicking with each motion while he smokes. He smokes the entire stick without anyone saying a word. When he finished, he finally continues, "I bet you're wondering why I brought you here."

I just stare at him, the question too stupid to offer a polite response. He fetches some gum from his pocket and disposes of the wrapper on the dirt. He points to the tower.

"Do you know what this is?"

"It's a tower," I say.

Billy smiles. "It's not just a tower, George. It's a cell phone tower. Do you know the range on this thing?"

"No. Should I?"

"37 miles. 37.25 miles actually. 196,680 feet. But who's counting?"

"So?"

"You got a problem with that?" Frank is suddenly in my face, unprompted and aggressive. He pulls me up by my collar. We stare at one another, me looking down at him in fear, Frank looking up at me in rage. Then he smiles. "I just kiddin' with you, Georgie." He pulls me toward him and kisses me, then puts me down and laughs. "Just playin'."

I stand there staring at him, defenseless, my hands still tied, and say nothing. What the hell is wrong with this guy? He definitely seems to have a screw loose. Billy walks toward us, stops, and slaps Frank in the back of the head.

"Fuck off," he says. "Go wait in the van."

Frank's face drops, but he does what he's told. He closes the rear doors of the van and disappears inside. He looks like a big kid who just got caught stealing another cookie.

"Why are we here?" I ask, now getting frustrated. "Where are we?"

Billy doesn't say anything. He spins me around and leads me toward the front of the van. He points out into the flatland at a small building. It looks like a tiny run-down house.

"There," Billy says, "that's where Snake hides out."

"Snake?"

"Yeah, Snake. Snake is the leader of the Zved's."

CHAPTER TEN

BILLY

"How was your date?" Frank asks as I sneak into the house and quietly close the door. It's late, just after midnight, so I'm surprised Frank is still awake. The light from the TV fills up the otherwise dark living room. He regularly watches TV with all the lights off, which I've never understood.

"Fine, but I'm going to bed now, though. I'll see you in the morning," I say.

"How'd it go?"

"Did you not hear what I just said? I'll tell you about it in the morning."

Frank doesn't respond and just continues to watch whatever movie or program he's indulged into this evening. He'll sulk about the rejection until morning.

Alicia is on board with my idea, now I just need to figure out how the hell to implement it. I quickly rip off my clothes and toss them in the laundry basket near the closet before sliding into bed without brushing my teeth. I can smell the warm beer on my own breath and I can taste the staleness in my mouth, but I ignore it. I close my eyes and block out the noise, hoping I'll find the answers subconsciously as I sleep.

IT'S MORNING AND FRANK is still asleep on the couch with the TV actually off. He sometimes puts it on a sleep timer so he has some background noise to fall asleep to, so I'm guessing that's the case here. I enjoy the silence. The spare bedroom has all of Frank's personal belongings in it, but he rarely sleeps in there. He hasn't handled our father's death very well, and I guess I can't blame him for that. Our father took him in after he was released from the hospital, and Frank was there until our father died. Our father was all he had.

I start a pot of coffee and try to be as quiet as possible so I don't wake Frank. I retrieve a pen and a notepad from one of the kitchen drawers and start jotting down the thoughts that came to me during sleep. My brainstorming session isn't much more than a jumbled mess of a web of ideas, but it helps me to see everything on paper. I do the same thing at work when trying to solve a case that's gone cold, or at least I used to. I may not ever be going back there, we'll see.

The pot of crushed grounds on the counter catches my nose when ready, and I pour myself a cup. I add a pinch of sugar and make my way back to the notepad on the table. Frank's nose catches the aroma too, as he wakes just moments later. His grunts and groans are distracting as he pulls himself up from the couch, his morning wood fully engaged. He staggers to the table and sits across from me. I look up at him but don't say anything.

"Mornin'," he grumbles.

"Morning. There's some coffee on the counter if you want some." I motion behind me to the fresh steaming pot.

Frank shakes his head. "How was last night?"

"Fine. Not much to say really."

"What did you talk about?"

"Not too much."

It's a lie.

"Do you like her?"

"Yes, I like her."

Frank smiles. "Does she like you?"

"I don't know Frank, we just had dinner," I snap. I'm sterner than needed, but I don't want to talk about it with him. Not yet.

Frank rubs the crust from his eyes before noticing the pad that I continue to make notes on during gaps in conversation. He leans in close to it and peeks at the upside down letters, then he glances back up at me. "What you doin'?"

I drop the pen on the table and lean back in my chair before looking at him. I study his groggy face while he tries to wake himself by blinking repeatedly. "Have you ever thought about us getting out of here?"

"What do you mean?"

"You and me, we could start over some place."

"Where would we go?"

I shrug. "We could go anywhere you want. We could go somewhere out of the country even."

Frank pauses for a moment, thinks about it, then smiles like he did when dad said we were going to Disney World when we were kids. "We could go to Mexico," he says. "I've always wanted to go there. That would be a fun vacation."

"I'm not talking about a vacation."

The smile falls from his face and he looks blankly at me, unsure of what I mean. "What you talkin' about then?"

"I'm talking about moving somewhere. Leaving Kansas and moving somewhere new, somewhere fresh, somewhere away from here."

"But why?"

"There's nothing here for us anymore. Dad's gone and mom's gone. What's left for us?"

Frank thinks about this and a look of sadness comes over his face. "I really miss dad," he says. He looks like he might cry.

"I know, me too."

I take a moment and think back to all the things we used to do together growing up, as a threesome, and I have to fight my lip from quivering. We were all so close back then and continued to be as we got older, but one night changed it all. It's all Snake's fault.

"But if we move away, what about your job and your house?" Frank says.

"I can find a new job and I can buy a new house."

"Sounds like that will cost a lot of money."

I pause and smile slowly. "I wouldn't worry about that. Money may not be an issue for too much longer."

CHAPTER ELEVEN

GEORGE

Billy opens the back doors of the van and ushers me inside. Frank is sulking, sitting on his hands on one of the benches. Billy motions in Frank's direction.

"Frank, grab that bag under your seat, will you?"

Frank pulls his legs in tight and looks to the left, then to the right, but he can't find the bag. He stands up and turns around to face the bench. He leans down for a closer look and bangs his head on the leather, groaning a bit. He rubs his forehead and looks for blood. Obviously, there is nothing there. Billy sighs behind me.

"Found it," Frank says as he grabs the bag and carries it to Billy. "Here you go, boss."

Billy takes the bag from Frank and drops it among the trash on the floor of the van. He unzips the top and separates the fabric. "Here." Billy hands me a nicely folded collared shirt and a baseball hat while still digging through the bag. I don't take it right away, so he looks up to me in frustration. "Take it." I raise my hands, showing him they're still tied together, and he nods. "Frank, take care of this."

Frank fishes a pocket knife from his jeans and saws me free. Blisters are forming just below my palms where the rope had been awkwardly rubbing. I reach for the shirt, now on the floor in front of me, and stretch it out, revealing an AT&T logo on the breast. The hat has the same familiar blue and white sphere.

"What's this for?" I ask.

"That's our in," Billy says.

"I don't understand."

"That cell tower is new. They just finished construction like a month ago."

"Okay."

"Network testing."

"Huh?"

"Put the shirt on, and the hat. Then you're going to walk down to that house, knock on the door, and invite yourself in." Billy hands me an iPhone from the bag, AT&T of course.

"And you expect it to be that easy? If this guy's the leader of some gang, why would he just let me in?"

There is a brief pause.

"You'll figure it out. Suck his dick or something."

Frank giggles in the background.

"And what if I don't?"

"I could kill you, but that'd be too easy. I do know of a pregnant lady that we can sacrifice in your place."

I can feel my throat beginning to tighten. He wins again. "Fine. Why me?"

"Because Snake would never suspect someone like you, and because he's probably armed. I mean, he's the leader of the fucking Zved's for Christ sakes." Billy forces himself to laugh, and Frank joins him. "Better you than me."

DRESSED IN MY NEW attire and with instructions on what to look for once inside, I make my way toward the small house in the distance. The dry blood in my nose from the earlier incident at the warehouse is crusted to the hair, but I don't think it's broken. The bleeding stopped quite a while ago, and the pain has just about gone away completely. I may have dodged a bullet there. I need to be more careful around these guys, that's a lesson learned the hard way.

The day is getting late and the sun is going down, but it's still bright. The flatlands are mostly sand and gravel, and it's exactly as its name describes: Flat. I could use this opportunity to make a run for it, but they have the van and, well, I do not. Looking around, there is nowhere for me to run and nowhere for me to hide anyway. Plus, Billy flashed me his gun before I left, just to keep me in check.

I can feel the sweat beading on the back of my neck as I approach the front door. The house is ordinary, just a little beat up, and it's literally in the middle of nowhere. I can't see anything else in the distance in any direction besides this house, the cell tower, and Billy's van. Maybe this makes the perfect hiding spot for someone like Snake.

There is no specific entrance, no walkway, nothing. Just dirt and gravel that leads up to the front door. My hands are trembling as I knock. I peek back toward the van, although I'm not sure why. I guess I was hoping it would be gone. The front door cracks open enough for the barrel of a shotgun to slide through and point in my face.

"Who the fuck are you and what do you want? You have five seconds," says the deep male voice from behind the door.

My mouth is suddenly dry and I can't breathe.

"Five...four...three..."

I'm completely frozen as the final seconds of my life are drowning down the barrel of a gun. I try to speak, but can't.

"Two..."

I can hear the gun being cocked from behind the door.

"One..."

"Network maintenance!" I scream, just in time. "I'm here for network maintenance! I work for AT&T. We just put that new tower up right over there." I point behind me.

The gun has not moved and the gunman hasn't said another word. I'm expecting my brains to be blown out all over the dirt at any second.

"It will just take a minute, Sir. I just need to come inside real quick and see how many bars I have, just to make sure the tower was installed properly."

"Get out of here. Go somewhere else," the man says, then he pulls the gun inside and closes the door.

"But there is no one else, Sir. You are the only house around here for miles." It's a final desperate attempt, and I hope I'm not pushing my luck.

Suddenly, the door swings open and a tall black man stares me in the face, his shotgun pointed under my chin. "I'm not fucking around. Get out of here or I'll blow your teeth into your stupid little brain." His perfect teeth shine through his well-maintained beard. He has short curly hair and he matches Billy's description perfectly. It must be Snake. He's thin too, real thin, like you have to wonder how someone like him became the leader of a gang thin.

It must be that gun that people fear.

I'm pushed back on my heels a bit, stretching my pants on my thighs. I feel a bulge in my pocket and it gives me an idea. "For your troubles, Sir, we are offering you a brand new iPhone." I pull the phone from my pocket and show it to him, my hands still trembling. He's not impressed. "And we'll cover your entire bill for your lifetime." I pause, still nothing. "And we'll do the same for up to ten of your closest friends. Plus, $10,000. For your troubles, Sir." I offer a cheap smile.

He presses the barrel of the gun deeper under my chin and puts his face next to mine, our noses nearly touching. "You have thirty seconds." He releases the pressure on the gun and pulls it away from me. He pushes me through the door.

Billy had told me to look for something or somewhere to store a lot of cash, somewhere hidden. I scan the room quickly while Snake closes the door behind us. The room is small and has a couch and a tube TV on a stand. There is a short hallway that leads to the kitchen at the end, and there is a single bedroom and bathroom off the wings. The walls are bare and are covered by some old wallpaper.

"Whose van is that?" Snake asks.

"That's mine, supplied by the company."

"What's your name?"

The question catches me off guard. I should have prepared something, but I didn't. "Bill Franks." As soon as I say it I regret it.

Snake doesn't say anything, and he just stares at me for a few seconds. "You have fifteen seconds."

I look down at the iPhone which is still in my hand, pretending to look at the bars of reception. I point down the hall. "Do you mind?"

He nods once.

The kitchen is practically empty. One folding chair lay on its side near the sink and it looks like the power cord to the refrigerator has been cut. The room smells of rotten garbage.

I quickly turn back down the hall and stick my arm in the bathroom, not bothering to turn on the light. A roll of toilet paper rests on the edge of the sink, and an old plunger is in the shower. I think I can see shit on it.

Back in the hallway, I head for the bedroom, but get cut off before I can enter.

"Not in there. Time's up," Snake says.

I glance in the room and catch a glimpse of a large painting hanging on the wall near a mattress that lay on the floor with no frame. It seems out of place.

Snake grabs my collar and pulls me toward him. "Not in there I said, motherfucker!" He rips the phone from my hand and pushes me toward the now open front door, my hat falling off in the process. "Now where's my money?"

"Call customer service and give them my name, they'll work out the payment details with you." I don't know if he believes me or not, but he doesn't raise the shotgun.

"Don't ever come back here again." Snake slams the door in my face. It's only a matter of time before he'll realize that the phone doesn't work, so I quickly turn and head back to the van, unsure if I should run or not.

I do make it back to the van, honestly surprised not to have a bullet in my back. I refuse to look behind me. I slide into the driver's side and start the van. Billy ducks in the passenger's seat next to me while Frank is still in the back. I move the van behind the tower, out of sight of the house, and stop. Billy sits up in his seat and looks at me.

"I see you're still alive, that's a good start," he says. "What did you find?"

Frank slides down to the end of the bench near us so he can hear.

"I don't know, I wasn't in there for very long. There is a painting hanging on the wall in the bedroom, that's the only place it could be. Maybe there's a safe behind there or something."

Billy nods. "Okay, good. That's good. That's perfect," he says. Relieved at his satisfaction with my effort, I slide in the back and sit across from Frank, close to the front. Billy slides over to the driver's side and turns to me. "Did you lose your hat while you were sucking Snake's dick?"

Frank laughs, loud and hysterically, with his mouth wide open. His voice cracks when it reaches its climax, and it makes my ears pop. Billy smirks and jams the van into gear. He waits for me to respond to his jab, but I don't find him humorous.

"Okay," he continues, "now for step two."

CHAPTER TWELVE

BILLY

It's 5:03 P.M. and I'm sitting in my van outside City Hall. I spent most of the day compiling my thoughts and creating what I think is a solid path forward. Frank didn't find any flaws, but his opinion needs to be taken with a grain of salt. I need someone else with an opinion that matters to take a look.

She'll be surprised to see me, I imagine, but this cannot wait until the weekend. I roll down my window by hand and wave at her as she exits from the building. She looks at me with uncertainty, but comes toward me anyway. She leans into the window. As she arrives and her blouse separates from her chest, I can't stop myself from peeking at her exposed cleavage. Just seeing the clasp of her pushup jamming her breasts toward me makes my heart race.

I need to stay focused.

"What are you doing here?" she asks. "I thought we weren't going to meet up until Saturday."

"Things have changed. I came up with a full plan today. I have it all laid out at my place. I need to discuss it with you."

Alicia looks behind her and whispers back to me, "You can't come here anymore, Billy."

I just stare back at her, showing her my dissatisfaction with her telling me what's right and wrong. "Are you coming or not?"

She sighs before quickly tiptoeing around the side of the van and sliding in the passenger's side. She jams her designer purse between her legs before she engages the safety belt. The sun shines on her legs, and I want nothing more than to reach over and feel them. They look like smooth butter, and I'm sure they feel the same way. Instead, I back out of the spot and glide into traffic, keeping my hands to myself. For now.

Thirty-two minutes later, we arrive at my house. I stop the engine and remove the keys from the ignition before turning to Alicia. "Frank's inside, you've been warned," I say.

She looks at me with concern. "Why do you say it like that? Is he dangerous? Last night you told me he was stable now."

"He is. He's just a little...different. Slow I guess."

"Is he dangerous?"

I pause. "No."

"You're doing a shitty job of convincing me."

"No, he's okay. Just be cautious. You never know for sure how people with his disorder will react to meeting new people. He may go off the rails a bit, or he might be fine. I don't really know for sure."

"Well if he tries anything with me or if I feel uncomfortable, I'm out."

I roll my eyes at her.

"I'm not kidding. I'll turn right around and walk out the front door and you'll never see me again. You need me more than I need you."

I glare at her. "Are you sure about that?"

She says nothing and looks away.

I quickly change my tone. "Okay, let's go." I open my door and hop onto the paved driveway beneath. Alicia repeats as I do and follows me toward the front door.

Frank is sitting in his usual spot on the sofa with his feet on the table as we enter the house. He's oblivious to the sound of the door as the high decibel level from the speakers on the TV fills the room.

"Get your feet off the table," I holler, which startles him. He immediately drops his feet to the floor and jumps up.

"My feet weren't on the table," he says to me.

"I saw them, don't lie to-"

"I didn't see them on the table," Alicia jumps in. Frank and I both turn to her. She approaches Frank and holds her hand out. "Hi, you must be Frank. Your brother has told me all about you. My name is Alicia."

Frank smiles widely and takes her hand. He turns to me. "See," he says, before turning his attention back to Alicia. "Hi. You're really pretty."

46

"Aww, thank you, Frank. You're really handsome too."

Frank blushes at her compliment. I study her as they release interlocked hands. The fact that she blatantly lied and completely discredited my authority pisses me off, but it was a nice gesture to win Frank over. I would never say it out loud, but it was a slick move by her. She smiles at me and I just shake my head with a small grin on my face. Her confidence helps me to justify my decision to even bring her here. I've always had the ability to judge people and their sincerity, and I still have it. This is going to be too easy.

I walk into the kitchen and retrieve the notepad from one of the drawers. I bring it to the table and open it up before sitting. Alicia notices and follows me to the table. She sits down across from me and tries to read my scribbles. Frank makes his way to the table as well and sits at the end, the three of us now in a triangle.

"Can I get you anything?" I direct the question to Alicia.

She shakes her head without looking up.

"Okay then, make yourself comfortable. We might be here for a while."

CHAPTER THIRTEEN

GEORGE

Back in the same empty warehouse, the two-way mirror stares back at me as I sit in the same bolted down wooden chair. I'm not strapped to the chair this time, which is nice, although my hands are still loosely tied in front of me. The light has been left on for me, so I'm able to get up and pace. I walk the perimeter of the room, counting my steps as I go. One of the cracked pipes has a slow drip and a damp spot is forming below it on the cement.

Across the room, the bulky door squeaks open. To my surprise, Alicia is pushed in and the door closes behind her. I immediately run in her direction.

"Alicia, I'm relieved you're okay! Are you okay?"

She offers me an exhausted smile and nods.

"Where have you been?"

She points to the two-way mirror behind me. "There, in that room. They locked me in and left for a while. I'm not sure how long it's been."

"It's been a couple hours at least."

"How do you know?"

"I saw the time when I was in the van."

"Huh?"

"They took me with them, in the van."

Alicia's face drops, and she turns a bit pale. "Oh no! What happened?"

"You don't want to know."

There is a pause. "I'm so sorry, George. I didn't mean to get you involved." She puts her right hand on her waist and grimaces. Her hands aren't tied and I don't see any blisters on her wrists, like I have.

"What's the matter, is everything okay?"

"I'm fine, just a little uncomfortable." Her clothes are loose and baggy, to cover her belly I guess.

I nod. "Sorry, I guess I'm not too sure how this all works."

"How all what works?"

"You know, this baby stuff."

She just looks at me and I can see in her eyes that this upsets her, but I don't know why. I'm not sure what to say, so I say nothing. After a few moments, I come up with something to break the awkward silence.

"How did you get here? How do you know these guys?"

She opens her mouth to speak but is cut off by the door thrusting open. Billy and Frank walk in, with Billy leading the way. Frank approaches Alicia from behind and grabs her arm, turning her toward him. He leads her out of the room. Billy stares at me silently for a few moments before speaking.

"Come with me." Billy motions for me follow, so I do. He leads me down the hall to another room, this one much smaller than the one I was just in. It's an old office maybe. Frank is sitting behind a table, playing with something in his lap. "Frank, let me have it."

Frank hands it to Billy, who puts it on the table.

"What is that?" I ask.

"That is for step two," Billy says.

"Okay, but what it is?"

"Take a look."

I raise my hands, showing the knot keeping them together. Frank stands and comes around the table, then cuts me free, much like he did in the van. The blisters on my wrists are worsening and calluses are beginning to form. I reach for the table and grab the item. It's a black hooded headpiece with two vents, one on each side, and a large square windshield of acrylic in the front. A few adjustable leather straps drape off the back. I think it's a gas mask.

"What are you going to do, gas him out?" I ask.

"No, we're not doing anything. You're going to do it. And it's not what you think it is."

"It's not a gas mask?"

49

"Well, kind of. It is technically a gas mask, but it only works for a certain type of gas."

"And what would that be?"

"Carbon monoxide."

CHAPTER FOURTEEN

BILLY

It's close to midnight and Alicia, Frank, and I are exhausted from long hours of discussion. An empty pizza box rests on the edge of the table, surely leaving a grease stain on the wood beneath. The remains of a now empty six pack are piled inside. Frank's head hangs off the back of his chair and his mouth open, snoring. Alicia has her head in her hands as she tries to put all of the pieces together. I'm mentally exhausted and could really use some sleep. I'm sure Alicia feels the same way.

"What do you think? Do you think it'll work?" I ask.

We've spent the entire night discussing our options and planning out the best path forward. But I don't feel like she's completely on board yet, especially with the last part. It's a little scary that Frank knows the plan in its entirety, but who's he going to tell? I just need to watch him carefully going forward.

"It's a lot to take in. I'm exhausted," Alicia admits.

"You can take my bed tonight if you want. I'll sleep in the guest room."

She smiles at me. "Thanks, that sounds nice. What about Frank?"

"He sleeps on the couch." Alicia raises her eyebrows at me. "By choice."

She nods. She seems to be putting off the question, so I press again.

"You never did answer the question. Are you in or out?"

Alicia stands and stretches before responding, "I can't make a decision right now. Can we talk about it in the morning? I need to sleep on it." She stands behind her chair, looking at me. I catch her hint and rise to my feet.

"Okay, well, I'll show you where you can crash." I make my way down the short hallway and lead Alicia into the bedroom. The bed is made and the floor is free of clutter, which seems to satisfy her. "Here you go. There is a bathroom down the hall and I'll be in the next room over if you need anything."

She looks at me and smiles. "Thanks, Billy. This is really sweet of you."

"It's no problem. Partners, right?"

She smiles again, but doesn't acknowledge the question. "Goodnight, Billy."

I nod to her and exit the room. She pushes the door closed, but it doesn't fully engage. I hesitate, but decide to peek into the crack in the door. Alicia's back is to me as she unzips her skirt from the rear, her backside protruding from underneath the lace as it loosens. She drops her skirt to the carpet and pulls her blouse over her head. My heart is racing from the thrill of the voyeur and I want to see more. I need to see more. She turns around and faces the door. In a panic, I scurry away and slide into the guest bedroom and quietly close the door. I can hear her close the door fully from across the hall.

I don't think she saw me, but part of me wishes she did. There is nothing wrong with looking at a beautiful woman, and I'm not ashamed for her to know that I'm attracted to her. I remove my clothes and hop into the bed, which hasn't been slept in for quite a while. The sheets are cool and crisp and fit snuggly on the pillow top mattress. I pleasure myself to the thought of Alicia being half-naked in my bed before falling asleep.

THE FAMILIAR AROMA OF grounded dark roast coffee beans wakes me. I pull on some pants and follow my nose into the kitchen. Alicia is wearing one of my t-shirts and some workout pants, both of which she must have found in my closet. The coffee pot is nearly full and she's washing something in the sink. Frank is surprisingly awake already, and he's sipping from a steaming cup. He notices me immediately as I enter the room.

"Mornin', Billy," he says.

"Morning," I respond.

Alicia stops the water and places something in the dish strainer that rests next to the sink before turning to face me.

"Hi," she says, smiling, "want some coffee?"

"Please."

She fumbles around in some of the cabinet drawers above her head until she finds the cups. She fills a mug and walks over to me, handing it to me with two hands. I flash her a quick smile in thanks.

"I found some clothes in your closet, I hope you don't mind," she says.

"I don't mind."

She smiles at me again and walks back to the sink. I grab a pinch of sugar from the glass jar on the counter and add it to my cup. I take a small sip before placing the cup on the counter. It's time to get down to business.

"So we've all had a night to sleep on it," I continue. "What are we thinking?"

"I'm in," Frank says.

Of course he is, the question was really directed to Alicia. Frank and I both look to her. She catches us staring and realizes she can't avoid the question any longer.

"I guess you're waiting on me, huh?" she says, trying to lighten the mood. It doesn't work. "I think it's a good plan that should work for the most part. I'm just not sure about the whole-"

"Mexico?" I interrupt.

"Yeah," she says, "we barely even know each other."

I nod in agreement. I hesitate before proceeding, "I'll tell you what, I'll leave it up to you. We can go forward with the plan as is, and if you really don't want to do it when the time comes, we don't have to. Okay?"

Alicia smiles widely and breathes a sigh of relief. "Are you sure?"

"Yeah, it's fine. We'll figure something out."

She walks over to me and pulls me into an embrace. She squeezes me with a heavy heart and I can tell she really means it. I'm not concerned about her apprehension. I'll convince her to go forward with it when the time comes. One way or another, it's going to happen, whether she wants it to or not.

"Thank you," she whispers in my ear before releasing me. She backs up a couple of steps so she can look into my eyes.

"Does that mean you're in?" I say.

"When do we start?

CHAPTER FIFTEEN

GEORGE

Back in the van outside Snake's place, we wait in silence. The warm afternoon sun beats on the van as Billy, Frank, and I rest in the stationary spot behind the tower. I sit in the back across from Frank as usual. Billy sits alone in the front with his left arm hanging out the window, smoking a cigarette. He peers at his watch and mumbles something to himself in which I can't make out. He takes one big drag and flicks the cigarette out the window. He fetches some gum from the center console with his right hand while cranking the window closed with his left. He turns to us and tosses the wrapper at my feet.

"It's time," Billy says.

Frank perks up like a well-trained dog and cuts my hands free. The callus on my left wrist has split open by the thumb, so I apply pressure to stop the flow of blood. The back door opens and Billy motions for me to follow. Frank starts toward the door too, but is stopped by Billy.

"Not you," Billy says. "Stay here and be the lookout. Can you do that?"

Frank's face drops, but he nods and sits back on the bench. Billy leads me around the van, bag in hand. Frank is suddenly in the driver's seat as we pass by the window. Billy raises his arms as if to question Frank's new position. The window rolls down a crack, and Frank pushes his face up to the hole.

"I can't be the lookout in the back, there ain't any windows," Frank says, smirking with pride like he's just won a bet.

Billy shakes his head. "Honk the horn if you see anything."

"Okay, boss."

AS WE APPROACH SNAKE'S house, Billy breaks the long silence between us, "I'll go around the back and you take care of the front. Work your way to the right, and we'll meet in the middle."

He debriefed me on the plan earlier, so I have clear instructions on what to do. Snake is gone for a while, but we still have to move quickly. Billy stops and drops the bag in the sand. He pulls out thick strips of foam and hands them to me, piling one on top of the other. He scoops up the bag and disappears around the back. I look to either side of me, and there's not a thing in sight. The van rests in the distance next to the cell tower, but that's it. Could I outrun him? Maybe, but where would I run to? I can't outrun a van, I know that much, so what choice do I have? I scan the house and locate the first vent on the corner near the foundation.

The strips of foam are cut to size. The metal vent casing houses two horizontal bars that are separated by a few inches of airspace above and below each, with the two bars sharing the middle space. I slide the first piece of foam in the middle slot, pinching it slightly to ensure it fits, leaving a slight bow in the center. Each piece of foam is about six inches too tall, which is by design. I slide the other two pieces into the remaining slots: Bottom first, followed by the top. As explained to me earlier by Billy, I'm able to manually close each horizontal vent bar a bit so that they tightly pinch the foam pieces, ensuring no air can get in or out; that's why the pieces of foam are a little big, to ensure that all of the gaps are covered.

I make my way along the right side of the house and do the same for the next two vents. I walk around the back expecting to find Billy, but don't. I peer around the left side corner, but he's not there either. He's nowhere to be found.

"All done?" Billy's voice behind me is startling.

"Where did you go?" I ask.

He's surprised by my questioning. He points to the ground next him at a bulkhead. "It was unlocked, so I figured I would speed up the process."

"What do you mean?"

"I made some puncture holes in the pipes."

"Which pipes?"

"All of them. What does it matter?"

"You're going to blow the whole place down." I chuckle to myself. "No money then."

Billy reaches behind his back and pulls a gun from his belt. He walks toward me and jams it into my forehead, shutting me up. "Fuck off. I know what I'm doing."

I put my hands up in surrender, but not in a panic like I would have just hours earlier. He's not going to kill me, he won't do this alone.

"Fine," I say.

Billy puts the gun back in his belt. Then, suddenly, a horn bellows in the distance. Billy's eyes open wide, almost stunned. He turns back to me. "Be cool." He reaches for his gun again and motions for me to follow him around the front. We creep around the house and I spot some flashing lights near the van.

"Fuck!" Billy says, then he turns to me. "Don't say a fucking word."

"Put down your weapon and put your hands up!" a weak voice shouts from the front.

I immediately throw my hands in the air, but Billy rips them back down and grabs a hold of my left wrist. I wince in pain as he strangles my open callus. Billy raises his weapon above his head in a non-threatening manner and hollers out to the voice.

"Don't shoot, I'm a cop."

A young uniformed officer crawls out into the open, looking relieved, though still pointing his weapon in our direction.

Billy continues, "I'll show you. I'm going to reach for my badge. Don't shoot, okay?"

The officer doesn't say anything and I can see the gun shaking in his hand as he tries to steady it. He's really young, right out of the academy I assume. His shirt collar is soaked with perspiration and his uniform is a crisp black with a newly ironed crease on the pants. I wonder if it's ever been washed. Billy releases my wrist and slowly retrieves his wallet from his back pocket. He flips open the vertical leather cover and flashes a badge.

"I'm Officer William Lewis, Topeka Police Department."

The young officer leans in for a closer look with his gun still pointed. Satisfied with what he sees, he drops the gun to his side and lets out a sigh. Billy flips his badge closed and puts it back in his pocket.

"Boy, am I glad to hear that," the young officer says. "I'm Officer Jimmy Jones, Jefferson PD."

"Jefferson? What are you doing in Topeka?"

Jimmy is embarrassed. "Quite honestly, today is my first day, and I'm actually a little lost. I'm not from here, I moved in from Oklahoma a couple of weeks ago for the job. I thought I knew a shortcut, but I must be going the wrong direction."

"Where you headed?"

"I'm trying to go back to the station. My shift is over. Today is, was my first day."

"Where's your partner?"

Jimmy shrugs. "No partner today, he'll be back tomorrow I'm told."

Billy nods. "Don't you have GPS in your car?"

"Budget cuts."

"Typical."

There is a brief silence. Jimmy looks at me suspiciously and catches my eye. I look away.

"Is he a cop too?"

Billy nods, then looks at me.

"Where are your uniforms?" Jimmy's hand starts to tense up on the handle of his gun, and I think Billy notices too.

"We're undercover, staking this place out." Billy motions to the house next to us. "But listen, we can't really stay and fiddly-fuck around here, especially not with you in uniform. If he comes home we're all dead."

This lights up Jimmy's eyes and the tension is released from his hand.

"You gotta go, newbie. This is our jurisdiction anyway." Jimmy tries to put his gun in his holster, but struggles. "Take a right when you get out of here. The main drag will lead you right into Jefferson."

"Thanks," Jimmy says, head down, fidgeting with the holster. Finally secured, he looks back up at us and gives us a nod. "Good day, officers."

Billy nods back and we stand in silence watching Jimmy scamper back to his car. Jimmy peeks in the window of the van before he gets in his car, flicks off the lights, and peels out of sight.

As Jimmy pulls away, Frank makes his way from the back of the van and into the front and honks the horn. Even from this distance, I can tell that he has a big grin on his face while he offers a childish wave. Billy waves back, more so of a confirmation that he sees him and less so that he's willing to admit he actually did something right. We start back toward the van.

"Are you really a cop?" I ask.

He doesn't look at me, but I can see him grin. "Game changer, isn't it?"

CHAPTER SIXTEEN

BILLY

Alicia, Frank, and I take rotating showers, throw some clothes on, and pile into the van. I agree to stop by Alicia's apartment downtown so she can gather up some clothes and various other feminine needs. Frank and I wait in the van for nearly twenty minutes before she reemerges, wearing a fresh outfit and carrying a leather bag filled with whatever it is she thinks she needs. She hops in the passenger's side and tosses the bag in the back, nearly hitting Frank with it. I wait for the apology for the time it takes, but it doesn't come.

"Are we going?" she asks.

I start the engine without responding. I pull into the busy street from the on-street parking spot in front of the apartment complex and head east toward the public library.

It's midday on a Saturday afternoon and the library is relatively quiet, just as I expected it would be. I'm looking for a specific type of person for the job at hand. We need someone who is intellectual enough to keep up, but not more intelligent than I am. He needs to be easy to manipulate and control, but strong enough to handle himself. Finally and perhaps most importantly, we need someone lonely who would do just about anything for the companionship of a woman.

That's where Alicia comes in.

She needs to seduce and hook the unsuspecting victim, then I'll reel him in. I have no doubt in her ability to hook someone, even if it's just on physical attraction alone. As for me and my role, well, that's really the least of my worries. The difficult part will be finding the right guy.

The three of us sit at a round table near the perimeter of the library and scan the room. The library is grand and the shelves are stocked full of books of all sizes, shapes, and genres. There are high ceilings and large windows, which brings heaps of natural light into the center of the room and disperses it throughout the isles. I grab a stack of books from the shelf behind me and spread them across the table.

"Look busy," I say, handing a book to Frank. Alicia also takes one from the stack, as do I. We hold the books up to our faces and pretend to read while we people-watch.

A young couple sits across from us at a similar table, holding hands and whispering to one another. A middle-aged mother and her two children wander around the young adult section. A group of women browse the romance section near the counter. In the fiction section near the corner of the library is a single guy. He's reasonably physically attractive I guess, average height and medium build. He looks like any regular guy you'd pass on the street and not even notice. He could have something to offer with a reasonable effort. Either he doesn't care or he doesn't get it. He looks almost lost over there by himself, and I may feel bad for him under different circumstance.

This could be our guy.

"Hey, look," I say quietly, getting Alicia's attention. "Check it out." I motion in the direction of the loner in the corner. Alicia checks him out from head to toe and I can tell she's considering him.

"He's not too bad," she says, nodding. "He might be worth a shot." She puts her book down and rises from her seat. She smoothens her jeans with her palms and straightens the light jacket that covers her blouse. "Wish me luck." She glides across the carpeted floor with confidence and heads toward the target. Her hips sway with each step, and she looks like a model strutting down the runway toward the photographers at the other end. Frank and I lower our books slightly and observe the action.

IT'S BEEN A LONG day. I knew Alicia was going to be good, but I didn't know she was going to be this good. She has really embraced her role. She spends the entire afternoon with this guy in the library, and she almost seems to be genuinely interested in him. By the early evening, the conversation moves out of the library and into a coffee shop across the street.

Frank and I had planned to wait outside the library in the van until Alicia came out, but it's gone on for too long. By 7:00 P.M. we're both famished, so we enter the coffee shop and order ourselves some grub. It looks like Alicia might have a stroke when she sees us enter the coffee shop and sit in the booth connected to hers. Frank and I eat in silence and eavesdrop on the conversation behind us.

We eat as slowly as we can, but pastries and homemade baked goods only last for so long. We leave the shop and wait in the van for another hour before Alicia finally emerges. It feels like we're staking out the joint while we sit in the parking lot of the library with the lights off in the van.

While in the coffee shop, Alicia used our guy's name during the conversation, strategically I think, so it gives me something to do while waiting for her.

George Sanders has no criminal record, no speeding tickets, and no negative marks on his credit report. I run his name and plates through the police database that I'm able to link to from my mobile phone that is paid for by the taxpayers. I discover that he doesn't appear to have any family around and he doesn't participate it any of the popular social networking sites. He's a banker with a college degree and a lifelong resident of the city. As far as I can tell, this guy is a nobody.

He's ordinary, dull, and forgettable.

He's perfect.

Across the street, Alicia slides into George's car and he pulls away shortly thereafter. I start the van and trail the Honda Civic, keeping a good distance between us as it obeys all traffic laws until it arrives at a sprawled out housing community a few miles from the center of town. I drive by the compact ranch and get a visual of Alicia without stopping. I park the van a few hundred feet past the driveway and wait.

A FEW HOURS LATER, Frank's snores wake me, bringing me to the realization that I too had fallen asleep. The illuminated clock in the center console provides a small glimpse of light in the van. It's 2:33 A.M. I check my phone: No messages from Alicia. She apparently has decided to make herself comfortable and is staying the night. That wasn't part of the plan, and quite frankly, it isn't necessary. I'm a little perplexed at her for thinking she has the authority to make these types of decisions. Or maybe it's jealousy, or envy. Maybe I want her to give me the attention George is getting, even if it's not sincere.

I'll give her another couple hours before I send her a message. For all I know, they could still be up talking, so I can't risk blowing this opportunity. I set myself an alarm as a reminder before trying to fall back asleep. She needs to be out of there before George wakes up in the morning, and she will be.

I'll make sure of it.

CHAPTER SEVENTEEN

GEORGE

The ride back to the warehouse has become routine. I sit in the back of the van across from Frank while Billy drives, mostly in silence. My hands are tied in front of me more loosely than usual, per my granted request. This allows me to slide the rope down my forearms a bit, thereby reducing the aggravation on my callused wrists.

Despite there being no windows in the back of the van, Frank uses an old necktie to blindfold me as we're about halfway back, I presume. The tie isn't quite wide enough to cover my eyes, so I can see the floor of the van through a small slit on the bottom. I imagine the idea is that I can't see where we're going, but there's nowhere to look out anyway, so it's actually rather pointless. I play along just as Billy does I'm sure, as a way to keep Frank feeling involved.

As we come to a stop, I can hear a steel roller opening a garage door then closing it again as we pull forward. After going through the usual motions of Billy opening the back doors of the van and Frank escorting me out, they lead me through some doorways and down some corridors, then into a familiar smelling empty room. Frank removes the makeshift blindfold and leaves.

"Get some rest," Billy says. "It's going down tonight."

He leaves, slamming the door behind him. In the corner of the room, opposite that of the wet spot from the leaky ceiling, is a flat pillow and wool blanket. It wasn't there before, but I'll take it. The old wooden chair from in front of the two-way mirror is still there, so I know it's the same room. Ignoring the hunger growls in my empty stomach, I lie down on the pillow and close my eyes. The cement is cold beneath me, but the blanket helps to mask it slightly. I fall asleep almost instantly.

MY DEEP SLEEP IS interrupted by the door opening and closing. It's dark, but I can hear soft footsteps approaching me. A figure is standing above me, but my eyes aren't adjusting quickly enough to make out who or what it is. A quiet whisper comes from the figure.

"Are you awake?" it's a woman's voice.

I grunt.

"George, it's me."

"Alicia?"

Suddenly remembering where I am, I pop up to the sitting position and the blood rushes to head, making me dizzy. I ignore it.

"I just wanted to see how you are," Alicia says.

"I'm fine, don't worry about me. How are you doing?"

"I'm okay, tired. How's your setup?" She smoothens the blanket with one hand, making contact with mine as she does so. "It's not much, but it's all I could find."

"It's great, it's more than enough. Thank you."

"I found this stuff in a closet in one of these rooms when you guys were gone. They didn't lock my door so I could use the bathroom. You know, the baby thing. So I wandered around for a bit and came across this. I thought you could use it."

"What else did you find?"

"Not much really. It's mostly just some old rooms, offices maybe, with some dusty desks and file cabinets and stuff."

"Did you try to escape?"

There's a long silence. "Uh, no. I didn't think about it I guess. I didn't want to take the chance, you know? I didn't want to put the baby at risk."

"That's understandable I guess." There's another long awkward silence before I continue, "Did you know that Billy's a cop?"

"Yeah, I know."

"What about that other guy, Frank?"

"What do you mean?"

"He can't be a cop too, right? Is there something wrong with him?"

"Frank is Billy's younger brother. He has BPD."

"BPD?"

"Borderline personality disorder."

"Is he dangerous?"

"Dangerous? I don't think so. He's a little unstable sometimes, but he seems harmless enough."

"Good to know. How do you know all this stuff about them?"

Suddenly, she grabs my wrist, grasping hard around my callus. I clench my jaw tightly and try to fight off the pain.

"Do you hear that? I think they're coming. I've got to go, I don't want to get caught. I'll come see you later." Just like that, she pops to her feet, runs to the door and slides out, and the door closes behind her.

I'm not left in the dark for long, though, as just moments later the lights engage and brighten up the room. I shield my face to avoid the brightness. The door opens and I can hear Billy enter.

"Get up, it's go time," he says.

I slowly rise to my feet and start toward the door, my hand still shading my eyes as I move. As I reach the door, Billy puts his hand on my shoulder and leads me down the corridor.

"Okay, so here's the plan."

CHAPTER EIGHTEEN

BILLY

The melody of my phone's alarm startles me from a light sleep. It takes a moment for me to react, but I do eventually dismiss the alarm and pull my seat to the sitting position. Frank is a deep sleeper, so the commotion doesn't stir him. After a moment of letting my eyes adjust to the illuminated background of my phone, I type a brief message to Alicia and send it across the airwaves.

It takes her less than a minute to respond.

I turn the key that dangles from the ignition and start the engine. I back the van out without looking and pull into the deserted street, heading back in the direction of George's ranch. I slow the van to a crawl and stop it in front of the driveway. I try to wake Frank, but he grumbles and refuses to move, so I guess he's staying where he is. He's far too large for me to try and move myself.

I hand crank my window to lower it then I light up a cigarette. I take a few drags and blow the smoke into the night before tossing it to the ground outside. The stimulation of the nicotine in my lungs wakes me fully.

In the distance, a door faintly closes, so I look through the dark toward the sound. A motion-activated light engages and lights up George's driveway. Alicia gallops toward us, shoes in hand. I motion to the back doors as she approaches, and she slides in the back, gently closing the doors behind her. I pull the van forward no more than a few hundred feet, just enough to be out of view from George's house, and pull to the side of the road. I throw the transmission into park and spin around to face Alicia.

"What the hell are you doing?" I snap at her.

She's taken aback at my aggressiveness, and she goes on the defensive. "What's wrong?"

"I don't want any bullshit, I'm not playing games. This was not part of the plan."

"Listen, I'm responsible for getting him hooked." She uses her fingers as air quotes around "hooked". "I'm just doing what I have to do."

"It wasn't necessary. None of it was needed. We don't need him to fall in love with you for Christ sakes. We just need him to want more."

Alicia looks away for an extended period of time. Something is wrong.

"Oh shit."

She looks back to me. "What?"

"You're falling for this guy, aren't you?"

She chuckles, but I can see her cheeks getting flush. "Don't be ridiculous."

I roll my eyes. My blood starts to boil. "What happened in there tonight?"

She looks away again, hoping I will ignore the question. I won't. I just stare at her and wait for the response.

"Nothing much, just talked mostly," she says.

I continue staring at her, waiting for something else. I can see her shame, but she's not going to say it, so I will. "You fucked him, didn't you?"

She snaps her head up and looks at me. "Does it matter?"

"It matters to me."

"Well too bad!" she snaps.

I shake my head in disgust, almost shunning her. Her defensiveness gives me all the information I need.

She sighs and forces herself to relax. "I'm not sure I want to do this. Maybe I'm not the right person for the job. I thought I was, but I don't think I can do this."

I shake my head. "It's too late for that."

"What if I say no? What if I just don't do it?"

I smile at her, although I'm not being friendly. I turn back toward the cabin of the van and open the glove box. I have to push Frank's tree stump legs out of the way to open the door fully, which stirs him. I slam the door and turn back to Alicia. I show her the gun. I don't point it at her, but I show it to her as a threat. I don't say anything as I watch her eyes widen and her face stricken with fear. She keeps her eyes on the gun and slides down the bench toward the back doors.

"Relax, I'm not going to shoot you," I say.

The tension doesn't release from her muscles as she continues to slide down the bench until she reaches the end. The doors are locked from the inside, so she has no way out and she knows it. She cowers in fear.

I think I've proven my point for now, so I turn back around and face the cabin. Frank is awake and staring at me. He gives me the same look that Alicia was, and he pushes his back up against the glass.

"What did I miss?" he says, his voice trembling.

I push his legs aside and toss the unloaded gun back into the glove box. I switch the transmission into drive and pull back into the still empty street. I can feel Frank's eyes watching me, and I'm sure Alicia is doing the same. I fight myself from smiling as I head toward home.

I'm in control here, and now they both know it.

CHAPTER NINETEEN

GEORGE

Billy, Frank, and I are outside the van, which is in its usual spot next to the cell tower in front of Snake's house. It's 2:30 A.M. and the air is chilly, although I'm still perspiring. A three-quarter crescent moon lights up a path for us as we make our way toward the house. Families of crickets make conversation under the stars as we walk.

"Stick with the plan. No funny business," Billy says, carrying a duffle bag in one hand.

"I'm ready, boss," Frank says.

I don't respond and just keep walking.

Billy faces me. "What about you?"

"What about me?" I say.

"You're not going to fuck anything up, right? Do what I say and nobody gets hurt."

"Let's just get this over with so I can go home."

The house is completely dark as we approach it. Billy does a perimeter check while Frank and I wait in the front. Frank is jittery, anxious or nervous I cannot tell. He twirls his thumbs and bounces back and forth between his feet. He looks like a child.

"Gunna be fun, Georgie," he says to me. I don't respond. He reaches over to me and wraps his arms around my shoulders and squeezes, lifting me into the air. "Georgieeee!" I can barely breathe as he squeezes me too aggressively.

"Put him down for Christ sakes," Billy's voice emerges from the darkness. Frank releases me and I fall the three inches back to the safety of the ground.

"Uh, sorry, boss," Frank says, embarrassed. Billy walks up behind him and smacks him in the back of the head.

"Calm the fuck down, you idiot."

Frank just stares into space as Billy glares at him. The trance is broken when Frank looks away, followed by Billy tossing the duffel bag on the ground. He kneels next to it, unzips it, and reaches inside. He pulls out two masks, the same carbon monoxide masks as from back at the warehouse, and hands them to Frank and me. I slip mine over my head and onto my nose and mouth. I feel around my neckline and cheekbone to make sure it's sealed properly, then I pull the straps tight. Frank is struggling to get his mask over his head. Billy, now too wearing a mask, hands me a steel bar and a rubber mallet. He slips two vials, one containing a reddish black powder and one containing a solid metallic substance, into his pocket before standing. He helps Frank adjust his mask before we head for the door.

Billy tries to open the front door, but the locking mechanism is engaged, so he grabs a crowbar from the duffel bag. He jams it in between the door and the frame just above the knob, giving his best guess to where the deadbolt is positioned. He wiggles the crowbar back and forth, trying to pry the door open, but it won't budge. While keeping one hand on the crowbar to hold it in position, he holds his open hand out behind him. Frank snatches the mallet from my hand and places it in Billy's open palm.

Frank smiles proudly.

Billy uses the mallet to wedge the crowbar in deeper, and he does the same on a few different spots on the door. The frame eventually splits through the center, but the door still won't open. Billy turns to Frank and nods, then Frank walks past me and toward the direction of the van.

"You may want to move out of the way," Billy says while yanking the crowbar out of the doorframe. Before I can respond, I catch a glimpse of Frank stampeding toward me.

"AAARRRGGGHHHH!" Frank screams like a mad man. His face is flushed and full of fury. He looks like he could kill someone.

I leap out of the way, falling to the dirt just in time as Frank plows through the door, shoulder first. The door is torn off its hinges and lands on the carpet beneath Frank's quivering body. The rest of the doorframe crumbles into ash in the doorway. The friction from the impact shakes the ground, and it feels like the beginning of an earthquake.

Billy brushes past me and tends to Frank, who moans on the ground. He whispers something into Frank's ear then pats him on the head like a dog. Frank pushes himself to the sitting position, then he slowly climbs to his feet with a big smile on his face. Billy must have said something nice to him for once. Maybe he praised him for his contribution.

Snake's motionless body is face down in the hallway. I've never seen a dead body before, but I read somewhere that it's supposed to release its bowels upon death, so I expect to see a puddle of urine or smell a pile of feces as I get closer to the body. I do not. Billy crouches beside Snake's body and searches for a pulse.

"Well, he's not dead yet," he says. "But he's barely alive."

"You want me to take care of him?" Frank asks.

Billy hesitates a bit, seeming unsure. I'm guessing he expected Snake would already be dead. "No, not yet. I'll tell you when." Billy's voice fades toward the end as he walks over the body and enters the bedroom. Frank and I follow him.

Everything is basically the same as I remember it. The mattress still rests on the floor without a frame and has a dirty sheet half falling off of it. An old wooden nightstand rests in the corner with a vintage alarm clock on top. The giant canvas still hangs on the wall on the other side of the room. I've never been much into art, but now that I'm able to actually look at it, this one has my attention. It's a farmland landscape, which is basically everywhere everyday Kansas, or at least the area that I'm from. There is a cow drinking from a small lake or a big pond in the background, which I've never actually seen before. The artist must not be local. The piece is comforting, though; it reminds me of where I've been and where I want to go.

Facing the wall, Billy wraps his hands around the sides of the mural and lifts it up, removing it from its hook and exposing a small stainless steel safe behind it. It seems rather small, probably not much more than a foot long. I'm not sure how much cash can fit in something that size, but it can't be that much. It has a combination dial on the right side with a steel handle just to the right of that. Billy fiddles with the dial briefly before turning to leave. I approach the safe with the steel bar that I've had in my hand and wait for the signal.

From outside, I see the light from Billy's flashlight shine into the room. He knocks it on the glass, which tells me he's ready. Using the steel bar, I repeatedly hit the front of the safe so it pings through the wall. I do this until I hear a tap from outside, confirming that Billy has found the location. I make my way outside to join him.

By the time I get to Billy, most of the vinyl paneling has already been torn off the side of the house and the wooden studs are being chipped away. Frank is out front on guard duty. Billy tosses the last of the panels to the ground, which exposes the rear end of the safe. He removes the first vial from his pocket and pours some of the reddish black powder into the palm of his hand. I observe as he begins to rub the powder on the exposed safe.

The powder, as was explained to me, is thermite. It's not an explosive material, but it can get hot enough to burn through steel. In a larger quantity, it's powerful enough to completely collapse a skyscraper that has steel beams or to cut through railroad tracks. How he got his hands on the stuff, I don't know, and I don't ask. It's probably better if I don't know.

"This thing is going to ignite when I touch the magnesium to it, so I'd back up a few steps," Billy says as he rubs on the last of the thermite powder.

"Can't you just use a lighter?"

"No, it's not hot enough. It needs to get to about 2500 degrees."

I step back as Billy removes the strip of magnesium from the second vial. He pulls out some gloves from his back pocket and puts them on for protection. He crouches down low and holds his hand above his head with the magnesium strip aimed toward the thermite powder. As the two make contact, a spark forms and is quickly followed by a bright red flash of light. Billy drops the magnesium and runs toward me as the flame ignites.

We watch as the safe begins to melt.

It takes a few minutes, but the liquid steel from the safe begins to drip down the vinyl paneling that remains and onto the grass below. A cloud of white smoke forms above the house as the rear of the safe slowly caves in on itself until the flame dies out.

Hearing the commotion, Frank joins us on the side of the house. Billy uses the mallet to smash over the cracks of the warped steel, which breaks off small chunks at a time until there is a hole big enough for him to slip his arm inside. He reaches in, appears to feel around a bit, then pulls out a small box. He shines his flashlight into the hole for a second look.

"Where's all the cash, boss?" Frank asks.

Billy holds up his hand to shush him. All eyes are infatuated with the box that sits in the palm of Billy's hand. After a brief pause, Billy opens the lid and exposes a brass key and a small ripped piece of paper. He reads the note aloud, "282w53s."

"Uh, what does that mean?" Frank mutters.

Billy snaps the box shut and slides it in his pocket. Without saying anything, he pushes past us and barrels around the side of the house. Frank and I chase after him.

Billy goes on a rampage inside the house, tearing apart and flipping over every piece of furniture in his path. "Bullshit! This is fucking bullshit! There has got to be another safe in this shit hole," he yells. He tosses furniture wherever there is space until everything in the house has been touched. "I know he has the cash, I know he does. He just took another job. Fuck!"

Frank and I watch Billy in awe.

With nothing left to destroy, Billy settles down. He scans the room and assesses the damage. He looks like he feels better now that that's out of his system. Before leaving, Billy whips the mallet across the living room and implants it into the drywall. Exhausted, he points to Snake's body, which is still face down on the carpet. "Get rid of him."

He walks out.

Frank struggles, but he's able to scoop up Snake's limp body and toss him over his shoulder. He opens the door in the hallway and hurls Snake down the wooden steps and into the basement. Snake's lifeless body lands on the cement floor at the bottom of the stairs and a pool of blood forms beneath his fractured skull. I listen for the release of his bowels, but it never comes. Frank slams the door and we leave out the opening where the front door used to be. Billy is already half way back to the van.

No one checks the body, but I'm sure Snake's dead. If he wasn't already dead from the extended exposure to the carbon monoxide, he surely would have died from the impact of the cement floor on his head.

He must be dead. I'm sure of it.

CHAPTER TWENTY

BILLY

By Monday morning, everyone has calmed down and things have gone back to the way they were before. No one has spoken of the incident, if that's what you want to call it, and we work on preparations for the next phase of the plan. Alicia is distant, which I'm sure is a combination of the realization of what she has gotten herself into and her trying to come up with a way out of it. What she doesn't know is that there is no way out, not alive anyway. She'll figure that out sooner or later.

Alicia has essentially moved in with Frank and me as a way for me to keep her under my supervision. She has to earn back my trust before I'll let her be that far away from me now. It's difficult for me to let her go into work this morning as usual, but it's a necessity to progress everything forward. I drive her into town for 8:00 A.M. and drop her off a couple of blocks away from City Hall. We need to keep things as normal as possible to avoid people trying to snoop around and blow everything up, so it needs to look like she's still walking into work. I don't watch her walk up the steps and go into the building, but I call the office every few hours during the day and hang up at the sound of her voice just to make sure she's still there.

At 4:30 P.M., I drive back into town and park the van in front of her apartment complex. I arrive a few minutes before 5:00 P.M. and wait for her. She needs to gather some more personal items from her apartment if she's going to be staying with me, she told me, which I find to be a reasonable request. After twelve minutes of waiting, I finally see Alicia approaching the complex as I peer in the mirror outside my window. We make eye contact as she walks past me, and I wait five more minutes before exiting the van and entering the building behind her.

Inside the building, I buzz her apartment, number twenty-three, and she unlocks the security door without saying anything over the loud speaker. I open the door to a long hallway and make my way up three flights of stairs which sit to my left. The hallways are all carpeted and are home to numerous stains and tears. The stairs are soft and rubbery like those in a high school, and the soles of my shoes squeak with each step as I climb them. A single fire hydrant hangs on the wall about halfway down each hallway, and the air is stale. As I reach the third floor, I can smell someone burning their dinner behind one of the locked doors. The building lacks care, as evident by the strong aroma of Indian food that fills the entry ways.

Number twenty-three is the last door on the left. There is another door which is held open by a door stop just past Alicia's door, which leads to another staircase on the other end of the complex. I stumble over a pair of children's sneakers as I walk past, which prompts me to kick the pair halfway down the hall. With my knuckle, I lightly knock on the door where the crooked two and three hang, and I expect the three to fall right off the door. It doesn't. Moments later, footsteps approach behind the door and I can feel an eyeball looking at me through the small peephole. The dead bolt disengages and the door is cracked. I push it open the rest of the way and slide inside.

Alicia's apartment is small and nearly empty, but it's orderly. It has a tiny bedroom and bathroom that are attached to the eat-in kitchen, which has outdated finishes and appliances. One of the linoleum tiles on the floor has a cigarette a burn in the center. There is no nice way to put it, the place is a piece of shit.

"It's not much, I realize," Alicia says, her tone implying I have a look of dissatisfaction on my face, "but it's cheap and close to work. It was only supposed to be temporary."

I nod and try not to laugh at the ever-worsening cosmetics, but I can't resist. I burst out laughing and toss saliva all over the kitchen. I lean forward and place my hands on my knees to help my balance. Most people would be offended at my lack of self-control, but Alicia soon joins in and starts to laugh too. It's the first time I've seen her smile like this, and it's the first time I've laughed so hard since my father died. It helps to release some of the unspoken tension between us. We take turns pointing out the flaws of the place, everything from the ceiling fan with a missing light bulb, to the busted sliding door that barely covers a ripped screen. It's a good laugh that feels great, and it's needed. I wipe the tears from my eyes as I regain myself and my composure.

"What is it that you needed again?" I ask.

Alicia wipes her face as well, although much less aggressively than I as to avoid smudging her makeup. "Just the rest of my clothes mostly."

"Show me where they are, I'll grab them."

She walks across the linoleum and into the carpeted bedroom, leading me to a pile of clothes that are on plastic hangers and neatly stacked on the bed. I brush past her and haul the clothes from the bed, tossing them over my shoulder. I quickly turn around and nearly bump right into Alicia, who is standing much closer to me that I thought. Our faces are close, although hers significantly lower than mine due to the height difference, and we hold the position for a moment. Her chilled breath steadies against my neck and it makes me tingle. I wonder what she is thinking at this moment, and I'm hopeful she has put George right out of her mind. A part of me wants to toss the pile of clothes back on the bed, throw her on top and tear hers off, but I resist. She's still trying to wrap her mind around all of this, and I really need to get her back on my side if this is going to work. There will be a time for me to make my move, but now's not it, despite the desires that reside within me. Instead, I smile at her with sincerity, which she returns with the same.

"Ready to go?" I ask.

Alicia nods.

With the pile of organized chaos draped over my shoulder, I follow Alicia down the long hallway and into the same stairwell that I entered from earlier. We pass a group of black teenagers on the way out the door, and all four of them look her up and down. She pretends not to see them as she makes her way to the van. Based on her reaction, I wonder if they've had some sort of altercation in recent days, perhaps they tried to come on to her and she rejected them. I catch the eyes of the tallest one with acne scars and we stare at one another as I walk past.

Without a confrontation, I make it safely to the parking lot and join Alicia near the van. She opens the back doors and I toss the clothes inside, disregarding the mess that covers the floor. She hops in the passenger's side and buckles herself in, then I hop in the driver's side and do the same. I catch the eyes of the same kid one more time before I pull away.

"How did today go?" I ask as we pull up to a four-way stoplight.

"It went fine. Everything's in place, just as we planned. I have the deed in my purse."

I PULL THE VAN into the driveway and park it in the center. I grab Alicia's clothes from the back and lead her into the house. I bring the pile of clothes into my bedroom, which will continue to be hers for a while, and toss them on the bed. Alicia has the small stack of papers already prepared on the table when I re-enter the kitchen. I take the pen from her hand and sign Sheriff Jack Hearns' name on the lines after the x's. I flip through the stack and try to make the signatures as clean and as consistent as possible in case it's audited. I'm not authorized to sign for anything on behalf of the Police Department, and someone would certainly recognize my name if I did.

You can add forgery to my soon to be lengthy list of wrongdoings.

It's common knowledge around town that my father was the Sheriff and that his son of the same name didn't follow in his footsteps after he passed. I guess that's one of the negatives of having a well-respected man for a father and having certain expectations to live up to. The truth is, I never wanted to follow in his footsteps and pursue a career in law enforcement, but with no plan and constant nagging, I begrudgingly obliged and went to the police academy when I graduated from high school. I did reasonably well in the classroom and was at a near expert level with the accuracy of a firearm, and it was good enough I guess.

Shortly after I graduated, a veteran officer retired in Topeka, so naturally, my father offered me the position and I've been there ever since. The local news loved the father-son heartwarming story initially, but it soon dissipated and I basically fell off the radar. I had a few questionable arrests when I first started, and my father had to make more than one deal with the prosecutors so they wouldn't sue the entire Police Department. Most officers would have been fired certainly, but my situation was different with my father being the Sheriff and all, so I was just assigned to basic traffic duty for much of the last twelve years instead. It was only in the last two when I started doing some actual police work and moved inside and off the streets.

I ONLY SCAN THE documents for keywords as I sign: Grantor, grantee, notary, deed, Topeka Police Department, State of Kansas. I'm not a lawyer, but the documents look official enough to me. I'm going to give Alicia the benefit of the doubt and trust that she knows what she's doing. Frank enters the room just as I finish signing the Sheriff's name on the final page.

"What you guys doin'?" Frank asks.

"We had to take care of some administrative things," I say, brushing it off.

"Like what?"

"Just some paperwork, boring stuff."

He looks at me like he is expecting more, but I plan to end it with that.

Alicia jumps in, "We just had to get the property transferred over so we have access to it."

Frank nods.

I glare at Alicia, who pretends not to notice. Frank knows the plan as he was awake and semi-engaged when we were going over it, but he doesn't know specific details. The fewer details he knows, the better, as it reduces the chance of a slip-up.

"What do we do now?" Franks asks.

It's a good question.

I look to Alicia and wait for her to respond, as this is one of her parts of the arrangement.

"I'll complete the property transfer in the system in the morning and we'll be good to go," she says. "I'll intentionally misfile the documents just to be sure, which will buy us some time."

"Tell me again," I begin, "what are the chances this gets back to the Sheriff?"

"It will eventually, I have no doubt about that. The city has over 125,000 people in it, though, and property tax time is just around the corner, so that'll keep everyone busy for a while. I'm sure the City Administrator will find it and question it during audit time. She'll ask the Sheriff about it and then an investigation will ensue. The Mayor will likely get involved too. It'll be a big mess for the city."

"How long is a while?"

"Three or four months anyway, minimum. Audits are typically done quarterly, so it could be longer than that before they actually figure out what happened. But by then, we'll be long gone."

I nod and smile. "Corruption in City Hall."

"And in the Sheriff's Office."

CHAPTER TWENTY-ONE

GEORGE

"**W**here we goin', boss?" Frank asks as Billy drives through the night streets. He sits alone in the front while Frank and I ride in the back. "Hey, boss, where we-"

"I heard you."

Frank looks like he wants to ask again, but he thinks better of it. It's not long before Billy pulls up to the Topeka Police Department. Frank catches a glimpse of the illuminated sign hanging on the brick building and panics.

"Woah! What's goin' on, boss? What we doin' here?"

"Relax, stay in the van," Billy says as he turns off the engine and slides out the door. He creeps around the side and opens the rear doors. He points to me. "Come with me."

Inside the station, we casually stroll past the empty desks and offices and slide into Billy's cubicle. He waves to a couple of graveyard shift officers as they sip coffee in the office adjacent to his cube. He turns on his computer and we wait for it to power up. Billy's cubicle is nearly empty and is impersonalized. There are no pictures of his family, no cute dog calendar, and no dirty coffee cup. The office necessities are lined up in a straight line, evenly spaced and dust free. The phone on the corner of the desk is blinking with a new message or two.

"What are we doing here?" I whisper.

"Don't whisper, it'll bring attention to us," Billy responds. He enters his password when prompted and logs into a database from the icon on his desktop. "Ah fuck, he's coming over."

I slide up in my chair and peek over the top of the cubicle wall and see a uniformed officer walking toward us.

"Billy! How goes it, baby?" the officer says as he approached. He's youthful and high on caffeine and clearly doesn't have an issue with working the night shift.

"Hi, Dave, how are you doing tonight?"

"Doing good, man, slow out there tonight. What are you doing here?"

Dave slips his thumb into the front of his pants behind his belt. He holds a cup of steaming coffee with his other hand and blows on it. The aroma of freshly roasted hazelnuts makes my mouth water.

"I've got to take a look at my notes on this case I've been working."

"Now? It's one in the morning, man."

"Yeah, I know. You know what it's like when you have a breakthrough." Billy smiles.

Dave takes a long sip of his coffee and nods his head in agreement. "Hey, I thought I heard you were off for a few days?"

"I was. I'm back now."

Dave nods and takes another sip of his coffee. "Well, welcome back then. Have a good night."

"Thanks. You too, Dave."

Before leaving, Dave acknowledges me by giving me a subtle nod in which I gladly return. Billy turns his attention back to his computer and begins typing in the search bar in the database that has finally loaded on his machine.

A few minutes go by and he still hasn't offered up any details on what he's looking for. He has the torn up piece of paper from the safe on his desk and he types the numbers in different combinations in the database. I can tell by the way he holds his spot on the paper with one finger while typing one character at a time with another on the opposite hand. I do the same thing.

"Are you going to tell me what we're doing here?" I finally ask.

Billy leans back in his chair, puts his hands behind his head, and sighs. He hands me the paper. "What do you see?"

I study at the paper. "What are you asking?"

"It's not a trick question, what do you see when you look at it? What's your first instinct?"

I study the paper again, not sure what I'm missing. "I don't know. A code or something. Five numbers, two letters."

"What has seven characters? I've scanned the entire police database for every license plate combination with these numbers in the whole fucking county."

"And?"

"Nothing, fucking nothing."

"Nothing at all?"

"Nothing useful. There was one Ford pickup that had six of the numbers, and a Volkswagen Beetle that had all seven, but not in the same order."

"Okay, maybe that's something to work with. The Volkswagen, I mean."

"It's registered to an 18-year-old girl, that's not it."

"What about the truck?"

Billy enters a combination into the database and reads back the results, "1989 Ford F-250, registered to a Reginald Washington, 89 years old and white. Unless you think Snake is tight with an 89-year-old white guy, he's not our guy."

Point taken.

I lean back in my chair and try to come up with something else, but draw a blank.

We bounce ideas back and forth for nearly an hour, things like partial VINs, dates, and other personal references from Snake's lengthy file. We scan through all of Snake's known aliases, previous cellmates, family members, and his known associates for any link to the number combination.

Nothing.

We're exhausted, out of ideas, and can barely stay awake anymore, so Billy gathers up all the files he can find and compiles them in a box to sort through again later. With the files in hand, we walk out the back door to avoid getting stopped and questioned by another officer. We make our way around the front of the building and slide into the van. Frank is passed out in the back, snoring like a buffalo. I sit down on the bench across from him and lean my head back as Billy reverses the van into the empty street. The plan is to just rest my eyes until we get back to the warehouse.

When I wake up it's morning.

CHAPTER TWENTY-TWO

BILLY

I drop off Alicia just before 8:00 A.M. at the usual spot a few blocks away from City Hall. Once I arrive back home, I make a call to the electric company to turn the power on at the property. I tell them that I'm the Sheriff and that it's for urgent police matters. The service representative asks very few questions and agrees to send a technician out to read the meter so they can turn it back on immediately. They promise that I'll be up and running by noon. I give them my personal post office box number to send the usage bills to.

I receive a call from Alicia just before lunch telling me the city is sending someone to the property for a walkthrough and inspection. It's standard procedure apparently before they'll hand over the keys to a commercial property that's owned by the city. Someone needs to be there to get the keys and to accompany the inspector on the walkthrough, so that sounds like a job for me. I go to my bedroom, now Alicia's, and pull out my uniform from the closet. As I button my shirt, I catch a glimpse of Alicia's bag resting unzipped on the floor next to the bed. An orange strap hangs out the side of the bag, and it tempts me to look through it. I lift the flap of the bag and look inside without touching anything. Various colors and styles of underwear and camisoles fill it, including an all-orange brassiere which caught my attention in the first place. I see nothing of importance, no weapons or anything, so I put the flap back where it was and leave the house, leaving Frank by himself inside. I hop into the van and head toward the property on 12th Street.

I park the van in a parking garage a couple of blocks from the property and head the rest of the way on foot, not wanting to pull up in a van and raise some eyebrows. I bring the van instead of my squad car so I don't risk the GPS alerting dispatch that I'm in it when I shouldn't be. As I approach the building, I see a tall white man with round glasses and a bald head holding a clipboard, waiting near the entrance. He's looking up at the side of the brick building and taking some notes on the pad on his clipboard. He turns to me as I approach.

"Hello there," he says, "you must be Sheriff Hearns."

I take his hand and shake it firmly. "No, I'm not the Sheriff," I say.

He makes a humming sound and looks down at his clipboard. "Oh, I was expecting the Sheriff."

"Yeah, I know. He got caught up in something this afternoon, so he asked me to fill in for him."

The man nods. "Oh, okay. Well, my name is Maury Levenestein. I'm one of the commercial property building inspectors for the city of Topeka."

"It's nice to meet you, Maury. My name is Bill Lewis."

Maury turns his head slightly and looks to be deep in serious thought. "Lewis...Lewis...that name sounds familiar." Suddenly, he thrusts his hand in the air and points his pen at me. "Any relation to William Lewis? He used to be the Sheriff around here."

"He was my father."

Maury smiles to himself, this seemingly being a proud moment for him, then he seems to remember. "Sorry about your loss," he says. "Your father was a good man. I never actually met him, but from the people I know who did, they had nothing but nice things to say about him." He offers me a weak smile.

I appreciate his sincerity. "Thanks."

Maury fetches a key from the string that is attached to his clipboard and motions toward the door. "Shall we begin?"

The old police station is dusty, cold, and likely full of mold. It's been nine years since the city agreed to build a new station, and seven since everyone moved out. It's a safe bet that no one has stepped foot in here since then. It's been in possession of the city ever since the move, and there are no plans that have been made public to do anything with the building. It's an eyesore to the already run-down area surrounding 12th Street, but it seems people have learned to ignore it. Everything about it makes it the perfect location for what we're going to use it for.

There is a long corridor that is lined with old offices, meeting rooms, and interrogation rooms. Many of the rooms still have furniture that was left behind from before the move. At the other end of the hall is another door which leads to the garage in the back of the building. Arresting officers would bring in the arrestees through the garage almost one hundred percent of the time, enabling the front door to be used for all other non-criminal civilian complaints or public visits.

I FOLLOW MAURY INTO the large holding cell room where he begins his evaluation. It's not a holding cell like you would expect in a modern jail; there are no bars, toilets, or separate rooms. It's one big empty room that used to house all of the accused while they awaited processing. The walls have been stripped of the benches that used to line the perimeter. The new police station is more tra- ditional and modern, and I'm sure they used this room as a big rea- son why the move was needed. A wide two-way mirror rests in its original place between the walls across the room.

"So," Maury says as he tries to make small talk while he takes notes, "what do you guys need to use this place for anyway? It's been locked up for years."

"Just a special project we're working on. We need some more space."

"Oh yeah, like what?"

"I can't really say."

"Are you planning to take down a big operation or something?" He chuckles to himself. "Maybe it's the Mafia. That's it, maybe there's a branch of the Mafia in Topeka."

He's overly enthusiastic about the thought of this, and his face lights up at this possibility. He's clearly searching for some excite- ment in his life. He wears a gold wedding ring on his left ring finger that looks rustic, so I'm guessing his wife of many years doesn't put out anymore, based on his need for excitement. Poor guy.

"Something like that," I say.

Maury makes his way around the perimeter of the room and stops at a faded water stain on the cement floor in the corner. He looks up and jots something down on his notepad. I follow behind him as he weaves in and out of the old offices, conference rooms, and interrogation rooms, making notes as we enter each room. Af- ter hitting each of the rooms, he leads me back out the front door and onto the sidewalk.

"Well," Maury begins, "the place is filthy and disgusting, but it's safe. I would advise hiring a cleaning crew before anyone moves in, but I can't force you to. I'll type up a full report and send it over to the Sheriff directly."

"Actually, the Sheriff is out of the office this afternoon, and this is really of high importance. I need to swing by City Hall later this afternoon anyway, so would you mind just sending it over to the clerk there? I can pick the report up on my way through and will hand deliver it myself."

Maury shakes his head in agreement. "That works for me. I'll have the report completed and sent across by four o'clock this afternoon."

"Perfect."

Maury unties the loose knot that attaches the key to his clipboard and hands the key to me. I clench it tightly in my hand.

"Before I forget," he continues, "you'll need to ask the Sheriff to fix the leak in the ceiling in that open room. It's a small leak, but it's still a leak. I'll be back in ninety days to make sure it's done. It'll be in the report in case you forget."

"Okay, no problem."

We shake hands and Maury slides into his Toyota that's parked on the street in front of the building. He waves as he drives away. I unclench my hand and look at the key with satisfaction. Ninety days is more than enough time.

CHAPTER TWENTY-THREE

GEORGE

It's morning and we're all in the one of the offices in the warehouse: Billy, Frank, Alicia, and me. Billy says he spent the early morning hours sorting through Snake's files again but came up empty. A tabletop map of the county is spread out across the desk. The ripped note and the brass key from the safe rest on the corner of the desk while Billy closely inspects the map.

"There is no intersection between 282 West Street and 53 South Street anywhere in this county," Billy says. "There is no 282 West Street period." He bows his head in frustration. "Any other ideas?"

Billy looks to each of us, but no one answers. He stares right at me, but I pretend not to see him. Out of nowhere, he swipes his arm across the table and knocks everything on the floor, startling everyone.

"Ideas people!" Billy continues. "There's ten million bucks out there somewhere that's going to belong to me!" He looks around the table again and still gets no reaction. "I see it's going to have to go another way then. Fine with me."

He bends down and unzips the duffel bag that's on the floor. He rises with a metal rod in his hand, the same metal rod that I used back at Snake's house. He walks around the table and stands behind Alicia.

She's reactionless as he wraps his arm around her neck and lifts her to her feet. Billy towers over her as he spins her around and leans her against the table so she faces him. She bends her head back and gazes at me, still without expression. Billy raises the bar over his head and winds up in the direction of her belly. Alicia clenches her eyes shut and braces for what's about to come.

Frank covers his face with his hands.

"The key," I say, holding off the assault. "There's got to be something with the key."

Billy looks at me but doesn't lower the bar. "Like what?"

"What about a safety deposit box?"

Billy lowers the bar a bit and Frank widens his fingers so he can see through the slits. Alicia's eyes are still clenched shut.

Billy asks, "Which bank?"

"I don't know."

"Not good enough."

Billy raises the bar back above his head and prepares to swing it toward my unborn child. Frank closes his fingers, completely covering his face again. Billy cocks his arm and starts to swing it toward Alicia. I jump from my seat.

"Wait!"

Billy rolls his eyes and lowers the bar. "What now?"

"Just hold on a second." I brush past Frank, whose face is now uncovered, and walk around the side of the table toward the map. I pick it up from the floor and toss it on the table. I intently scan the streets of Topeka on the map until I find it. I spin the map toward Billy and point at the spot. "There."

Billy lowers the rod completely and releases Alicia from his grasp. She finally opens her eyes and lets out a deep sigh of relief. Billy follows my finger on the map with his eyes.

"What am I looking at?" he asks.

"Right there," I say, tapping on the spot repeatedly. "Shawnee County Savings Bank is located on 53rd Street."

Billy whips his head from the map and looks at me. He's glowing with excitement. "And 282w would be the safety deposit box number?"

"That's what I'm thinking."

Billy looks at his watch. "It's eight o'clock, let's go. They'll be open by the time we get there."

Billy and I start for the door. Frank pops up from his chair and runs after us. Alicia is left in the room mumbling something to herself.

CHAPTER TWENTY-FOUR

BILLY

I t's been almost six weeks since everything was put in place, and I'm still waiting for the next job to go down. I've been back to work for just under three weeks now, and I'm trying to act as normal as possible. I've split my time between investigating a burglary on Chestnut Street and a bomb threat at the local high school. Sheriff Jack Hearns has kept me away from any homicides, but I always have one eye on what the Zved's are up to. There was a suspicious murder in Wichita, a car bomb, and one over the border in Kansas City, a drive-by shooting. Both occurred last week, and I suspect the group is involved.

The Zved's are back at it.

It is one of their patterns to back off for a while if the police are doing too much sniffing around, so they laid low for a while. It's nothing new. Either they sense that the heat has cooled, or they are running out of cash. Either way, they're back at it and I'm all over them.

Alicia has been doing her best to keep the deed transfer under wraps at the office, and she tells me that no one has been snooping around that she knows of. She received and immediately deleted the inspection report from Maury Levenestein when expected, and she cleans out her inbox's recycle bin weekly to make sure it's gone. Once the state gets wind of some sketchy activity internally, they'll hire an IT contractor to look through all of the records. They will find it eventually, hidden somewhere on her hard drive, but it buys us more time.

Before he died, my father used to get anonymous emails from an unknown informant in regards to the activity of the Zved's. The sender's IP address was always untraceable as each message bounced through multiple servers and was unique every time. There was always speculation that it was from someone with inside knowledge of the Zved's doings, whether a current or former member, or maybe a family member of one of them that wanted to put a stop to it. There was never an indication of motive and the details weren't always completely accurate, but my father took what he could get. There were rumblings inside the department that someone was playing with him and was intentionally trying to defer him or distract him from other pressing matters, but he never believed it.

When he died, I automatically forwarded all of the emails from his account to mine. Despite the sender always sending the messages anonymously, he or she always used the same subject line, so I forwarded just the messages containing the subject keyword. I still log in to his email account monthly without anyone knowing so the account doesn't automatically close. The IT department is pretty slow around here, so the account should stay safely open for a while. All other messages have been routed to Jack Hearns' account.

IT'S LUNCH TIME AND I'm sitting at my desk enjoying a sandwich. I wash each bite down with a sip of warm bottled water and read through my vague notes about the burglary on Chestnut Street. It was a home invasion that occurred, well after midnight, and the owner scared the perpetrators away with a baseball bat. The two intruders were wearing dark ski masks and gloves. They got away with some electronic video equipment and some sports memorabilia, but that's about all we know. The owner, a middle-aged bachelor, thinks the intruders may have been black, but he cannot be certain since it was dark. That's all he remembers about their physical appearances. We found no traces of DNA, no fingerprints, and no unidentified hair follicles at the property. As far as cold cases go, this one is about as cold of a trail as you will find.

My computer screen is dark and on standby, but a gentle chime sounds through the speakers. I flick the mouse to re-engage the screen and wait for the color to come back in the form of pixels. I drop my sandwich on the short stack of case files as I read the subject line: URGENT. I stumble around to find the mouse and quickly open the message. It reads:

7.9 1900 10m

Deciphered, it means the Zved's next hit is going down on July 9th at 19:00 hours for a purse of ten million dollars. I glance at my calendar, which confirms my uncertainty.

Today is July 9th.

Under normal circumstances, I would run into Jack's office and tell him what I've learned, but the thought doesn't even enter my mind today. I'm not going to say anything to anyone yet. Some things are better left unsaid. I pick up my sandwich from the stacked reports and wipe the crumbs away. I munch on the remainder of the crust and stare at the computer screen.

Things are about to get interesting.

THE FOLLOWING DAY, I arrive at the office before 8:00 A.M. I turn on my machine and immediately log in to the county database. I scan through the police reports from last night until I stumble across something that fits the usual pattern. One report in particular catches my eye. The report was filed shortly after midnight, although the incident notes a time of just after 9:00 P.M. According to the report, last night on Colonel Avenue, a luxury sedan heading west ran off the road and smashed head-on into a tree. Speed is expected to be the cause of the accident, but I know better than that.

The driver of the sedan was a veteran Shawnee County attorney, which could explain why someone could have wanted him dead. If I were to dig into his files, I bet I'd find some incriminating information on someone important in there, probably a politician. He was probably getting close to the truth about something they had done, so they hired someone to plug the hole before the water filled up and sank the boat.

It happens all the time.

The incident was made to look like an accident, but trust me when I say it was no accident. To the investigators, it just looks like the driver might have been drunk or fell asleep at the wheel. The report even says as much. If I had to guess, I'd put my money on the coroner's office finding that alcohol was not the cause of the accident, and that they'll settle on sleep deprivation being more likely. The accident will be viewed as tragic, and it is, and the Zved's will walk away without any blood on their hands once again.

And ten million dollars richer.

Unless I get to them.

The Zved's are professionals and they know what they're doing. A more likely scenario is that someone from the Zved's ran him off the road and tried to make it look like an accident. There is money involved here, which means it wasn't about a personal beef with someone on the inside. Ten million is a lot of money for a contract slaying, so someone important must have had something important to hide. An indictment would have been in the short term I'd imagine, so that's where the police will start when trying to figure out what really happened.

I spin out of my chair and march down the hall to Jack Hearns' office. I whip the door open without knocking. Jack is here early, as he surely must have been notified of what happened last night. I startle him, and he nearly spills his coffee all over himself.

"What the hell, Bill?" he says.

"We need to talk."

"This better not be about that accident last night. The guys on the scene say it was definitely an accident, no foul play. Bill, this shit has got to-"

"That's not what I'm here about."

Jack is taken aback. "It's not? Well, good then. Come on in and sit down."

I sit in the soft chair across from his desk.

He continues, "What can I do for you?"

"I need a few days off."

Jack sits up straight in his chair, now looking concerned. "What's going on? Is everything okay?"

"Everything will be fine. I just need to take a few days." Jack studies me, and I can tell he's about to dig for details. I offer up more rehearsed information before he can meddle. "It's Frank. He's had a...setback I guess you could say. I need to bring him back to the hospital over in Hays."

Jack sinks a bit in his chair. "Oh, Bill, I'm sorry to hear that. When did it happen?"

"Late last night."

"You should have just called me at home. You didn't need to come in to talk to me."

"It's okay, I have a friend staying with him for now. And I just had some time off, so I just wanted to make sure you're okay with it."

"Bill, don't worry about it, okay? Go take care of what you need to take care of, and come back when you can."

I stand up from the chair before he changes his mind. "Thanks, Jack. I owe you one."

I leave his office and walk over to my desk. I turn the monitor off but leave the machine running in case I need to log in remotely again. I turn the corner, weave around the cubes, and head for the front door. I glance at my father's commemoration plaque for what I expect will be the final time.

I will finish what you started, dad. I will get revenge.

CHAPTER TWENTY-FIVE

GEORGE

5³ʳᵈ Street is crowded at 8:45 A.M. on a Friday morning. The doors to the coffee shops are constantly revolving with people filing in and out to get what they need to make it to the weekend. People are scrambling on the sidewalks in their business suits. We're right in the center of the business district, Billy and me, so the risk couldn't be higher. The van is parked behind an old parking garage for easy access back to the freeway when we're gone. Frank is waiting there for us.

We have to walk a couple of blocks to get to the bank, and we make a pit stop on the way. Billy drags me into a men's clothing store and pays for some business casual slacks and a dress shirt for each of us in cash. He leaves an extra hundred for the young salesman so he doesn't have to wait for him to make change, although he won't budge on the dress socks buy-one-get-one deal of the day. Go figure. We change in the dressing room and wear the new clothes out. We toss our old clothes in one of the trash cans outside.

"I don't know if I can do this," I say as we make our way into the bank. I try to flatten one stubborn wrinkle on the chest of my new shirt. "I work at a bank, what if someone recognizes me?"

"You used to work at a bank," Billy says.

It's a good point, as I'm sure I've been terminated by now. Although it still doesn't solve the problem of potential recognition.

"Just follow my lead."

We enter the bank and head right for the main desk. On the wall to the right is a framed headshot of a man in an expensive suit. I can't read the name plate beneath it, but I recognize the face. I sat in on a compliance conference hosted by him recently, I think. I doubt he'd even recognize me if he saw me, but I'd rather not find out. I keep my head down and follow Billy as he brushes past everyone waiting in line and approaches the teller.

"Excuse me, ma'am," he interrupts.

"I'm sorry, Sir, you'll have to wait in line just like everyone else," the middle-aged teller says, dismissing him.

Billy grabs his wallet and flips it open, showing her his badge. "Official police business. I need access to one of the safety deposit boxes."

Concern takes over her face and she asks the customer to step aside, although she immediately starts shaking her head. "No, I'm sorry, I can't do that."

"I'm not asking."

"I can't. I could lose my job."

Billy leans in. "I don't think you understand the gravity of the situation," Billy searches for and finds the name tag on her blouse, "Barbara. We've received a report of a potential bomb on the premises and we need access to this box."

Barbara gasps and covers her mouth with her hands. "A bomb?" she whispers in an attempt to block the conversation from the line of agitated customers.

I look around me. It seems no one has heard the conversation.

"That's right, a bomb. Now, box number 282w. Please."

Barbara hits some keys on her computer and gazes blankly at the screen. "That's an invalid box number," she says.

"Check again."

Barbara hits some more keys and shakes her head. Nothing. "I'll go get the manager, maybe he can help."

I step forward, fearing the man from the photo will recognize me and blow our cover. "No, we don't have time to wait for the manager."

I can tell Billy's surprised at my tone, but he tries not to show it.

"I don't know what you want me to do, the number is invalid," she says.

"What about without the 'W'?"

Barbara hits some more keys and waits for her machine to load. She shakes her head again. She's starting to look rattled and overwhelmed, and she soon begins to cry. Most of the customers have vacated the line behind me, but a few do still remain. One older man sees Barbara crying and looks especially concerned.

This is the last thing we need.

I need to come up with something quickly or this whole thing is going to be busted. Thinking back, I once had a safety deposit box that had five digits. Come to think of it, so did the ones at the bank that I work in, or is it worked now? That must be the problem.

"We're missing a digit," I say. Billy and Barbara both look at me simultaneously. "Most boxes have five digits, not four. Maybe the 'W' is code for something."

There is a brief silence, then Barbara's face lights up. "I got it!" she says excitedly. "'W' could be the location code of the box." She wipes the tears from her cheek and goes back to work on her computer. "Our boxes are sorted by aisle number with each aisle matching with the corresponding alphabetic letter code."

Billy looks at me for approval, but I have no idea what she is talking about; this bank is much larger than what I'm used to.

"Huh?" I say.

"The 'W' represents the twenty-third letter of the alphabet, so if I replace the 'W' with the twenty-three, we might have something." She hits one final button on her computer and waits. "That's it! I can't believe I didn't think of it earlier." She disappears in the back office and returns with a giant looped key ring and walks around the counter. "Follow me." She motions for us to follow her toward the vault, but she stops suddenly. "I almost forgot. The box can't be opened without a second key. The bank has one and the box owner has one."

Billy grins and reaches his hand in his pocket. "That won't be a problem," he says as he proudly shows off the brass key from Snake's safe.

Barbara leads us through a heavily secured door at the back of the bank and into an open room. Metal shelves line the perimeter of the soundproof room from floor to ceiling. Similar longer metal shelves run wall to wall in the opposite direction. Small signs hang from each aisle, each one containing a two digit number. The numbers are in numerical order starting at one and stretching to twenty-six, just as she described.

In aisle twenty-three, about halfway down are the boxes in the two hundreds. Barbara fingers through the boxes until she comes upon 282.

"Here we are," she says as she pulls out the box from the shelf. She brings the compact steel box to her chest and inserts her key into the hole closest to her. She twists the key and disengages the lock on her side. Billy tries to slide his key into the other hole, but it doesn't fit. He flips it upside down and tries again, but it's far too large for the hole. It looks nothing like the key that Barbara has, so it not fitting doesn't surprise me in the least.

Barbara opens her mouth to speak, but Billy cuts her off by tearing the box from her hands. He smashes it against the concrete floor and without warning, pulls out his gun. Barbara shrieks and runs past me, rubbing my shoulder with hers. She and I both bail around the corner just as Billy opens fire on the box.

Six rounds explode before the gun clicks. Barbara covers her ears and sits in the corner, crying hysterically. My ears are ringing from the blasts, but I'm otherwise unharmed. My hands are trembling from the shock of the near miss. I force myself to peek around the corner and inspect the damage Billy has caused.

Below Billy's feet is the box, torn to shreds. All six bullets pierced the box, each one just above the empty keyhole. Barbara's key is still engaged on the other side. I didn't think Billy would ever actually use the gun that he carries around, so this is a real eye opener for me. I fear he might be more dangerous that I had originally thought.

Gauging by his reaction, I can tell that this is not what we were looking for. I'm frightened at what he might do next if and when the pressure intensifies and the heat gets turned up. I watch as Billy is able to pry open what remains of the busted box and sift through the contents. There is a foreign passport belonging to a Chinese man plus a few thousand Yuan wrapped with an elastic band. He tosses the contents to the cement and walks out. Barbara meets him at the doorway.

"What the hell is wrong with you?" she says. "What if there was a bomb in there?"

"It's all clear," Billy replies coldly as he brushes past her and makes his way back into the now empty main lobby of the bank.

Barbara throws her hands on her hips in disbelief at the officer's rudeness. I don't say anything to her as I leave, although I'm tempted to apologize. I hear footsteps running in the background as we exit through the front door of the bank. I turn back and catch a glimpse of Barbara pointing in our direction with a man beside her, probably the manager from the picture frame.

"Don't look back," Billy says as he turns me with a tug on my arm. The quietness from the bank is washed out by the busyness of the morning rush. We turn right onto 53rd Street and blend in with the crowd.

Maybe we're overthinking this whole thing.

CHAPTER TWENTY-SIX

BILLY

Wilson Memorial Psychiatric Hospital is in Hays, Kansas, which is about three hours west of Topeka. We're not going there. Frank was a permanent resident at the facility for four and a half years, starting when he was seventeen. He was involved in a physical altercation with a customer while he was working the register at a fast food restaurant at the time. The guy went nuts over a mistake with his order and Frank just snapped. He went ballistic and threw hot oil all over the guy's face and nearly beat him to death. He was restrained by a group of bystanders in the restaurant until the cops showed up. It was clear as day on the restaurant surveillance, which included audio.

Several witnesses testified at his trial that he looked like he was possessed, like he needed an exorcist or something, and some of the things that were recognizable in the audio recording were actually quite disturbing. The prosecution played the audio over and over for the jury, and it never got any easier to listen to. Our father had hired the best defense team in the state, and they were able to get Frank off reasonably well. He was facing ten to twelve for various charges, and he was being tried as an adult. The jury agreed with the plea of insanity and he was sentenced to five years in Wilson's inpatient care facility instead of prison. The victim's face was pretty badly scarred from the burns, but his vision was unaffected. We never saw or heard from him again after the trial.

Frank was diagnosed early on in his stay with a Borderline Personality Disorder. The most shocking thing about it was that no one even knew there was anything wrong with him before. Sure, he was a little peculiar growing up, but it was just assumed to be social awkwardness. The hospital had told us that BPD patients typically aren't aggressive toward others, but in rare cases they can be. Frank is a rare case. Most BPD patients do the most physical damage to themselves, usually cutting, but Frank never showed signs of wanting to hurt himself. They put him on some combination of medications and enrolled him in various therapy sessions, which helped them find the root cause of his troubles. Our mother's death many years prior probably had something to do with it, although the hospital never did share their findings with dad and me. Frank doesn't like to talk about it.

The hospital felt Frank was ready to be released six months shy of his completed five-year sentence, and the judge agreed. It may have just been an overcrowding situation, but we didn't ask many questions. No one did. Our father agreed to take Frank in and watch over him, so that might have helped, considering his status in the community at the time. When he died, I couldn't just let Frank try to survive on his own. His symptoms are manageable with prescription medication, and social awkwardness is really the only lasting indicator of the disorder. He's a little slow, certain people make him feel uncomfortable, and certain activities can over-stimulate him, but for the most part, he's fairly normal. Whatever normal is.

IT'S 8:15 A.M. AND I'm walking up the stairs of City Hall and making my way toward Alicia's desk. I push past the line of customers and nudge an old lady aside, then I press my face close to the glass that separates Alicia's desk from me. Alicia's eyes bulge and she's apologetic to the line of people, especially to the old woman who I nearly knocked to the floor.

"What are you doing here?" Alicia sternly whispers to me through the glass.

"We have to go, now. It's time."

Alicia's face lights up and she reacts without hesitation. I turn around, rush out of the building, and down the steps. I pull the van in front of the steps and wait with the engine running. It doesn't matter if anyone sees us anymore as we'll be out of here in a matter of days. Alicia comes storming out of the front door less than one minute later and she's in the van moments after. I peel away as the door closes and head home to pick up Frank.

I whip the van into the driveway and park it halfway on the grass. Alicia and I open our doors, jump out, and run inside.

"Frank!" I yell as I kick open the door. "Get up, we've got to move!"

Frank falls off the couch at the startle. It takes him a moment, but he does slowly get to his feet and look to me. "What's goin' on?" he asks, still shaken from his surprise wake up call.

"It's happening, get your stuff together."

A giant smile comes across Frank's face and he quickly rushes past me and into the spare bedroom, his bedroom, or mine depending on how you look at it, and disappears. He almost slips and falls again as his twisted sock catches the corner of the doorframe. Alicia makes her way to the end of the hall and slides into the bedroom. I pull my phone from my pocket and dial the number that is written on the open notepad on the table. It rings four or five times then goes directly to voicemail. I hang up and dial again. He answers before the second ring.

"Hello."

"Is this George Sanders?" I ask.

"Yeah, who's this?" his voice is deeper than I remember, although I didn't hear too much about him besides what I overheard at the coffee shop.

"Do you know an Alicia Diaz?"

"Who is this?"

"Do you know an Alicia Diaz?"

"Who the hell is this?"

"Do you know an Alicia Diaz?"

"Tell me who this is."

"If you know an Alicia Diaz, meet me at Josie's Bar and Pub in thirty minutes."

"What the hell is going on? How did you get this number?"

"I'll be waiting." I hang up before he can counter. I place the phone on the table and turn around. Alicia and Frank are both standing behind me, waiting. Alicia has changed her clothes and Frank has put some on. Alicia hands me a change of clothes and I take them from her. I strip off my uniform and put on the chosen outfit. "Kiss this place goodbye. We can never come back here again."

I take one final look at my first home before leaving for good. I lead the way out the front door with Alicia and Frank trailing closely behind. They both carry some bags of personal belongings and supplies, and I have similar ones waiting for me in the van that I've had prepared for weeks. I kill the lights and lock the front door on the way out, leaving my uniform in a wrinkled mess in the middle of the kitchen floor for whoever to find.

CHAPTER TWENTY-SEVEN

GEORGE

Back to square one.

Billy, Frank, and I are back at Snake's house, searching for something we missed. We're wearing our masks again just in case, although the busted front door should have aired the house out to a safe level by now. Billy is working on the side of the house, peeling more siding off near the hole where the safe is. Frank is sorting through the destroyed interior of the house again. I'm outside, walking the perimeter of the small yard.

Much of the grass is uncared for and burnt. I can tell the soil is sandy, so it's probably difficult to grow anything. Clumps of weeds crumble beneath me as I step. I scan the flatlands as I make my way around the perimeter, searching for the unknown. My shoes sink in the occasional weak spot as I make small squares inside of larger squares as I pace. A young garter snake slithers past me at one point, but nothing else catches my attention.

When my squares have covered the entire yard, I make my way toward the side of the house to check in on the progress Billy has made. The right side of the house is almost completely stripped of the vinyl siding, much of it broken into pieces on the ground below. Some of the wooden studs are rotted and splitting, which could be the result of termite damage. Billy's not there, so I head inside.

The upstairs is empty and Billy and Frank are nowhere to be found. I can spot the van through the window in the living room, confirming they haven't gone anywhere. It would've been nice if they had. The door in the hallway is cracked open slightly and I hear a noise from behind it. I approach it, pull it open, and head down the stairs. I hold onto the railing as I climb down so I don't slip on the fluids left behind. Snake's body still lays on the concrete below. The mask conceals the smell of the decomposing body a bit, but my stomach still churns as I get closer to it. I shield myself and refuse to look directly at it for fear I may vomit in my own face. Billy notices me right away as I stumble around the corpse.

"What did you find out?" he asks.

I shrug. "Nothing, what about you?"

Billy shakes his head, then Frank does the same. Billy lets out a long sigh. He sounds exhausted. The basement is musty and dry and has a cracked window that leads out to the backyard. Some light is shining through the bulkhead stairway. Billy and Frank stand next to one another and talk quietly, trying to come up with a new idea I suppose.

Many of the pipes overhead are separated and cracked, probably from when Billy did his damage previously. A stack of collapsed moving boxes fill one of the corners and a nest of dead spiders fills another. Standard yard maintenance tools line the wall to my left: a rake, shovel, push-style lawn mower, and a garbage barrel full of grass clippings. It seems as if someone actually did care about this place at one point in time. That must have been before Snake moved in.

As the sun changes its direction outside, the small window moves a shadow away from the stairway leading to the bulkhead. I didn't notice before, but a thin trail of something, maybe a water stain or line of animal droppings, lead toward the wall of landscaping tools. As I move closer to get a better look, it becomes apparent that the trail is actually a line of dirt. The dirt path leads directly to the barrel with the grass clippings. It looks like the barrel was dragged from the bulkhead staircase to its current position resting against the foundation wall. I'm no expert by any means, but it must be relatively fresh, or it would have been kicked around at some point from people walking through it. Curious, I crouch down next to the shovel and rub my finger across the blade. A line of dirt wipes onto my fingertip.

"Hey," I say, capturing the attention of Billy and Frank, "check this out."

They approach and Billy crouches next to me. "What is it?" he asks.

"This shovel has some dirt on it."

Billy looks at me, dumbfounded. "Yeah, that's because it's a shovel."

Frank giggles, and the sarcasm pisses me off. I'm the one doing all the work here. I push it away. "So does the barrel. It feels kind of fresh."

Billy swipes his finger across the blade of the shovel, just as I did, and a line of dirt imprints his fingertip. Billy stands and passes the shovel over to Frank, who grabs it by the wooden handle. Billy motions in the direction of the barrel, then Frank jams the head of the shovel inside. He tosses the first layer of grass clippings to the cement floor. Billy watches intently as Frank repeats the process three times over. On the fourth toss, a pile of dirt falls on top of the pile of grass clippings on the floor. Billy approaches the mess and looks into the barrel.

"The rest is full of dirt," he says.

I stand and look into the barrel myself, confirming what Billy has just announced. Frank takes a peek too, feeling left out. Billy turns to me and meets my eyes; we're both thinking the same thing I think.

"Why would there be a barrel full of dirt?" Frank asks.

"Maybe someone dug a hole and there was some leftover dirt," Billy says.

I nod in agreement.

He continues, "And they had to put the extra dirt somewhere."

Frank nods, but he doesn't look like he understands.

Billy turns to me. "Okay, so where?"

I think about it for a moment and come up with an idea. "Can I see that note?"

Billy fetches the torn paper from his pocket and hands it to me. I study it briefly and hand it back to him.

"Do you have a compass?"

CHAPTER TWENTY-EIGHT

BILLY

Alicia, Frank, and I wait in the van across the street from Josie's Bar and Pub with an eye on the parking lot. Alicia is sitting next to me in the front while Frank is in the back, preparing for action.

Alicia and I are together now, as in a couple, and we're most certainly on the same page. Our relationship has grown over the last six weeks, and I trust her completely. We haven't slept together yet, but I'm working on that. Our relationship is still new, and we've had some arguments and disagreements, but I expect those to fade out over time as we spend more time together. I know she's still having a hard time with having to do this to George, but it's what needs to be done. She's still not convinced about what should happen when this is all over, but there is no time to deal with that now. We'll have to figure it out when the time comes.

It's been just about thirty minutes since the call, so I expect George will be rolling in at any moment. Just as this thought crosses my mind, I catch his car whirling around the corner.

"Here he comes," I say. "Right on time."

Alicia tenses as she spots the car and Frank makes a strange noise in celebration from the back. I observe as George gets out of his car and makes his way toward the pub. I start the engine as George pulls on the double doors across the street.

"Okay, let's go," I say. "Hang on tight back there."

I jam the van into gear and take off toward the parking lot. The tires squeal as I whip around the corner and speed toward George as he approaches his car. He stops and turns to face the van, then I slam on the brakes and spin the wheel hard to the left, whirling the back end toward him. The van comes to a stop and Frank pushes open the back doors. He reaches his arm out toward George, grabs his collar, and pulls him into the van. Before George can even process what has happened, Frank grabs my unloaded gun from the bench behind him and slams it into the back of George's head. George falls face first onto the floor of the van and is knocked out cold.

Alicia gasps at the sound of the thud of George's head hitting the floor.

WE HAVE MADE A few of changes to the old police station while we waited for the need to use it. With Frank's help, I had installed one of those sensors in the back that will open the garage door when a vehicle drives over it. There is a minimum weight threshold needed to engage the sensor, which the van does meet.

To keep Frank busy and involved, I had him clean up the place a bit. I wasn't going to hire a cleaning company, obviously, as the inspector suggested, but I agreed that it needed to be cleaned up a bit. We're going to be spending quite a bit of time here for the next handful of days, so it needs to be livable. The final addition we made to the building is being tested out right now. Frank spent a couple days tearing up a section of the floor in the open holding area and installing a chair. He used a rented jackhammer and a chair we found in one of the old offices and cemented it to the floor.

ALICIA, FRANK, AND I are looking through a two-way mirror that separates the holding area that George is in from the old interrogation room that we are in. Even though the lights are off in the room, we can see him pretty well thanks to the reflection of the light from our room against the mirror. George is strapped to the chair, his wrists and ankles tied to the arms and legs. He's been unconscious for a couple of hours since Frank knocked him out in the van. The idea wasn't to hurt him, but we needed to make sure he cooperated. We struggled to carry his limp body inside through the garage and keep him upright long enough to strap him down. He was breathing then, and I can see he still is now as the rhythm of his chest compressions have been regular and consistent.

Finally, George begins to stir. He gathers himself and looks around in a panic. It takes him a few minutes to realize that he's strapped down, and he screams out for help when he does. I look to Frank and motion toward the door of the interrogation room. He leaves and heads toward the holding room. When Alicia and I are alone, I pull out a knife from my pocket and open it up.

"Wait," Alicia says.

"What?" I hold the knife still as I wait for further information.

"I can't do this."

"Jesus Christ, I thought we talked about this," I snap.

"I know. We did. I thought I would be okay with it, but seeing him like this, I just can't do it."

"Well too bad. We've made it this far, there's no turning back now."

"But-"

"No. Not buts. You don't have any choice in the matter any-more. You will do as I say or-"

"Or what, Billy? Are you going to shoot me?" She stares at me, challenging me.

"Don't test me." I stare back at her, and she backs down. "Now sit down so we can do this. Please."

Alicia reluctantly sits in the chair that is in front of the two-way mirror and crosses her arms. I kneel down and stretch her blouse out in front of her. I use the knife to cut a jagged sliver into the ma-terial to make it look like it was torn in a struggle. I grab a handful of dirt and dust from the floor and rub it onto her knees. While still crouched in front of her, I loosely tie her ankles to the legs of the chair. I don't tighten the knots, so she can move her legs freely if she wants, but it looks the part. I rise to my feet and do the same thing to her wrists.

"I'll be back in a few minutes," I say, then I take a handful of her hair from the back and push it over her face before leaving the room.

A few minutes later, I head back to the interrogation room, steaming from George trying to attack me. He saw Alicia through the mirror and flipped. It served its purpose, but I didn't expect him to act so aggressively that quickly. As I enter the room, I see that Alicia has freed herself from the chair and is violently pacing the room. She has tears streaming down her face.

"You son of a bitch!" she says, then she runs over to me and starts pounding on my upper torso with her open hands as she screams profanities at me. I catch her wrists and overpower her, pushing her against the wall with her arms above her head.

"Calm down."

"You said you weren't going to hurt him!"

"I had no choice, he was going for my weapon."

Tears continue to pour down her cheeks and her makeup is starting to run. I take a deep breath and slowly release some tension from my grasp of her wrists. I move one hand down to her face to wipe the tears, but she slaps my hand away with her free one.

"I'm done. I can't do this. I want out."

Her resistance is starting to push me over the edge, and now is not the time to have this conversation. I grab her wrists again and push her with a greater degree of force into the wall. I can see the fear in her eyes as the frustration pours out of me.

"Stop," she says, "you're hurting me!"

"Shut up!" I grab the knife from my pocket and flip the blade out. I bring it close to her neck and I move my face close to hers. "The only way you get out is in a body bag. If you say another thing about it, I will cut your fucking throat and leave you to bleed to death on the floor. You got that?"

She looks helpless, and I feel a little guilty for that, but I need her to understand that I'm not screwing around. Not anymore. I pull the blade away from her neck and fold it before putting it back in my pocket. I slide my hand from her wrists and grab her around the waist.

I struggle to restrain her as she fights while I drag her down the hallway. She's kicking my legs and screaming at me, but it's all just noise. I swing open the closet door near the holding room and throw Alicia inside where George is already waiting.

"Two minutes," I say. I think she falls to the floor when I push her, but I slam the door without getting a good look to confirm.

I pace up and down the hallway for a couple of minutes and try to regain my composure. I thought she had come around and was on my side and I thought that I could trust her. Obviously, I cannot. I'm going to have to take extra precautions to ensure she stays in line. I was hoping to avoid this, but I've been preparing for the possibility of it. I'll now have to treat her like a prisoner and not a partner in this. I hate to do it, but I can't risk her trying to run. She has just made double the work for me.

Two minutes is up, or close to it, so I go back to the closet and whip the door open. I reach inside and grab Alicia's arm, pulling her into the hallway. I slam the door in George's face.

"Did you say it?" I demand.

She's still frantic, so she doesn't respond right away. I squeeze her arm tighter and ask again. She shakes her head.

"Say it right now or you're dead."

She wails at the force of my grip, but she does eventually yell out to George as I pull her away.

"George, I'm pregnant!"

CHAPTER TWENTY-NINE

GEORGE

The yard surrounding Snake's house looks like a war zone. Frank has spent the last hour digging shallow holes with no apparent logical pattern. Holes are scattered across the lawn with patches of untouched square footage left between them. Stacks of dirt are piled up in various places. As there is only one shovel, Billy takes me for a drive to go find a compass while Frank puts his physical frame to good use.

I must be gaining Billy's trust. He lets me sit in the front seat without my wrists being tied or without a blindfold covering my eyes as he drives. It's nice to not have the rope tear open my calluses again. Billy's attitude has changed. I can hear the excitement in his voice as he talks about the next step after we find the money. He lets his guard down a bit and is a little careless probably, which is unlike him. I do my best not to make it look obvious that I'm taking mental snapshots and studying the surroundings. I don't think he notices. He's too busy talking.

Billy tells me that has to make a pit stop at the warehouse before swinging by the local outdoor store to pick up a compass. He doesn't say for what, and I don't ask. He runs inside and leaves me alone in the van with the key still in the ignition and the engine running. I might be giving him too much credit, but the possibility of this being a test does cross my mind. I consider making a break for it in the van, but the finish line seems near, so I think better of it. Instead, I try to figure out where I am.

Once I see the rusty outline of letters on the side of the building, I can't believe I didn't put things together before. Years ago, the Topeka Police Department built and moved to a new station. The old unit was on 12ᵗʰ Street, which is where we are now and where we've been hiding out in, and it's just a few miles from my house. Billy must have kept a key to the old place without them knowing all this time. Strangely, as I think about it, the electricity is working, hence the lights and garage door, so someone must be paying for that. How the city hasn't picked up on that is a different question, perhaps one that will be answered down the line. Something strange is definitely going on, though, I know that much.

A slamming car door breaks my concentration. I look over and Billy is sitting next to me in the van. I didn't even see him come back outside. He studies me intently and he clenches his teeth. I can see his jawbone through his face as he tightens the muscle. He must have seen me staring at the building and I wonder if he realizes his mistake. I get my answer as we drive the rest of the way in silence.

FRANK IS SITTING IN the shade holding the shovel between his legs when we return. The sweat has saturated his shirt and a dark stain protrudes from under his armpits. His productivity is impressive, but exhaustion and dehydration have taken him over. Billy tosses him an unopened bottle of water, and Frank guzzles it down. He gags a little toward the end from drinking it too quickly.

"Find anything?" Billy asks, directed to Frank.

"Nothin', boss."

Billy nods as he uses a pocket knife to cut through the plastic packaging that holds a plastic compass. "Does anyone know how to use one of these?"

Frank shrugs.

"I'll take a look," I say as I hold out my hand.

Billy cuts through the rest of the package and hands me the compass. I used one once before when my college roommate and I got lost during a camping trip in Michigan, but it's been a few years. I place the compass in the palm of my hand and spin myself around until the needle points into the western quadrant. I maneuver myself so the arrow rests on the 282.

"This is 282 degrees west," I continue.

Billy removes the note from his pocket and reads it aloud, "282w53s. What about the 53? Add 53 to the 282, what do you get?"

I close my eyes and add it up, then peek at the compass. "335, but that's northwest. That doesn't make sense."

Billy grunts. "Subtract it then."

I close my eyes again and make the calculation. "229." I look down at the compass. "That's southwest. That could work."

Billy turns to Frank. "Check it."

Frank jumps to his feet and moves toward us with the shovel. "Where?"

"Right here," Billy says. "This is 229 degrees southwest."

Frank pauses and looks like he wants to say something, but he doesn't. He starts to dig. Billy stands with his hands on his hips and supervises.

As Frank digs I begin to question myself. Holding the compass still, I walk backward a few steps, then back forward and around Frank. The compass doesn't change.

"I don't think is right," I say.

Frank stops, and Billy looks at me.

"What do you mean?" Billy asks.

"229 degrees southwest is this entire path." I pendulum my arm back and forth, drawing an invisible line in midair. "229 degrees extends for an infinite distance. It's never ending."

Billy brings his hand to his face and rubs his chin. "You might be right."

"Plus, why would it be written that way?"

"Written what way?"

"The 282 west, then 53 south. That's just a little strange, don't you think? The 53 would come first if it was southwest."

"Unless he wanted to make it difficult for someone to find."

"Maybe."

There is a brief silence.

"What do you suggest?" Billy says, ending it.

"I don't know, maybe it's a measurement or something. 282 degrees west, then 53 something."

"But what?"

I shake my head. "Not sure. You know these people better than I do, you tell me."

We stand in silence while the sun beats down on us. Frank's skin is burning from being in the heat all day.

"I got it!" Frank blurts. "Centimeters! 53 centimeters."

Billy rolls his eyes. "No, that's not it."

"How do you know?"

"Because centimeters starts with a 'C' and not an 'S', you fucking idiot."

Frank's head drops in disappointment. "Oh."

Sensing Billy's frustration, I turn around and begin walking the path, keeping the compass steady at 282 degrees. I look up as I approach the side of the house. I peer at the compass, then back at the house. 282 degrees is pointing directly at the torn up exterior wall of the house where the safe is.

I holler to Billy, "Hey, come here."

Billy makes his way toward me, slowly, with Frank following closely behind. "What is it?" Billy says when he gets close enough to hear.

"What about steps? 53 steps," I say.

"53 steps from where?"

I point toward the side of the house. "Look. The compass is pointing directly to the safe at 282 degrees."

Billy cocks his head slightly to read the compass. He yanks it from my hand to check himself. "Holy shit."

WITH HIS BACK AGAINST the siding, Billy walks toward Frank and me, counting each step aloud as he moves. He counts out fifty-two steps then slams his feet together on the last.

"Here," he says.

Frank hustles over to him and starts to dig. He stacks piles of dirt to the side as he quickly begins and widens a hole. He thrusts the shovel into the hole and it hits something solid, and the shovel vibrates in his hands.

"What was that?" Billy asks, fully alert.

Frank jams the head of the shovel into the dirt again and the vibration returns. Billy rips the shovel from Frank's hands and pushes him aside. He pushes some dirt around with the shovel then drops to his knees. Using his hands, he wipes dirt to the side until a wooden box peeks through the earth. He flicks dirt behind him like a playing dog until most of the box is visible. He reaches down and pulls on the box, but it doesn't budge. Frank jumps in and grabs the back side, and they pull on it again, which frees it from the hole. They drop it on the ground beside us.

The box has thick walls and a secured lid, and it looks fairly new. It's three feet wide and three feet tall with an oversized lock on the lid. Billy takes the key from the safe out of his pocket, jams it into the lock, and turns. The lock clicks and snaps open. Billy removes it and tosses it to the side. He lifts the lid and slides it to the back so the hinges hold it in place. Billy and Frank both look inside and their jaws drop. I poke my head around the side and also peek inside.

Stacked top to bottom and covering the entire surface area is what we've been looking for, the holy grail of criminal activity. My eyes widen and my heart begins to pound. Frank reaches his hand in, but it's swatted away by Billy.

"We fucking did it," Billy says as he drops to his rear. Frank pulls Billy toward him and squeezes him. Typically, Billy would have cussed him out and swung at him probably, but he doesn't seem to notice. Not right now. He can't remove his eyes from the box, and neither can I.

I have never seen that much cash before.

CHAPTER THIRTY

BILLY

Alicia hates me for making her say that to George, she told me. It worked, though, as he said he would help. I expected nothing less, although I didn't have an alternative plan in case he refused, so I'm secretly relieved. I guess I would have offed him if he declined.

Then what would we have done?

Regardless, he's on board now, so we go right to work. I lock Alicia in the interrogation room with the two-way mirror, despite her resistance. She kicks and screams, but I'm eventually able to force her in the room with Frank's help and lock the door. Now what the hell do I do with her? It's an issue to deal with later, though; there are more pressing issues at hand.

In the van on top of the hill overlooking Snake's house, I give vague instructions to George on what to look for once he gets into the house. Equipped with an AT&T polo shirt and ball cap that I swiped from a giveaway at the mall last week, I advise him to play the network maintenance card. "Tell him you work for the company and that you need to check the network," I tell him. I don't know if it's going to work, but George's innocence and non-threatening demeanor should get him in the door at least. Snake isn't stupid, but I'm hoping he'll fall for it.

Please fall for it.

Once inside, George is to look for somewhere that Snake could be hiding all the money. I don't know specific details on when the transfer of the cash happened or where it occurred, but I can't imagine he would wait more than twenty-four hours to pick up the loot. Some of it was likely paid up front, so there should be cash in the house already since people like Snake don't use banks. It won't be out in the open, but it will be somewhere accessible for a quick escape if needed.

We'll see what George can find.

Frank and I sit alone, nervously. There is a cell tower to my left, and I smoke a cigarette out the window. The nicotine numbs my lungs and gives me the high that I need to help me relax. We watch as George slowly makes his way toward Snake's front door. He turns to face us before knocking on the door.

"Come on, George," I whisper to no one as we wait for the action. The door appears to crack open slightly, so I crouch down and out of sight. Frank is in the back and is easily hidden. I'm able to peek around the mirror on my door and continue to watch the action. Moments later, Snake is outside the door and face to face with George, pointing a gun in his face. It's tough to see his face from here, but it sure looks like the Adrian that I know. Part of me wants to take aim and end this all right now, but there is something I need from him first.

"What are they talkin' about?" Frank asks from the back.

It's a rhetorical question, so I don't respond. He asks again, so I shush him, as if I am trying to eavesdrop on the conversation from a few hundred feet away. I can hear nothing, but I try to concentrate in case I'm needed as backup.

"He's in!" I blurt excitedly as Snake pushes George into the house and closes the door. I must admit, I'm impressed with George's ability to think on his feet. It's amazing what people can do when their life is on the line.

Less than a minute later, George is pushed out the front door and is soon walking back toward us. His hat is gone, but he appears to be in one piece. I don't know what he said in there to piss Snake off, but I can hear the echoes of Snake yelling, even from this distance. George has no idea how lucky he is to be alive.

I've seen Snake kill for much less.

Staying low and out of sight in case Snake is watching, which he probably is, I slide across the bench and into the passenger's seat. George approaches the van and enters in through the driver's side. He starts it up and moves it behind the cell tower, just out of sight of the house. I keep a hand on my gun on my hip since he's in control of the van, just in case.

The ride back to the old police station goes quickly, and I do my best to organize my thoughts with the confirmed information that George discovered inside the house. I wasn't expecting the safe to be inside the wall, but it does make sense. Having some familiarity with criminals and how their minds work, it was a near certainty that Snake had a safe somewhere. I was expecting it would be built into an end table or a bureau or something, but having it inside the wall could be quicker to access for an emergency withdrawal. Luckily, I did my homework, so I'm fully prepared to crack the safe.

Almost.

When we're a few miles out from the old police station, Frank ties George's hands together in front of him and loosely covers his eyes with his own tie. I consider telling him that it isn't necessary since the windows in the back of the van are tinted and covered with a sheet, but I decide to let it go. He could use something to keep him busy. I pull the van in through the rear of the station and close the garage behind us.

I had engaged the child safety lock on the back doors to the van when we brought George inside when he was unconscious earlier, so I have to get out and open the doors from the outside. I can't risk him trying to get away. I pull Frank aside before he leads George out of the van.

"Bring him inside and toss him back in the holding area, "I say. "Cut him loose when he's in there, we don't want him to feel like he's being held against his will."

"Where you goin'?"

"I have some supplies I need to go pickup."

"Right now?"

"Right now."

Frank nods, but he looks a little uneasy about the idea.

"Just keep the doors locked and you'll be fine. I won't be long." I consider giving him my gun for protection, but he's proven that he can't be trusted with it. I know what kind of damage he's capable of inflicting, and although he takes his medicine every morning, I just can't have that. Just ask the guy from the fast food place if Frank's capable of causing harm. He'll tell you.

Frank leans in the back of the van and guides George out while he holds onto the rope between his wrists. He closes the doors and leads them into the station through the side door.

"One more thing," I say before they make their way through the doorway. "Don't let the girl out until I get back."

CHAPTER THIRTY-ONE

GEORGE

Everything that was in the black duffel bag that Billy's been carrying around is scattered across the lawn: a handgun, steel bar, police badge, and the three gas masks, among other things. The wooden box that was unearthed from the dirt is now empty and the contents are in the bag. Billy sniffs the final stack of cash before placing it into the duffel bag. He zips it, throws it over his shoulder, and points in the direction of the scattered contents on the ground.

"Pick that stuff up, will you?"

Frank reacts immediately and gathers the items as Billy and I make our way back toward the van.

"What now?" I ask.

"Yeah, what now, boss?" Frank's breath is heavy as he hustles to catch up to us.

"We're done. I guess that's it," Billy says.

"So I can go home then?"

Billy nods.

"With Alicia?"

He hesitates. "With Alicia."

"What about us, boss?" Frank interrupts.

"We'll leave in the morning."

"Where you guys going?" I ask.

Billy looks at me but doesn't say anything. He's made one mistake too many by letting me see where they've been keeping me, so he won't make another.

"Mexico, baby!" Frank blurts out.

Billy snaps his head around at Frank and smacks him in the back of the head.

"What was that for?"

Billy pauses, smiles, then he wraps his arm around Frank. He pulls him ahead of me so they're alone. I can't make out what he's saying, but Billy whispers something in Frank's ear, which Frank seems to enjoy. They're glowing as they walk the rest of the way to the van, Billy's arm still casually dangling around Frank's shoulder the entire time.

I can't help but smile too.

THE CASH IS BURSTING out of the unzipped bag as it rests on the tabletop. The three of us are sitting around the table in one of the offices back at the old police station. Frank is falling asleep in the chair from physical exhaustion, and Billy is doing the same from mental. Billy holds a stack of hundreds in his hands while he fights his body's urge to sleep. I'm wide awake, still high on an adrenaline rush, and ready to go home. The door behind me creaks open and Alicia enters the room. Her mouth drops and her pupils dilate when she sees the bag on the table.

"Oh my God," she says, "you actually did it! I can't believe it!"

Billy and Frank both startle at the sound of her voice and awaken from their trances. I pop up from my chair and run over to her. I grab her hand.

"It's over," I say. "We can go home now." She musters a weak smile and almost starts to cry. I turn to Billy. "When are we leaving?"

"In the morning."

"What? No, I want to leave now. You have your money."

"In the morning I said."

"We had a deal."

Billy rolls his eyes. "Did you not hear me say, 'in the fucking morning'?" His frustration is obvious.

"No, the hell with that. We had a deal and I did my part. You have your fucking money, so I'm leaving now whether you like it or not." I put my hand on the base of Alicia's back and lead her out the door. We'll walk back to Josie's and pick my car up from there.

She gasps before we can exit the room.

I turn around and look toward Billy, who's suddenly standing next to us. His left hand is wrapped around Alicia's wrist and his right hand holds a gun, which is pointed in my face. The barrel digs into the bone above my nose. Billy's bloodshot eyes are locked in on mine and the vein in his forehead is pulsating.

"You're not going anywhere."

CHAPTER THIRTY-TWO

BILLY

It's almost 8:30 P.M. by the time I arrive at the self-storage unit across town. The facility is outdoors and is open for twenty-four hours a day, so I'm able to weave through the narrow driving paths in the van. The posted speed limit is five miles per hour, and I can't go much quicker than that anyway due to the sharp corners and wide vehicle frame. I rented the unit out four or five weeks ago now, and I've visited periodically since then with the new items that had arrived from overseas.

Inside the unit rests a single worn out plastic storage container without a lid. I had ordered a few masks online from a company in Sweden that specializes in zombie apocalypse survival goods, and a gas mask apparently is included in those supplies. There are companies all across the United States that offer the same type of products, but I was looking for a specific type of mask, one that I could only find outside of the country. The masks need to filter out carbon monoxide specifically, and that is something that is a bit difficult to find, I discovered. Carbon monoxide is odorless and colorless, which is perfect for what we're trying to do, but it could be extremely dangerous for us if we're not protected properly.

Also in the box are some short pieces of foam, each cut in lengths of exactly six inches, from which I had picked up at the local home improvement store. The foam is cut from a spool of weather stripping, so it's made to block the outside air from going in and the air inside from going out.

Lastly, and perhaps most importantly, are two small rounded Tupperware containers, each enclosing a separate substance. The first is a small amount of a reddish black powder that looks like a mixture of paprika and cinnamon, but it's far from it. It's thermite, and it's powerful. It won't explode, which is critical, but it can and will burn through steel. The tricky part is that most igniters don't get hot enough to light the thermite, so that's where the magnesium comes into play; that's what's in the other container, a few thin metallic strips of magnesium.

Since thermite is not an explosive, it's not illegal to own, but it was a bitch to find. I did some digging around and made some calls, and I did eventually find some locally. I found the guy online but never did find out his name. He got his hands on a big chunk of the material from somewhere, he wouldn't say where, and I didn't ask many questions. I met him after hours one night in street clothes, and we made the cash transaction quickly and seamlessly.

After fingering through the supplies in the box, I pick it up and load it into the back of the van. I leave the padlock hanging from the storage unit, unlocked, and make my way back around the rows of units and toward the exit. I leased the unit on a month-to-month basis, and I already paid for July, so I'll just leave the lock for the next person. I have no use for it anymore.

I WAIT FOR THE garage door to open while the front tires of the van rest on the sensor. When it does, I pull into the empty garage and close the door behind me. With the box in hand, I struggle with the door handle of the old station, but I am eventually able to get it open. The hallway is empty and the lights are dim, and it's silent. I peek in a couple of the old offices near the doorway, but Frank is nowhere to be found. At the other end of the hallway, I catch a glimpse of a shadowy figure weaving through the offices.

"Frank, is that you?" I yell out to the figure. My voice echoes in the emptiness.

No response.

I enter one of the offices and place the box of goods on the table before making my way down the hall. "Frank?"

There is some shuffling in the room adjacent to my position in the hallway, but still no response from Frank. I slide my hand down to my hip before entering the room, enabling myself for quick action if the gun is needed. To my delight, the racket is coming from

Frank, who is shuffling furniture around the room. I allow myself to relax.

"What the hell are you doing?" I ask.

Frank is startled and quickly turns to me. "Jeez, you scared me."

"I've been calling your name. What the hell are you doing in here?"

"I'm looking for something."

"I can see that." I wait, but he doesn't seem too keen on offering more information voluntarily, so I press further. "What are you looking for?"

"Uh...well, not something. More like someone."

My face drops and I'm instantly concerned. "What do you mean? Who?"

"Well...the girl may have got out."

Concern is replaced with anger, and I walk toward Frank. I get in his face. "You better be messing around. Tell me you're messing around."

"Sorry, boss."

Not knowing what else to do, I grab one of the many chairs that are scattered across the room and throw it. It smashes into a rusty file cabinet and one of the legs snaps off. Frank leaps back and covers his head as the metal on metal clashes.

"What the hell happened, Frank? I told you not to let her out until I got back."

She was yelling, so I went in there, and she said she really had to pee. She said the baby was pushing on her bladder."

I slide my hand down and retrieve the gun from my hip and begin to pace the room. I shake my head in disgust and try to decide whether to put a bullet in Frank's head or not. He had one job, and he fucked it up, of course. How stupid can someone be? I take a moment to gather myself and put the gun back in the holster on my hip before I do something stupid. I will need Frank down the line, so I needn't overreact. How far could she have gone?

"Frank, my brother," I speak slowly to keep myself relaxed, "Alicia is not really pregnant."

Frank's jaw drops as if this is news to him.

"It was just a trick to get George to play along. Now, I need you to think for me. Tell me exactly what happened."

Frank pauses and looks at the ceiling, trying to retrace what happened in his mind. I move next to him and put my arm around his shoulders.

"Okay. I went in there, and she said she had to pee-"

"I got that part. What happened after that?"

"Right, okay. So I let her out and walked with her to the bathroom, then she said she needed some privacy, so I waited outside. She came out when she was done, and I started walking her back. She asked where you were and I said you'd be back soon. She told me she would go back to the room and wait for you because she wanted to talk to you about something."

"Did she say what it was?"

"No. She wasn't crying anymore, though, she seemed happier than she was before."

I nod. "Okay, so what happened after that?"

"She seemed better, so I went back into one of the other rooms to wait for you and she went back to where she was. Then I heard a door close. That's it."

"How did you find out she was missing?"

"I thought I heard her talking to someone, so I went to check it out. But when I got there she was gone."

I ponder this for a moment, and that's all it takes for me to figure out what happened. I'm relieved, and I smile at the realization. "Did you happen to look at the big two-way mirror on the wall when you went in there?"

Frank shrugs.

I continue, "I didn't think so. There's no way you could have heard that door close. You would have never heard it through the walls. That room is on the other side of the building. The sound would have been muffled by the surrounding rooms."

"I heard a door close, I swear."

"I believe you."

Frank is shocked. "You do?"

"I believe you heard a door close, but not *that* door close."

Frank just stares at me, dumbfounded.

"Did you check the room George is in?"

"No."

"Why not?"

"It's locked."

I roll my eyes at his stupidity. Maybe he will be more of a liability than I thought. "Yeah, from the inside, you fucking idiot."

Frank hangs his head, obviously embarrassed. I turn and leave the room. Frank follows. I make my way to the holding cell where George is being held and open the door. George and Alicia are both standing there, having a discussion, and they're startled at the sound of the door. I turn to Frank, who avoids my eyes.

"Go get her," I say. "Bring her to the room and close the door yourself. Make sure it's closed. Then meet me in the first office next to the back door, I have some stuff to show you."

Frank doesn't say anything as he walks past me and approaches Alicia. He grabs her arm from behind and leads her out of the room. I give Frank a head start by having a staring contest with George. What were they talking about I wonder? He looks exhausted already, as his eyes are heavy and glazed over.

"Come with me," I say, motioning for George to follow.

He does.

I lead him into the office where I put the box of supplies from the storage unit. Frank is already inside and has moved the box to the floor. He is playing with one of the gas masks in his lap, most certainly trying to figure out its purpose. I trust Alicia is in the same interrogation room as before, waiting to speak with me about something. It better be an apology.

CHAPTER THIRTY-THREE

GEORGE

I spend the evening alone in the empty room with the leaky ceiling. The pillow and blanket are gone from the corner, so I have nothing but the cold cement to keep me company. I can hear someone sitting by and guarding outside the door the whole night. At one point I hear some snoring, which actually gave me some comfort and allows me to relax for a while. I don't sleep much as I'm on high alert, but I must have fallen asleep at some point, because the sound of Billy's voice wakes me.

"We can go now," he says.

Once I compose myself, I drag my stiff body from the cement floor and wobble to the door, trying to gather myself after a rough night. Billy seems to be in a better mood already, well-rested and with clear eyes.

"They're waiting for us in the van," he continues.

I follow Billy down the long corridor for the last time, knowing my life will never be the same again. Frank and Alicia are waiting in the van as expected when we arrive. I hop in the back and sit next to Alicia on the bench while Billy jumps in the front. Frank is sitting opposite us on the other bench. Alicia doesn't look up when I sit next to her, but does when I place my hand on her naked forearm. She offers a simple smile. Something is bothering her, but I can't tell what it is. She's probably just exhausted. I realize now that I don't really even know her that well, and this new life together is going to be challenging. Challenging but rewarding I hope. I think about this and our unborn child as we ride in silence, my hand resting on her forearm the entire time.

After a few right turns and stops and restarts, the van comes to a complete stop and the parking brake engages. The front door opens and I can hear Billy walking around the side of the van. The back door slides open and the morning sun shines in, forcing me to shield my eyes from the brightness.

"You can go," Billy says to me from outside the van.

Surprised it's this easy, I stand from the bench and head for the door. I catch a glance of Frank, who is sitting with his head down, looking a little sad. He doesn't look up so I don't say anything. I reach back, expecting Alicia to grab my hand, then leap onto the pavement next to Billy.

My Civic rests in the same parking spot I left it a few days prior, just before all of this happened. A yellow piece of paper is wedged between the windshield and the wiper, a parking ticket I assume. I can't tell for certain from here, but there might be a boot on the passenger's side wheel too. I see these things and they would have bothered me in the past and completely ruined my day. But now, it all seems so trivial. Nothing else I can experience in my life from this point forward can be as difficult as what I've gone through and survived in the last three days. Even the thought of having to try to figure out how to be a dad on the fly seems to be no big deal. That, in combination with trying to build a relationship and co-parent with Alicia, this woman that I barely know, at the same time seems like a minute task at this point.

I turn back into the van to help Alicia step down, but she's still sitting on the bench across from Frank.

"Come on, let's go," I say to her, but she stays sitting. I look to Billy, who stares back at me, emotionless. Frank still has his head down. "What are you doing?"

Tears fill her eyes as she starts to speak, "George, I-"

A few loud bangs interrupt her thoughts, one right after the next. Billy's head spins around and he scans the parking lot. He throws himself to the ground and shields his head as the echoes continue to fill the sky. He pulls me down so I'm crouched next to him.

"What the hell's going on?" I ask.

"We've got to get out of here!"

"What's going on?"

"They're shooting at us!"

"What? Who is?"

"Snake's men, they must have found us."

Billy waits for the next shot then hops in the back of the van, where Frank and Alicia are now on high alert.

"What's going on? What's happening?" Alicia asks frantically.

"We've got to go." Billy slides his way to the front and stays low as he puts the van in drive. "Get in the van!"

I'm still crouched down, torn between making a run for my car or listening to the voice inside the van.

"Get in the van," he repeats. "We're leaving in two seconds."

Frank offers his hand out to me. "Come on, Georgie!"

I see Alicia inside the van, and she has a panicked look on her face, and I make up my mind. I can't leave her, not like this.

"Now!" Billy yells from the front.

I reach up and grab Frank's extended hand. With one smooth yank, he pulls me into the van and releases my hand. I fall to my knees. He slams the back doors using the handles on the inside and the sunlight disappears between the cracks. The van peels away from the parking lot, the tires squealing and the engine revving, as Frank reaches into one of the two duffel bags on the floor and fetches out a gun. He places it in the passenger's seat as Billy swerves into oncoming traffic. The recurring gun shots in the background are masked by the bellowing car horns and screeching brakes from the street.

Alicia screams as she fights to keep herself on the bench, and Frank is fumbling through the same bag on the floor. I'm still on the floor of the van and I'm tossed around from side-to-side with each hard steer.

After what I expect is a few miles of sharp turns and high speeds, the van finally slows down and comes to a stop. Billy climbs into the back and starts tossing the contents of one of the bags, the one with the supplies, across the van.

"Where is it?" he demands. He tosses items in every which direction, determined to find whatever he's looking for.

"Where's what, boss?"

I try my best to dodge the flying objects, but something soft hits me square in the face. Billy grabs the bag from its base and pours the remainder of the contents on the floor.

"Where's my badge?" Billy looks up and stares right at Frank.

"Uh-"

"Where's my fucking badge?"

"Uh, I dunno, boss. It should be in the bag. I grabbed everything like you told me to and put it in the bag."

"Well guess what? It's not here. How'd that happen?"

It's a rhetorical question.

Billy continues before Frank has the chance to respond, "Because you, you fucking idiot," Billy stands over Frank, who is trying to pull himself off the ground after falling during the ride, "left it on the fucking ground, you fucking moron!"

Frank starts to open his mouth to speak, but Billy won't allow it.

"The one fucking thing that can track us to this whole thing you left behind. Are you a fucking retard?"

It's another rhetorical question.

Billy closes his fists and begins to clobber Frank repeatedly across the head. Frank tries to cover his head with his arms, but Billy grabs one of them and pulls it away, allowing a small gap for Billy to keep hitting him. Frank doesn't try to fight back as he just does his best to protect himself.

He cries out to Billy, "Stop! Stop! Please stop!" Frank's pleas are ineffective and just enrage Billy further. Billy grabs a handful of Frank's hair and pulls him to his feet. Frank puts his hands on top of his head, trying to free himself from Billy's grasp, which exposes his face. Billy uses his other hand to throw more short-armed, forceful blows into Frank's face. Frank's eyes roll back in his head and he falls to the floor. Alicia screams in the corner and covers her eyes.

I do nothing as I watch Billy kick the consciousness out of Frank.

CHAPTER THIRTY-FOUR

BILLY

George is toying with one of the masks in his hands as he tries to process what's going on. It's getting late, and everyone is hungry and exhausted. I walk around the desk and reach inside the box from the storage unit. I toss a couple strips of weather stripping foam on the table. I leave the containers of thermite powder and magnesium strips in the box for now. Frank and George look between the foam and the masks and try to put the pieces together.

"Here's the deal," I begin, "there are five exhaust vents around the perimeter of Snake's house. Each one is less than a foot wide and is barely noticeable if you weren't looking for it. There's no chimney, so the toxins need to escape the house somewhere, which is why there are vents." I take a breath and pick up one of the pieces of foam. I use the foam to demonstrate what I mean in the air. "These pieces are cut perfectly to fit inside the arms of the vents. Once you push them in, slide the vent closed and the excess material will jam up the vent holes."

George nods. I think he's following me so far. Frank, not so much.

I continue, "No air will be able to get in, and no air can get out. Snake won't even realize something is wrong, and he'll simply fall asleep and never wake up." I grin. I'm admittedly proud of myself for coming up with the idea, and I'm fully convinced it'll work to perfection.

"And that's where the gas masks come in," George says, still nodding.

"That's right. Once Snake is out, dead, we just go in, open the safe, and walk out the front door. The fumes won't affect us since we'll be wearing the masks."

"What fumes?" Franks asks, confused.

"Lots of things produce carbon monoxide, Frank. If he runs the gas on the stove or washes his clothes, that will do it. Using the heat would be perfect, but he won't need that this time of year," I say.

"It does get pretty cold at night sometimes," Frank says.

"Not that cold."

"How long is this going to take?" George asks.

"Why, going somewhere?" I stare at him, and he stares back. "It depends, a day or two maybe."

"What about the safe?" George asks.

"What about it?"

"How are you going to crack it?"

"Let me worry about that."

I could mention the thermite, but some things are better off left unsaid. The last thing I need is to give him any ideas.

"What makes you so sure it's behind that painting?"

"Trust me, it fits. Even if it's not there, although it is, we'll find it. Do you worry about that." I pause. "You guys got all that?"

George nods, Frank doesn't. I was really only asking the question to George.

"What do we do now?" George asks.

"We sleep. Tomorrow is going to be a long day." I turn to Frank. "Take him back into the room."

Frank reacts quickly and walks over to George. He leads him out of the room without tying his hands and without any resistance. When I hear the big steel door from the holding area open and close, I make my way into the hallway and head toward the interrogation room where Alicia is being held. I quickly whip the door open in an effort to catch her doing something mischievous, but she's just sitting in the chair, watching George through the two-way mirror when I enter.

"You wanted to see me?" I say.

Alicia stands from the chair and walks over to me. I'm defensive, preparing myself to be attacked again. Instead, she loosely wraps her arms around me and lays her head on my chest. The affection is infrequent, so I enjoy it for a moment and soak in her warmth.

She whispers to me, "I'm sorry. I'm really sorry."

I pull away from the embrace and take a step back so I can look into her eyes. They're beginning to pool with tears.

"What happened to you earlier? I thought we were on the same page?"

"We are, I'm sorry. It just all hit me at once and seeing George again made me feel sorry for him. He's a nice person and he doesn't deserve this."

"Listen, I get it, but we have to stay focused. In a few days, we'll be sailing to freedom, rich as hell, and we'll be laughing about this. You'll forget all about him then."

She smiles and nods in agreement. "You're right, I'm sorry, baby," she says. It's unconvincing, but I'll take it.

I'm pleased she hasn't asked me about threatening her again, because I don't regret it. I had to do what was necessary to keep everything on the right track, and I'll do it again if it's needed. I'm in charge of this operation, and it's going to go according to plan. I'll make sure of that.

Alicia bends her neck back slightly so her face points up at me. I place my hand on her cheekbone and plant my lips on hers. My entire body tingles as her thick lips suffocate me. We separate and I smile at her, placing my arm around her shoulder as she turns. We spin ourselves and slide out the door sideways so we can stay embraced. We leave the room together and head toward the garage. We'll sleep in the front seats of the van tonight, and Frank will sleep in the back. I'm willing to bet he's already sound asleep and filling the van with snores.

"Do you think he believes what I said?" she says.

"Who?"

"George, about the baby."

"Oh yeah, he believes you. Trust me on that. I could practically see the thought bubbles floating above his head when I was talking to him. You did it, you hooked him. Now I just have to reel him in so we can collect our reward."

"Poor guy."

CHAPTER THIRTY-FIVE

GEORGE

"Is he dead?" Alicia asks with tears in her eyes. Billy, sweating and breathing heavily, is sitting on the bench next to me.

"No," Billy says with conviction.

"How do you know?" she says.

"Because I know."

Alicia looks across the van at me as I stumble over Frank's body and sit next to her.

"Is he breathing?" Alicia asks.

I look over to Billy, who turns his head and looks away. Although he said Frank's alive, I have to wonder if he does have a slight doubt about that. He went too far and he knows it. I slide off the bench and crouch down next to Frank's motionless body on the floor of the van. I kneel on an empty soda can, which pinches my skin. I grab it in disgust and toss it to the side before placing my ear against Frank's chest. It's subtle, but there is a heartbeat. Either Billy knew how far he could push it, or he got lucky.

My vote is lucky.

"He's breathing," I say.

Alicia lets out a long sigh of relief. "Oh, thank God."

Some tension releases from Billy's body too. He tries not to show it, but I can see right through him. He definitely got lucky this time.

A few minutes go by without anyone speaking. No one looks at each other and the tension is heavy. Now that my heart has stopped racing, I'm able to gather my thoughts. Something is going on with Alicia, something major I suspect. She was about to say something before, to explain what's going on I suppose, but I may never know what that was. Is she really pregnant or did something happen to the baby? Was she going to come with me? Maybe they won't let her, maybe they're not going to let her go like they promised. My thoughts are interrupted by Billy's words scissoring through the tension.

"Well, we can't go back and we can't stay here," he says. "We need somewhere else to go while I figure out what the hell we're going to do next." Billy's eyes lock onto mine. "Somewhere unexpected."

I toss my arms in the air, I've got nothing. I'm done coming up with ideas. But he continues to stare at me like it's my responsibility.

"What?" I snap.

"Your place."

I shake my head furiously. "No, absolutely not. Not happening."

"Do you want to live, or do you want to die?"

I continue to shake my head. "No, anywhere but there. If they find us I'll never be able to go back there again."

Billy shrugs, not caring in the least. "I expect it will take them at least a day to figure out who you are and where you live," he says. "We'll be safe there until tomorrow."

I say nothing and continue to shake my head. Billy reaches in the front of the van and grabs the gun from the seat. He clouds the barrel with his breath and pretends to clean it. While still looking down at the gun and keeping his head steady, he looks up at me with just his devilish eyes.

"I'm not asking."

I DIDN'T WANT TO go to my house originally for obvious reasons, but at least the surroundings are familiar. Billy watches curiously as I struggle to find the right key from my keychain. I'm exhausted and can barely even think straight. It's only been a few days since I've been here, but it seems so much longer than that. I've missed being home.

Everything is exactly how I left it, except for the dust piling up on the end table next to the couch. That's new. The blue light illuminates on the dishwasher, letting me know the dishes are clean. My cereal bowl still rests in the sink with now crusted flakes on the perimeter. The three-day-old paper sits on the table where I left it in a rush.

After helping Billy carry Frank into the house, I make and quickly devour a couple of sandwiches. When done, I make my way down the hallway and slide into my bedroom. I throw myself on the wrinkle-free bedspread and sprawl out. I sink into the caved in outline of my backside and some tension releases from my body. The mattress is a little old and I've thought about replacing it recently, but it feels so perfect right now. It'll beat a cement floor any day.

A few minutes pass, and I'm nearly asleep when I can sense someone standing in the doorway. I struggle to force myself to turn around, but when I do, I see Alicia's silhouette standing above me. It startles me.

"Sorry, I didn't mean to scare you," she says.

"It's okay." I slide over to make some room and tap the bed beside me. "Sit down."

She does. "You're a good man, George. You really are."

This takes me by surprise. "Oh, well thanks."

"The way you've handled this whole situation has been...admirable. And to do it for me, you don't even know me that well."

"Us. I did it for us."

She smiles widely, like she did back when we first met.

"There it is. There's that smile," I say, playfully pointing at the dimple on her cheek. She blushes and turns away. "Where has that been?"

She shrugs. "There hasn't been a whole lot to smile about lately."

I nod in agreement.

Maybe that's all it was, maybe I've been overthinking this. Maybe she's just been struggling with this whole situation like I have.

"Anyway," she continues, "I just wanted to say thank you. So, thank you."

"Well it's not over yet, but you're welcome."

There is a brief silence, then Alicia stands. "I'll let you be alone, I just wanted to say that." She starts toward the door.

"No, stay." I spread my arm open and invite her to rejoin me. Although emotionless, she turns and comes back to the bed. She sits on the edge and slides herself up toward the pillows. I place my arm across her belly and pull her close to me, hoping I will feel the baby kick. Her belly is still quite small, much like her frame, and almost non-existent. Maybe it's too early to feel anything. I'm not too sure how this all works, but I'll figure it out.

I close my eyes and think back to the day we met and the night we spent together. We were almost in these very same positions. I doze off to the rhythm of Alicia's heartbeat, comforted by knowing that she'll definitely he here when I wake up this time.

CHAPTER THIRTY-SIX

BILLY

E arly in the morning, while still dark, I wake up and leave the old station on foot. I grab some coffee and doughnuts from a shop a block away and bring them back to share with the group. Between the four of us, we devour all but three of the two dozen doughnuts and empty the entire box of coffee. The initial sugar high wears off by late morning, and the three of us, the men only, struggle to stay awake in the van. I think we're all envious that Alicia is able to stay behind and sleep.

Frank, George, and I spend most of the day in the van outside Snake's house, just out of sight behind the tower. We wait until just after 5:00 P.M., when Snake finally leaves. An inconspicuous black sedan comes out of nowhere from behind his house and Snake hops inside. I watch intently as the car pulls away with Snake and some of his men inside before exiting the van. Frank is staying back and will be on the lookout for a sign of any unwanted company. He'll lay on the horn if someone shows up.

George and I make our way toward Snake's house on foot through the bright sunshine. I carry a light black duffel bag containing the foam for the vents. Once at the house, I drop the bag and pile the strips of foam into George's hands. I toss the bag back over my shoulder and head around the back of the house, looking for a way in.

I had watched Snake lock the front door before he hopped in the car that came by, so I don't even bother checking it. I check each of the windows as I walk around the perimeter of the house, and they're all locked too. All of the windows are at eye level, so I could break the glass and pull myself inside with some help, but that's not going to work. Why waste time on plugging the vents if I'm just going to leave a window open?

As I make my way around the back side of the house, an obvious entrance peers up at me from the lawn. I approach the rusted steel doors and toss the duffel bag to the side. The doors to the bulkhead are unlocked as I tug on them, so I open the right side and head down the rotting stairs. As I approach the bottom, a foul odor catches my nose, and I cover my face with my shirt. My backside blocks the sunlight as it tries to brighten a path for me, so I'm unable to see the source through the darkness. There must be a dead critter beneath the stairs, perhaps an opossum or a raccoon.

At the bottom of the stairs, I feel around for the doorknob on the wooden slab in front of me and grab it when I do find it. Like the main bulkhead doors at ground level, the door is unlocked, so I'm able to push inside. It's a stupid mistake on Snake's part, but I'll gladly take it. There is one tiny window that peeks through the foundation which provides me just enough light to find the string that hangs from the single light bulb on the ceiling. I pull on the frail string and the bulb shines.

The basement is ordinary. It's cool and smells of mold and the dead critter from under the stairs in the bulkhead. The ceiling is low and lanes of unorganized copper pipes hang above my head. I try to follow the paths of the pipes to find the sources, but they intersect in multiple places and all seem to end up in the same location next to the two tanks that are near the furnace. I remove the knife from my pocket and slide out the blade. I reach above my head and flex the pipes as much as possible before punching holes in them. I stab in multiple locations and move up and down the trail of copper until my arms ache. Most of the holes are small, no larger than that of a pinhole, due to the knife struggling to penetrate the tubes, but it'll do the trick.

Before heading upstairs, I scan the basement for a clothes dryer, and find one tucked away underneath the staircase. Its vent is cemented to the foundation, so I make multiple puncture wounds all over the duct until it's frayed enough to be torn in two. I turn the knob of the machine to the longest time allowed and push the button in to start the machine. It rumbles and shakes as I make my way up the stairs.

For all of the time that I've spent tracking and watching Snake, this is the first time I've seen the inside of his house. I'm almost giddy. The air is stale and the house nearly empty. It's hard to be-lieve that it has ten million dollars hidden somewhere inside, but it does. The floors are outdated and the walls are stained yellow where they meet the ceiling from the excess smoke. The walls in my house got this bad once, which is why I no longer smoke indoors. I've determined that it's less expensive to smoke outside.

Through one of the windows in the kitchen, I spot George as he fills the gaps of the vents with the foam as instructed. He doesn't look up from his work and doesn't notice me surveying him. I get a sense of satisfaction by watching him slave away at my direction.

I work my way down the hall and find the bedroom. I enter the room and immediately see the painting that George had mentioned hanging on the wall.

He was right, it's out of place.

The colors are bright and vibrant, and it most certainly doesn't fit in with the rest of the house. I approach the painting and lift the bottom of it up to take a peek at what rests behind.

Bingo.

Despite the enticement, I leave the painting on the wall and gently caress the front of the stainless steel safe with my finger. The safe is embedded into the wall, so I'm unable to tell how deep it is. The house is old and the walls are thin, so I should be able to access the backside of the safe from the side yard. We'll find out how big it is then.

I'm tempted to try and crack it now, but if Snake returns during the attempt, we'd all be screwed and there'd be a lot of bloodshed. I must be patient in order to do this properly, despite how strong the lure is.

I gently release the painting and allow it to blanket the face of the safe. I step back a few steps and measure for levelness in the form of an eyeball test. When satisfied, I leave the room and head back down the basement stairs. I ignore the temptation to turn on the gas on the stove for fear that it'll be too much and will explode once the fumes make their way upstairs through the vents in the floor. I restart the timer on the dryer before holding my breath and heading back above ground through the bulkhead.

WE'RE BACK IN THE van, heading toward the old police station while Snake's house slowly builds up enough toxicity to kill him. It'll hit him like a ton of bricks when he returns home, and he'll fall brutally ill shortly after he arrives. He'll go to bed early thinking he ate some bad sushi or something, and he'll die in his sleep.

That's what I'm hoping will happen anyway.

George hasn't made a peep from the back, as I'm sure his heart is still racing from our encounter with the newbie cop from Jefferson. How he didn't pick up on the fact that I'm an officer of the law will surely baffle him, maybe even more so than the fact that Jefferson now thinks he's one too. I chuckle to myself. I am truly enjoying watching him trying to catch up with me. I'm a step ahead and always will be. It'll be too late by the time he does finally figure out what is happening to him.

We pull into the garage shortly after 6:00 P.M. and Frank escorts George back to the holding area. I get out of the van and wander the halls looking for Alicia. I find her reading a paperback in one of the offices. She pops up from her chair when I enter the room.

"There you are. How'd it go?" she asks, rather excitedly. It's nice to see her enthusiasm has returned.

"Everything went great, maybe even better than planned. I was able to get inside."

Her face lights up. "Did you see it?"

"I saw the safe, yes. I have no doubt that's where the money is being kept."

She lets out a passionate yelp and runs toward me. She jumps into my arms and kisses me on the cheek. After savoring it for a moment, I release her.

"So, what does that mean for us then?"

"It means we're going back tonight. If all goes well, we could be sailing through the Gulf within a matter of days." I smile at her, and she returns the gesture.

"Are you hungry? You must be hungry. I got some food," she says, changing the subject. She turns around and bends over next to the chair she was sitting in. I gawk at her silently as the denim wraps itself tightly around her hips and reveals the outline of her thong.

My legs start to shake.

She tosses a few plastic bags on the desk and turns back to me. She catches me fantasizing and reddens. She walks over to me and whispers in my ear, "Not tonight. Let's wait until we're alone, sailing across the ocean, our bodies bouncing to the tides of the waves." She swings her hips slowly and provocatively to show me what she means. "I want it to be special." She smiles at me and kisses me on the cheek again.

Now she's just torturing me.

I twist my lower body to readjust my now bulging self as she backs away.

"I bought a bunch of snacks from the store," she says. "Help yourself."

I approach the table and look through the bags for something of substance. "When did you go to the store?"

"A little while ago. I had some money in my pocket, so I grabbed something to eat and that book over there." She motions to the paperback she was reading that now rests face down in the chair. "You guys were gone for a long time."

I nod in understanding, although I don't like the fact that she went out without my permission. I can't blame her, though, I suppose, but I don't have to like it. What if someone saw her come back here? What if she was followed? I want to ask her this, but I decide to let it go for now.

It's not long before Frank finds us and he and I scoff down the remainder of the contents in the bags of snacks. He tosses a few items he doesn't want to George, per Alicia's request, and I spend the next twenty minutes describing to them what happened at Snake's that neither one of them saw.

Shortly thereafter, we call it an early night and go back to our normal sleeping quarters in the van. Frank falls asleep and starts snoring almost immediately. I grimace and can hardly stand it.

I set an alarm on my phone for 2:00 A.M. so we can head over to Snake's while the night is at its darkest. That gives the fumes almost eight hours to fester in the house and build up enough toxicity to kill Snake. I had originally thought that it was going to take a few days to get this done, but me being able to get in the house and jumpstart the process should make it go much quicker than that. We're looking at less than a day now.

THE MELODIC CHIME WAKES me at exactly 2:00 A.M., and I struggle to find the button to dismiss it. My eyelids are heavy and I'm still sleep deprived, but I force myself to get up. I reach over to shake Alicia awake, but my hand falls flat on the seat next to me.

She's gone.

Lacking the energy to be concerned, I drag myself out of the van and walk into the station. The hallway is dark, but I find a light switch and flip it. The LEDs above my head brighten the path for me. As my eyes adjust, I see Alicia scurrying toward me, looking guilty.

"What are you doing?" I ask.

"I had to pee."

I nod, satisfied with her answer.

"What are *you* doing?" she asks.

"It's two o'clock, it's time to go."

"Already?"

I nod again. "The next time you see me we'll be ten million dollars richer."

She smiles weakly. "I hope so."

She moves past me without saying another word and drags her feet into the same office I had found her in earlier. She's not a morning person I guess. That's just another thing we'll learn about each other as we build our new life together.

I flip the lights on inside the holding area, and I can hear George shuffling around as I open the door. He's shielding his face from the light as I enter the room.

"Get up, it's go time," I say.

George slowly rises to his feet and staggers toward me. I put my hand on his shoulder and lead him out of the room.

"Okay, so here's the plan."

CHAPTER THIRTY-SEVEN

GEORGE

The sound of a rapid hammering from the basement wakes me. The sun is beginning to go down, which means I slept for most of the day. It could be a kind gesture from Billy, or it could just be that he was distracted. Either way, I'll take it. I do my best to slide off the bed quietly so I don't wake Alicia, who is still sleeping in the bed. The floor squeaks as I tiptoe into the hallway.

The basement door is cracked open and I can see the light on downstairs. The hammering grows louder as I make my way down the steps. I hold onto the railing as I try to wake myself completely. In the middle of the floor is my toolbox, which Billy must have found in the closet in the hallway upstairs. Billy is on his knees with his back to me and his arms are busy, although I can't tell what he's doing from my angle. He doesn't hear me come down the stairs, so I walk slowly and try not to make any noises that may startle him, as I don't know where his gun is. I stop when I reach him. I'm sure he senses me next to him, but he doesn't look up from his work.

"What are you doing?" I ask.

He has one of the tiles that is directly in the center of the floor nearly displaced from its original position. The grout is chipped away and scattered across the adjacent tiles. He has the bag of cash next to him and he uses a small chisel and hammer to try to separate the ceramic tile from the adhesive that keeps it suctioned to the subfloor. A bowl full of water and a wooden spoon rest a few feet away. He stops what he's doing and drops everything. He looks up at me from his knees.

"I think I've figured out a way out of this," he says.

I nod, not really believing him. "What are you doing to the floor?"

"We need a place to hide the money temporarily, and they won't even think to look in the floor. No one ever hides anything in the floor. The ceiling, yes. But not the floor."

It does cross my mind that Snake had hidden the money in the ground, so someone has thought of it before, but I figure it's best not to disagree.

Billy grabs the tools again and continues working his way around the tile as he does his best not to crack it. I stand in silence and watch the process for a few minutes until the tile successfully pops off, exposing the subfloor.

"Will you hand me that?" Billy asks.

I grab the shovel that leans against the wall across the room and hand it to him, now standing. "What are you going to do with that?"

"Stand back."

Billy straddles the exposed floor and raises the shovel above his head. He thrusts his arms toward the ground and jams the tip of the metal shovel into the wood. The tiles on the floor are good size, nine square feet each, so his target area is wide. He pulls the shovel back over his head and repeats. The rapid speed and downward force splits the wood quickly.

The ground beneath is dry and cool, but it doesn't take Billy much effort to break through it with the shovel. I hold a black industrial trash bag open while he piles the dirt inside as he digs. The bag is almost torn out of my hands by the weight of the dirt with every toss. He makes the hole in the earth shallow enough so the bag is still visible once dropped in, but deep enough so that the tile can lay back flat on top.

When the bag is full and beginning to tear, I drag it across the floor and leave it under the stairs. Billy walks to the corner of the room where a half-empty bag of grout rests from when the original floor installation happened. I hadn't even looked at it since I bought the house a few years ago. He drops in on the floor next to the hole.

"I saw this sitting over there, so I figured what the hell," Billy says.

He lifts the bag and pours a handful of the powder into the bowl of water. He uses the wooden spoon to mix it up while reading the directions on the bag. I just now realize he's using the bowl that my grandmother had handed down to me from her grandmother before she died. It's been in the family for over a hundred years. Of course that's the one he chose.

When the concoction in the antique bowl thickens, Billy uses the wooden spoon to rub material into the gaps around the tile.

"How are we going to remember which tile it is?" I ask.

Billy stops what he's doing and knocks on the tile with his knuckle. An empty echo sounds from beneath the tile. "It's hollow, but they won't be able to tell by just walking over it. They wouldn't know unless they were looking for it specifically, which they won't be."

"You keep saying 'they'. Who are they?"

"I don't know for sure who they are, but I know they're Snake's men. They're members of the Zved's."

"How do you know that?"

"I caught a glimpse of their faces when they were shooting at us. I recognized them, I think, but I can't place their names right now."

"How many are there?"

"Two, but the longer this goes on the more guys will be on our trail."

"When will it end?"

Billy pauses for a moment before responding. "Never. Not until we're dead."

I gulp. "What if we kill them first?"

Billy shakes his head. "Doesn't matter, they'll just send more guys until they find us and kill us."

"What do we do then?"

"There is only one thing to do. We get the money and we hide. Somewhere away from here, somewhere we can disappear."

"And that's why you and Frank were going to go to Mexico?" Billy nods.

Suddenly, I have a realization. "What about me?"

Billy shrugs.

"That's why you were going to let me go," I continue. "You knew that they'd find me and come after me. They'd kill me so you didn't have to. You'd get away with the money and you wouldn't have to worry about me going to the police."

Billy starts to spread the grout with the wooden spoon again, but he doesn't react otherwise. He meticulously fills in the remaining gap near the corner of the tile then tosses the spoon to the side. He stands up and meets my eyes.

"What about Alicia and the baby? Were you going to just let them get killed by these guys too? You're a real son of a bitch," I say.

Billy's mouth starts to widen into a smile, and then he begins to laugh. His chuckles gradually increase in intensity, and I'm taken aback a bit as he howls with hilarity.

"What's so funny?"

Billy, now leaning forward and resting his hands on his knees to keep himself from falling over, spreads his arms wide. "Take a look around you," he says. "Do you not see what's going on here?"

I fight the urge to physically look around me as I can see it's not meant to be taken literally. "Answer my question."

Billy's laughs settle and he wipes the tears from his eyes. "What question?"

"Were you just going to let Alicia and my unborn baby be killed too?"

He shakes his head. "You really don't know what's going on here, do you?"

"What are you talking about?"

"She's not pregnant. And she's with me."

I take this in for a moment, but begin shaking my head almost immediately. "No, that's not true. I don't believe you. We have a real connection."

Billy starts to laugh again. "Connection? Is that what you call a connection? Do you actually think she's pregnant? She's not."

"I don't believe you."

Billy points in the direction of the stairs without looking. "Go ask her yourself."

Without hesitation, I turn around and storm up the basement stairs. I don't want to believe Billy, but my heart already aches. I need to hear it straight from the horse's mouth. Once upstairs, I hurry down the hallway and whip the bedroom door open. Alicia is sitting on the edge of the bed as I enter.

"There you are," she says. "Listen, I've been thinking about it the whole night, and I could barely sleep. There is something I need to tell you."

"Are you really pregnant?"

She's surprised by my question and my sternness. "George-"

"Don't lie to me. Please. Are you pregnant?"

Alicia puts her head down and takes a deep breath. I can see the tears pool in her eyes, and it gives me the answer that I already know in my heart. I ask again before she has a chance to speak.

"Tell me the truth. Billy just told me everything."

She lifts her head up and looks at me, both eyes now completely filled with tears. "George, I'm so sorry. It was never supposed to-"

"How could you? I thought we had a real connection?"

She jumps to her feet and walks toward me. "We did have a real connection. We still do."

"What about Billy? He said you're with him."

"That was before."

"So that is true?"

She reaches for my hand with compassion, but I pull away. She sinks her glassy eyes into mine and I can't tell if she's being sincere or not. I don't know what to believe anymore. She reaches for my hand again. This time, I let her take it.

"He doesn't really care about you, you know," I say. "He would leave you to die in a second, just like he was going to do to me."

Footsteps from the hallway are approaching. I must have been too distracted by Alicia's gaze to have heard Billy coming up the stairs. He pops his head in and sees Alicia caressing my trembling hand.

"You can stop the act now," he says. "I told him everything." He begins to laugh again as he disappears down the hallway. The laughing is really starting to piss me off.

"Ignore him, Alicia says, "I have a plan."

I rip my hand from her grasp. "You have a plan? I'm tired of following everyone else's plan. Where has that got me? Dead, that's where. It's about time I make my own fucking plan." I spin around and rush toward the door.

Alicia reaches for me, but I ignore her and leave through the doorway and head down the hallway. I brush past the open bathroom door and catch a glimpse of Billy leaning his head back and taking a leak. I rush into the kitchen and pull open the cabinet drawer that's directly to the right of the dishwasher. I yank the entire cabinet off its track and watch as the contents go crashing down onto the linoleum floor. I bend down and grab the longest and sharpest butcher's knife I can find and make my way into the living room. Billy and Alicia arrive in the opening just moments after I do.

"What the hell is going on in here?" Billy says, still zipping his pants.

I stop once I get to the couch that Frank is still passed out on and stand over him, holding the knife above my head. Alicia's eyes widen in shock and she gasps. Billy is suddenly calm.

"Who's laughing now?" I say.

"What are you doing?" Billy asks calmly.

"I'm turning the tables in my favor. It's about time I have some leverage."

"There's no need to do anything stupid now."

"Stupid? You don't want me to do anything stupid? You said it yourself, I'm too stupid to see what's going on around me, so I must be stupid! Just another stupid person doing a stupid thing!" I look down at Frank's already bruised and battered body and I feel nothing.

"Let's talk about this," Billy pleads.

I look up and stare at Billy. "I think we're past that point, wouldn't you say?"

"Nobody has to get hurt."

"Funny how things change when the shoe is on the other foot, isn't it?" I look back down at Frank and raise the knife further above my head. I catch Billy feeling for his gun, but I can see it resting on the table beside me. My arm is quivering as I struggle to steady the blade. I take one final glance across the room and see Alicia covering her face in fear, much like she was in the van. I don't trust her anymore, but I can't stand to see her like this. I lean my head down and drop the knife to the floor.

I can't do it.

CHAPTER THIRTY-EIGHT

BILLY

It's a chilly summer night, which really isn't even chilly at all, and Snake's house is lifeless. I carry a black duffel bag which contains the three carbon monoxide masks, a crowbar, a rubber mallet, a thin steel rod, and two glass vials. I stand on my toes on the side of the house and peek inside the window. I use my hands to cup my eyes to try to help myself see through the darkness. There is evidence of some recent activity inside, as I'm able to faintly make out some figures on the kitchen counter, dishes perhaps, which were not there earlier. I drop to my feet and continue around the back side of the house and along to the western side, and I look in each of the windows like I did in the first.

I can hear Frank screwing around in the front as I make my way back toward him and George, and I scold him for that. After a brief confrontation, I drop the duffle bag to the ground and start pulling out the goods. I hand a mask each to George and Frank, then I strap mine around my face. I pull the straps tight and secure the ventilation filter over my nose and mouth. I slip the two vials into my pocket and hand the mallet and steel bar to George before standing and approaching the front door.

After a few unsuccessful attempts to pry the front door open by wedging the crowbar into the frame and knocking on it with the rubber mallet, I give Frank a subtle nod. I step back and suggest for George to do the same, and admire the damage as Frank throws his giant frame through the front door. Frank grunts on the floor inside the house with the door lying beneath him. I walk over to him and whisper in his ear.

"Nice job, Frank. You did good." I pat him on his head as I make my way into the house. I find the light embedded into the drywall near the door and flick on the lights. The living room fills with light and illuminates around Snake's lifeless body as it lays face first on the carpeted hallway.

I breathe slowly through my mask to ensure the filter is engaged properly, then I approach the body. My heart starts to race, and I hope the plan has worked. It looks like it has. To confirm, I crouch down next to Snake and reach for a pulse on his neck with two fingers. I feel around in multiple spots on his neck before finding a dull pulsation just below his cheekbone. Truthfully, I'm a little bit disappointed, but I try not to show it. I turn to Frank and George, both of whom are gazing at what they think is a dead body from across the room.

"Well, he's not dead yet, but he's barely alive," I say.

"You want me to take care of him?" Frank asks.

I pause for a moment, as I'm not quite sure of our next move yet. I had fully expected Snake would be dead from the exposure already. Considering how his body is in the hallway and the house was completely dark, I'm able to hypothesize what happened: Shortly after Snake got back home, he began to feel the effects of carbon monoxide poisoning. It started with a minor headache that gradually worsened and progressed into symptoms of nausea and dizziness. I figure he was getting ready for bed early and passed out on his way to the bathroom. Either that, or he didn't even make it halfway down the hall before succumbing to the toxicity shortly after his arrival back home. If the poison was strong enough to knock him unconscious so quickly, it should have been strong enough to kill him already too. Plus, that doesn't explain the total darkness. Who comes home and the leaves the lights off?

I'm sticking with scenario one.

"No, not yet. I'll tell you when," I say, then I walk over Snake's torso and into the bedroom. Knowing exactly what I'm looking for, I cross the room and lift the painting from the wall. I didn't get a long look at it before, so seeing the size of the safe takes me off guard. It's a lot smaller than I had expected, and concerns about it actually containing the cash do cross my mind. Putting those thoughts aside, I leave the room and head outside.

My police-issued flashlight leads the way out the busted front door and around to the side of the house. A few stars above my head try their best to help too. I knock on the glass of the lone window in the bedroom with the butt of the flashlight, and George responds by slowly knocking the steel bar on the front of the safe. I put my ear on the vinyl siding and listen for the ping. I slide to where I estimate the safe is on the wall, and when I hear the tinny ping, I tap on the wall.

I rest the flashlight on the windowsill and aim it in the direction of my target. The angle isn't perfect, but I'm not looking for a clean disassembly, so it's plenty good enough. I remove the crowbar from the duffel bag and aggressively jam it into the vinyl. It's not particularly difficult to remove vinyl siding, as it's flexible and tends to crack easily, so my progress is quick. It's not long before George joins me outside, and most of the siding is already removed from the area I need by the time he does.

The wooden studs are more difficult to chisel away, although the teeth of the crowbar do grab large chunks when enough force is applied. It only takes me a few good swings to chip away enough of the surrounding studs to gain access to the back of the safe. I recognize the brand as a common one from the stamp on the bottom left corner, and it's a good one. Most safes are protected from fire, and this is one is no different. No safe is protected from the heat that ignited thermite gives off, though.

Using the thermite from one of the glass vials, I carefully rub the powder along the edges of the safe, directly over the welds. I avoid putting any powder on the back of the safe itself, as the last thing I want to do is put the contents it contains at risk. If the powder burns through the center of the safe, it may just melt the entire thing, including the cash.

After warning George to step back, I remove safety gloves from my back pocket and put them on for protection. The heat this thing is going to give off might singe my hand right off if I'm not careful. I remove the magnesium strip from the second vial and crouch down so that my face isn't in the area when the contact occurs. I hold the metallic strip above my head and slowly move it toward the powder. I do my best to steady my hand, but I'm unable to stop it from shaking completely. Perspiration is beginning to bead on my forehead, so I rub it away with my left shoulder. I push the magnesium against the powder, and they immediately spark upon contact. I drop the magnesium when I hear the concoction engulf and run to where George is standing some feet away. We stand in silence and admire the scene as the rear of the safe slowly melts away.

Having heard the commotion, Frank joins us, and it only takes a few minutes until the rear of the safe has completely caved in on itself and only thin shards of steel remain in clumps. Using the rubber mallet, I knock on the sharp edges of the shards of steel that remain until I'm able to slide my arm inside without cutting myself.

The safe is not very deep, and I'm able to touch the back of the hinged door in the front with my fingertip before I get to my elbow. I bend my wrist down the hole and feel around until I make contact with a solid object. As I finger the edges, I can tell it's not a stack of bills, and the disappointment sets in. I grab the object and pull it out of the hole, and I'm careful not to make any contact with the still scorching edges of the safe.

A brass key and a note with seven digits written on it are all that the box contains, and I'm pissed. I thought that this was it and that Alicia and I would be sailing to freedom in a matter of days. As the three of us stare at the box and its contents, it's obvious now that this is going to involve a whole lot more than I was planning for. I'm going to be forced to utilize the people around me, and I can feel everything starting to slip through my fingers. My control of the situation is slowly dissipating, and I'm getting anxious just thinking about it.

Not knowing what else to do or where to go from here, I go back into the house and tear it up. I know there's no other place in the house that a second safe could be hidden, and I know Snake wouldn't keep the key to the thing in the same building if there was, so I'm at a loss. This key could go to anything and cracking the code to the safe is going to be like trying to find a needle in a haystack.

I flip over furniture in a rage and throw the mallet through the drywall before leaving, but not before telling Frank to get rid of Snake's body. How he makes sure he's dead and what he does with the body is up to him, I just never want to see him alive again.

On the bright side, at least Snake is out of the picture now, so part of the plot for revenge has been achieved. Not so encouraging is that we have no way of tracking where he's storing the cash now, and we're completely on our own to figure it out. I could keep him alive and try to beat it out of him, I suppose. Maybe the satisfaction of seeing him suffer, much like I have experienced since he took my father from me, would make the end result even sweeter. I consider telling Frank to forget it and to toss Snake in the van instead, but I hear a loud thump as I start to turn around.

So much for that.

I hope I won't regret this.

CHAPTER THIRTY-NINE

GEORGE

This is rock bottom for me, no doubt. I don't know what has gotten into me, as I honestly considered killing him. It's not his fault I suspect, none of this, but he's not innocent either. I think the combination of everything that has happened is just too much for me now. At least before I found out the truth I had something to believe in and something to work toward, a metaphorical light at the end of the tunnel so to speak. I had dreams of walking away from this whole thing clean and with Alicia and our baby by my side, but now that's all gone. A dream may not even be strong enough; I envisioned it as a near certainty. I've been played, lied to, scammed, and used and I feel like a fool. I was so blinded by this whole situation that I failed to see what was right in front of me.

I'm downstairs tidying up in an effort to calm myself and clear my mind after my outburst. It's been over an hour since that happened, and the downstairs is pretty much spotless now. I move the full garbage bag of earth, a half-empty bag of grout powder, and the rest of the supplies Billy used to hide the cash under the floor just outside the back door. I leave the toolbox under the stairs so I can remember to bring it back upstairs when this is all over. It's a long shot, but it gives me some hope that my life will one day resume with some sense of normalcy. The new grout around the tile is beginning to dry and it looks almost normal.

Billy was right, I don't think anyone would notice the difference if they weren't looking for it.

With my grandmother's bowl in hand, I make my way up the stairs and into the hallway. It's silent. I peek in the bedrooms, bathroom, and kitchen, then make my way into the living room. There is no sign of Billy or Alicia and Frank is gone from the couch. I move toward the front window and pinch the blinds open. The van is gone from the driveway. I don't know where they went, but I'm sure they'll be back soon. They probably just left me alone to let me cool down.

This could be really my chance to finally get away. Now that I know what's really going on and that they are just using me so they can lead the Zved's on my trail instead of theirs, I have no reason to stay. There is no baby and no Alicia on the other side of this.

It's just me. Alone, as always.

I just remembered that my car is still in the parking lot with the boot on it, so I'm not going to get very far on foot. Plus, Billy will undoubtedly find me and will probably kill me when he does. Either way, I'm dead, so does it really matter? If I stay, at least I won't be alone when I die. The thought of this is comforting, the not being alone part, so I decide to stay and take my chances and hope things turn around in my favor somehow.

The sun has nearly set and the street lights have started to turn on. A vehicle approaches from over the hill in the distance. As it gets closer, I can see that it's a van; a van, not *the* van. It's the same style as Billy's, at least in terms of cosmetics, but it's darker. It's tough to tell since the light is low, but it could be either dark blue or a shade of gray or black. The van slows up and stops as it approaches the house. Two unrecognizable men look my way and stare. My eyes meet with the driver's as he gazes at me through the window. Something about the way he watches me sends terror through me. I've never seen him before, but I wonder if these are the guys that Billy was talking about: Snake's men, the Zved's, the guys who've been looking for us.

I flick the blinds closed and try to not panic. My heart is racing.

I've been doing exactly what Billy has told me to do for the past few days and I suddenly feel almost lost without his guidance. If this is them, I don't know what to do. Is this where it ends? Are they going to kill me right here, right now? A thought crosses my mind and I can't actually believe it, but I wish Billy was here right now. He'd know what to do.

Slowly, I pinch open the blinds again and peek out through the glass. The street is empty. I quickly scan the street and look up over the hill. The van is gone. Whoever it was has left, so maybe it wasn't them after all. I think I'm starting to get paranoid. The knot of tension releases from my chest and I take a deep breath. The feeling is short-lived, though, as a car door slams from the driveway.

My gut reaction is to hide. As soon as I hear the door, I run from the window and go into the kitchen. I retrieve a knife from the counter, the same butcher's knife as before, and sneak into the bathroom. From inside the shower, I can hear the front door creak open.

My heart is pounding even faster and I'm sweating profusely. My anxiety has transitioned to legitimate terror and my chest is again tight. The tightness is squeezing my lungs and breathing is becoming difficult. I try to breathe in deeply through my nose and into the pit of my stomach, but the tension won't allow it. I can only take short breaths that are sharp, painful, and very loud. My cover has certainly been blown as I can hear footsteps approaching from the hallway.

Is it worse to die from a heart attack or from bleeding out from a bullet wound or two? The pain is equivalent I would guess, but there is something to be said about not having to suffer. I hope he just shoots me through the head so I go instantly.

The footsteps approach the bathroom and enter the room. I squeeze the handle of the knife with all I have. Someone's fingers curl around the edge of the shower curtain that I hide behind and whips it to the side. I shriek like I've seen a ghost in a haunted house as I fall to the floor of the bathtub. I close my eyes as a man leans over me and holds something in my direction. I grind my teeth and wait for it, but nothing happens. Slowly, I open my eyes and look up at the intruder. His hand is extended to me.

It's Billy.

"What the hell are you doing in there? And why do you have a knife?" Billy says.

I release my grip on the handle of the knife and let it fall onto the floor in front of him. I'm beyond relieved. I look down and notice that my hand is soaked with blood. The pressure from squeezing the handle so hard must have split open the calluses that had begun to scab over on my wrist. I wipe the blood on my shirt. I can feel the tension fully release from my body and I nearly start to cry as I'm overwhelmed with emotion. I reach for Billy's hand with my clean one and pull myself up and out of the tub.

"What the hell happened?" he asks.

"I thought that was it. I thought I was dead for sure," I speak quickly as I struggle to catch my breath.

"Calm down. What happened?"

"I think I saw them."

"Saw who?"

"The guys that have been following us."

"Why do you think that?"

"There was a van that drove by with two guys inside. They were staring at the house."

"Did they see you?"

"I think so."

Billy puts his hands on his head and paces in circles. "Shit. Okay. Are you sure it was them?"

"I don't know who they are, so no, I'm not sure! All I know is that these two guys were staring at me and that they looked like they wanted to kill me."

"What were they driving?"

"I already told you, a van. A van like yours. It was dark, maybe blue or black. It was like five minutes ago, maybe less."

Billy nods and peeks at his watch. "And you're sure they saw you?"

My breathing has slowed and I'm able to feel my chest deflating. I nod my head. "He was staring right at me."

"Okay, come with me. I have a plan to get us out of here." Billy starts toward the door and waits for me to follow.

I'm a bit reluctant, so I pause. That's how I play it off anyhow. I realize I have no better alternative than to follow his lead again, but I want to make him think I'm actually contemplating my options. I connect with Billy's eyes and hold for a moment as I try my best to maintain the suspense in regards to what I'll do next. It's all an act, though, as deep inside I know that is exactly what I was hoping he'd say.

CHAPTER FORTY

BILLY

After the dust settles and my mind clears, I start compiling a new plan. The next logical thing to do here is to figure out what the hell that seven digit number is all about. The number will lead us to the purpose of the key, I'm almost certain about that. I'm deep in thought, so I don't bother responding to Frank's question from the back in regards to where I'm taking us. I wish I had a notepad so I could jot down all of the things I want to look up, but I don't. Staying quiet will help me keep the information organized in my mind until we arrive, so I drive in silence.

I pull up in front of the new police station in the center of town and get out of the van. Frank panics as he doesn't have a clue on why I would bring us here, but he relaxes a bit when I tell him to stay in the van. George follows me inside to help me brainstorm while I do some research in the database.

After waiting a few minutes for the computer to turn on in my cubicle and shoeing away officer Dave with some unenthusiastic small talk, I'm ready to do some research. I had left my machine on when I left the office a couple of days ago, so it's peculiar that it's has been turned off, but I try to ignore the conspiracy theories that scroll through my brain.

The first search I do in the county database is for license plates. All non-vanity issued license plates have seven digits, so it's a logical place to start. There are no exact matches, so I scramble the digits and search again. I repeat the process until each of the digit combinations have been entered, and no exact matches occur. With no success, I go back and revisit the partial hits, which don't provide much in terms of useful information either.

A 1989 Ford F-250 matches six of the seven digits, albeit not in the same order, and the vehicle is registered to an elderly man. The second hit is more interesting as it matches all seven digits, not in order again, but the Volkswagen Beetle is registered to a young woman, so that doesn't help me either. I can tell by the clean records of these two individuals that they have no association with Snake or the Zved's. It would be clever for Snake to use someone like them to throw the police off track a bit, but Snake isn't as smart as he thinks he is. He has managed to get away many times over, but he wasn't able to get past me. Not this time. Without the restrictions put on the effort to capture him by the city, he would have been caught a long time ago, and I wouldn't even be in this situation.

I had been hopeful to find some sort of lead while scanning through the police database, but it turns out to be a colossal failure. The second scan I do includes searching for partial VINs for vehicle types known to be associated with the Zved's, plus those registered to known associates. After that search also yields nothing, George and I scan through some of Snake's files for less obvious ideas.

It hasn't been long since we arrived, and hour maybe, but I decide it's best if we go somewhere else to do this. I can sense people gossiping around the office, and the longer we stay here the worse it's going to get. The last thing I need right now is for Sheriff Jack Hearns to find out about this. With George's help, I gather up all the material into a single box and carry it out the back door when no one is watching.

FRANK AND GEORGE HAVE both fallen asleep in the back of the van, so I leave them there while I bring the box of files inside through the garage. Alicia is curled up in a chair, also sleeping, when I walk by, so I find the office with the biggest table and get started.

As I read through Snake's files, I realize there isn't much that I don't already know. Despite having no felonies on his record, he's been arrested over twenty times for numerous misdemeanors. He had the charges dropped in over half of those cases, and he's only spent a total of one year and twelve days in jail combined for all of his other offenses. Either he had the best defense lawyer money can buy, or he bribed some judges for their leniency with a cut of his dirty money.

I assume the latter.

As I continue to browse through the files, there are no obvious connections that jump off the page at me. I scroll through the records and look through past cellmates and those of other Zved members, jail inmate numbers and cell blocks, important dates, addresses, and even subliminal references made in his many tattoos.

I find nothing that even comes remotely close to referencing 282w53s.

There are stacks of manila folders and individual papers piled across the top of the table, and I've hit a dead end. After hours of searching, I'm exhausted and frustrated, and I really need some relief. I'm about to rise from my chair and pace around the room when Alicia shows up in the doorway.

"Hey, what are you doing?" her voice is raspy and she clears her throat.

I sigh.

She can tell something's not right, as I would have woken her up if I had the money. She senses my frustration. "Did something go wrong?" she asks.

"There was no money."

"What do you mean? What about the ten million?" She's suddenly awake and wide-eyed, and is fully engaged in the conversation.

"It's wasn't in the safe."

"If not the money, what was inside?"

I remove the key and note from my pocket and hand them to her. She studies them for a moment.

"I don't know what it means yet," I say. "I've looked through all these records and searched the police database for some reference, anything. But I've got nothing."

Alicia is suddenly pacing the room rapidly, and she seems quite nervous.

I continue, "Don't worry, we'll find it."

She shakes her head as she continues to pace. I can see the sweat forming on her neck. "We don't have much time," she says frantically.

I rise from the chair and walk over to her. I lightly grab her shoulders with my hands to stop her from pacing. "Relax, I'll find the money. I'll come up with something and we'll get out of here. I promise."

"No, you don't understand. I think they're on to us."

"What are you talking about? Who's on to us?"

"Everyone!" Tears are beginning to fill her eyes, and she's close to losing it. I guide her over to a chair and force her to sit.

"Calm down and talk to me. No one is on to us. Did something happen?"

She gazes into my eyes through the tears and nods at me. "I saw someone snooping around outside the building yesterday.

""What? Why didn't you say anything?"

"I thought you were going to get the money tonight, so we'd be gone by the time they came back."

My heart is pounding, and she now has me worried. "Okay, alright. Who was it? Do you know who it was?"

She shrugs. "I don't know. There were two guys. They were looking in the windows and they tried to break in through the back."

I back away from Alicia and start pacing in the same pattern she was before. The situation is getting urgent and there is no telling how much longer it will take for the Zved's to find out what's happening.

This is not going the way I had planned.

We need to find that money, and fast, before they find it and it's gone forever. I need to come up with a plan of attack, and I need to do it now.

"Okay," I say, "go to the garage and wake up the guys and meet me down the hall. We've got to figure out what the hell we're going to do."

In the small office near the garage door, I push the empty plastic bags and paperback that Alicia was reading earlier onto the floor. I spread a tabletop map of the county across the table and starting scanning it while I wait for Alicia to return with our friends. Moments later, she enters the room with Frank and George following behind her.

"Sit," I say, "both of you. No one sleeps until we figure out what the hell this means." I slam the key and note on the corner of the table and cross my arms as the groggy men flop into chairs.

Alicia stands in the doorway and blocks the exit.

CHAPTER FORTY-ONE

GEORGE

Alicia and Frank are standing side-by-side in the living room as Billy and I enter the room. They turn their attention to us right away. Alicia looks at me with concern, which is likely a combination of recalling my outburst from before and the bloody hand print across my chest. I avoid her eyes. Frank looks okay if you can ignore the swollen face and two black eyes. He appears to be standing on his own without any support from Alicia, so he must be feeling better.

"It's nice to see you awake," I say in Frank's direction. Even through his battered face, he still manages to smile at the attention.

"Thank you," Frank responds. "I got a headache and my face is a little sore, but I'm okay."

I nod, assuming he hasn't seen a mirror; I think he'd feel a little differently about it if he had.

He points to my shirt. "What happened to you?"

Alicia looks attentively at me, also curious to hear my answer.

I shrug. "Nothing. I'm fine." I quickly change the subject. Do you remember what happened to you?"

Frank looks to Billy before responding. "I slipped and fell in the van."

I catch a glimpse of Billy nodding subtly in confirmation. He has Frank wrapped around his finger and it's beginning to make me sick. Frank's not a bad guy. That doesn't make him innocent, but he's nothing like that tyrant brother of his. I can tell Alicia feels the same way, as I catch her rolling her eyes. I really do feel bad for almost killing him.

"I'm glad you all want to stand around and chat, but we have to go," Billy the tyrant chimes in, darkening the mood.

"What's going on?" Alicia asks.

"They know where we are. George saw them while we were gone."

Frank's eyes pop at the sound of this, although it's difficult to see through the swelling in his face.

"Speaking of that, where'd you guys go?" I ask.

"Nowhere," Billy mutters.

I want to press further, but we really do need to get out of here, so I let it go.

"Where we gunna go, boss?" Frank asks.

"I have a place in mind. Somewhere close by. We'll come back for the money in the morning, then we'll go."

Frank smiles. "Go where, boss?"

"You know where."

"I want you to say it." Frank is giddy.

"No, I'm not going to say it."

"Oh, come on. He already knows," Frank says, referring to me.

"I'm not saying it." Billy is stern, which disappoints Frank.

Frank leans in close to Alicia and whispers, although it's not very quiet, "Mexico, baby."

Alicia is unresponsive and I can hear Billy mumble something to himself. There is a brief silence before Billy speaks again.

"It's time to go. Everyone stay in here until I give you the signal that it's safe." Billy walks across the living room and over to the front door. He pinches open the blinds and peeks outside, much like I did before. After scanning the street, he reaches for the door.

"Hey, boss?" Frank startles everyone.

Billy turns and faces him as he holds onto the door handle. "What?"

"What's the signal?"

Billy rolls his eyes and sighs, obviously annoyed. "When I say it's safe, just come, okay?" Billy doesn't wait for a response and turns back to the door. "What a fucking moron." He turns the handle and pulls the door toward him, allowing some space for his head to slide out. He scans the street again before turning back to us. "Okay, come on. Hurry up." He opens the door fully and motions for us to follow.

Alicia goes first, followed by me, then Frank. Billy closes the door behind us and sneaks his way across the walkway and into the driver's side of the van. Alicia reaches the back of the van shortly thereafter, and she and I pile inside. I close one door and wait for Frank to hop in the other.

A moment passes and there is still no sign of Frank. He was right behind me, so he should already be in the van by now. He must have forgotten something and turned back. I slide toward the rear doors and start to poke my head out. Just as I do, multiple rounds of explosions and loud echoes fill the air.

Gun shots.

I recognize them as being the same sound as before in the parking lot of the pub. I pull my head back into the van, slam the doors, and throw myself on the floor and cover my head. It's like we're on the battlefield. Alicia shrieks from the bench behind Billy's seat and slides onto the floor next to me. Billy ducks in the front and covers his head. Someone is screaming, but I can't tell who it is or what they're saying.

Maybe it's me.

Then, suddenly, just as quickly as it started, the gun shots fade out and the faint sound of squealing tires are heard peeling away in the background. Billy lifts himself and looks back at us.

"You okay? Everyone okay?" he says. He's breathing heavily but is fairly calm. I look to Alicia, who looks back at me. She's quivering, like me. I turn to Billy and shake my head. "Where's Frank?"

My eyes sink as Billy's face turns to panic. His cheeks are rosy, but the paleness is beginning to overwhelm his face. He must have thought that Frank was already in the van.

Billy pushes his door open and runs around the front of the van. I lose him as he passes in front of the windshield. Moments later, I hear his screams. No words actually come out, just loud, murderous screams. I look to Alicia, who is sobbing in her hands, then I hop over the front seat and join Billy outside.

Frank's dead body is in the driveway, right next to the rear wheel of the van. Blood is streaming down the side of the uneven driveway and staining a path under the van. If I didn't know it was Frank, the body would be unrecognizable. Tens of rounds of ammunition tore through his upper torso, neck, and face, killing him instantly. Bullet casings litter the street.

I walk back around the van and sit on the rear bumper. My stomach churns and I can taste the acid of the bile starting to make its way up and out. I try to hold it back, but I can't. I vomit at my feet as I think about how easily that could have been me over there instead.

Billy's hands are covered in blood and he sits on his knees on the ground next to Frank, pounding the cement with his closed fists. I can't help but feel sorry for him as I know what it's like to lose someone who's close to you. He lacked the tolerance needed to deal with Frank and his apparent condition, but he didn't want him to die, that much is obvious.

Billy is becoming hysterical as he continues to pound his fists into the cement. I lift my feet over the vomit, open the back doors, and slide back into the van, letting him be. I move onto the bench on the passenger's side and rest my face in my hands. Alicia is doing the same on the bench opposite to me.

I try to think of another time that I've seen a grown man weep like that. I can't recall such an instance.

CHAPTER FORTY-TWO

BILLY

I park the van in the parking garage a few blocks from 53rd Street, then George and I start in that direction. Frank waits inside for us to return and Alicia is back at the old station. It's around 8:30 A.M. and the sidewalk is crowded. George and I walk in the opposite direction as most people.

Shawnee County Savings Bank is one of the largest privately owned banks in the city, and it's our target this morning. The note from the safe is secured in my pocket, as well as the brass key that I hope belongs to a safety deposit box inside the bank.

"Let's make a pit stop in here before we head over," I say to George as I lead him into an upscale men's business clothing store that stands alone by itself.

"What do we need in there?" George asks.

"We need a new wardrobe if we're going to look like cops. I'm buying."

We've been wearing the same clothes for a couple of days now, and they're dirty and a bit foul smelling, so we need a fresh look. I have my badge with me, but we need to look presentable too so there's no hesitation on the part of the bank employees.

I ignore the enthusiastic salesman as we enter the store, and I walk directly to the back wall. Crisp suits in various colors and styles line the wall, all hanging in perfect unison. The lighting is strategically placed so that the most expensive Italian ones are highlighted, and they grab my attention immediately. The suits are sharp, but they may be a bit of an overkill. All we really need is some new slacks and shirts and even blazers would be unnecessary. They'll just get in the way.

I reluctantly slide over to the section that has slacks and button-up shirts hanging individually, and we pick out some dark colors. The salesman follows closely behind us as we browse through the racks. We change into the new outfits in the designated rooms in the back, and I pay the salesman in cash before we leave.

Back on the sidewalk, the morning rush hasn't died down any, so it takes us a moment to cross the sidewalk to get to the trash cans. We toss our old clothes into the can and make our way toward the bank. It's still a block away, so I take the opportunity to go over the details one more time.

"Just follow my lead in there," I begin. "We're both cops and we need to access that box. We don't leave until we see what the contents are."

George doesn't react, and I can tell he's having anxiety over the whole situation.

I continue, "If this is it and there is cash inside the box, we're confiscating it as evidence. They'll probably catch on at that point, so be prepared to run. You come back this way and I'll go the long way around the other side of 53rd, and we'll meet at the van. You'll beat me there, so you tell Frank what's going on so he's ready to roll as soon as I arrive. Got it?"

George nods.

My heart rate is increasing as we approach the impressive stairwell to the bank, and the adrenaline rush fuels me. Things are about to get pretty exciting.

I fight through the apprehension and I blast us through the line of law-abiding citizens with confidence. I approach the teller and flash her my badge. Barbara, the teller, is obviously uncomfortable and unsure how to react. After some back and forth banter and some resistance from her to provide us access to the safety deposit box, I hit her with it.

"We've received a report of a potential bomb on the premises and we need access to this box."

She gasps and covers her mouth with her hands. She spends the next couple of minutes frantically searching through her computer for a hit on various combinations of the seven digits that I have memorized from the note in my pocket. There are no results. I back away from the counter and pace around in a small circle. Fuck. What the hell do we do now?

"I'll go get the manager," Barbara says. "Maybe he can help."

Before I can respond, George breaks his silence, "No, we don't have the time to wait for the manager," he says.

He's not following my lead like I told him, but maybe he has an idea, so I don't intervene. He worked in a bank before he joined me, so maybe there's something I'm missing. I stand back and watch him go to work.

It's not long before the two of them are in a deep discussion about there being too many digits and the labeling of the shelves that house the safety deposit boxes, or some shit like that. They lost me almost immediately, but George seems to know what's going on.

At least I hope he knows what's going on.

Barbara pounds some keys into her computer, and before I know it, the three of us are in the vault searching for a safety deposit box that contains a fictional explosive device. It all happens so fast and I'm not totally sure how we did it, but I like where this is headed. We're in business.

We're in aisle twenty-three and Barbara is holding a steel box with the number 282 engraved on the front. The brass key from the safe is in my hand, and I look at it with uncertainty. The key that Barbara is using looks nothing like the one that I'm holding, as hers is much smaller and is a glossy silver. Mine is brass and appears to be much too large. This isn't good.

She inserts her key into the designated hole on the box facing her, and the lock disengages with a click. She looks up and waits for me to do the same on my end. I slide the head of the key toward the hole on the box and try not to look concerned as the brass comes nowhere close to fitting. Now frustrated, I flip the key and try it again, but the results are the same.

Fuck. It's another dead end.

Barbara opens her mouth as if she's about to say something, but I don't want to hear it. Not knowing what else to do, I rip the box from her hands and smash it on the concrete floor below. I reach behind my back, pull out my gun, and begin emptying an entire clip into the box.

My accuracy has always been excellent, and today is no different. Each one of the six bullets hit the target and the clasp with the key hole is nearly blown off. My ears are ringing and the powder residue forms a small cloud in front of me. The smoke tickles the hair in my nose, but I refuse to wipe my face. I wait a moment for the heat to cool before crouching down to the level of the now shredded box. George creeps around the corner from where he and Barbara had hidden away to during my rampage, and I can sense him watching me meticulously as I pry open the remainder of the box and sort through the contents.

Unless Snake knows some Chinese guy named Li Yong and has made a currency exchange from dollars to yuan, this is not what we're looking for. There is a small wad of Chinese yuan tied together with an elastic band in which I pick up and quickly count. I stop counting after I reach the one thousand mark, which is about halfway through the stack. The contents are minimal and the cash can't be valued at much more than three or four hundred US dollars. I toss Li Yong's passport and a wad of yuan next to the severed lid of the safety deposit box and push myself to my feet.

Barbara tries to stop me on the way out, but I stay in character and offer an explanation of a false alarm before brushing past her. I look straight ahead and fight with my peripheral vision to avoid observing my surroundings as George and I walk toward the front doors of the bank. I'm not sure if the room is sound proof or not, but I doubt it would matter if it was. From the reflection on the windows, I can see the bank manager in an animated discussion with Barbara back near the vault. She's clearly trying to convince him to call the police.

It will only be a matter of minutes before the police are dispatched and are arriving at the scene to interrogate Barbara and any other witnesses who may have stuck around in the line to discuss what happened. Mr. Yong will be notified that his belongings may have been compromised, and he'll probably file a lawsuit against the bank for their lack of security after he's questioned about any possible terrorist connection. He'll never bank with Shawnee again.

The bank manager will be forced to terminate Barbara after her carelessness, but he may fight for her to at least get a severance package. The surveillance footage will be scrutinized but the police will find no clear images of our faces as we kept our heads down and away from the lenses of the cameras. It's going to be a big hassle for the institution and some policy changes will probably be enforced within a matter of weeks, and it's all for not. The key didn't fit and the money wasn't there, and we're no closer to being out of Kansas.

"Don't look back," I say to George as he's about to do just that as we approach the front doors. We slip down the stairs and onto the sidewalk and blend into the crowd. Police sirens are rapidly approaching from the other side of 53rd Street and George is getting tense. "Stay cool." We walk at a rapid pace, but we do not run. I find a shortcut through an alley that attaches to the rear of a grocery store that is across the street from the parking garage.

Frank is sitting in the driver's seat as we approach the van. I walk around and open the rear doors and George hops inside. Frank shuffles across the seat and into the passenger's side as I open the front door. He looks between George and me before speaking.

"Did you get the cash, boss?"

I slowly turn to face him as I try to figure out how he became to be so stupid. If we had the cash we would have arrived at the van at different times and there would be a little bit more enthusiasm involved. We would have had the box with us and we'd already be back on the interstate. This is usually my time to tear into Frank and his lack of intelligence, but I decide to spare him the humiliation this one time.

"No, no cash," I say. "That wasn't it."

I start the ignition and head toward the exit of the parking garage. I take a left out of the garage and head back in the same direction we came from on 53rd Street.

Five police cars with their lights flashing line the street just outside of the bank as we drive by. The lane closest to the bank is barricaded by the squad cars and an officer is forcing people away from the entrance of the bank. I recognize his face from a distance, but his name slips past me. I met him only once in passing as he was hired for the graveyard shift during my first leave of absence. It's after 9:00 A.M. now, so his shift should have ended an hour ago. You're welcome for the overtime, Mr. Nameless.

"What do we do now?" George asks from the back.

"We're going back to Snake's place. We must have missed something."

"What are we looking for this time?"

"We're going to search every square inch of that property until we find something we can use. I'm all ears if you have another idea."

I can't go back to Alicia with nothing. She's getting concerned and I'm afraid she may crack under the mounting pressure if I bring her more bad news. I won't tell her about what happened in the bank, as she'll become paranoid that we'll be tracked and found. She won't understand that we avoided the cameras. Even if we didn't, Sheriff Hearns thinks I'm at the hospital in Hays with Frank, so it'd be a clear case of mistaken identity. It happens all the time. Plus, nothing even happened inside the bank beside a little damage to the one safety deposit box. Nothing was taken and nobody was hurt, and the cops are not on to us. Alicia won't understand any of this.

She already thinks the Zved's have found us, and she might be right, so that's why we need to find the cash before they do. Time is running out. Every phone call that goes unanswered to Snake will just raise more suspicion that something is wrong. I figure we have less than twenty-four hours before someone heads over to his house and finds him dead, and less than eight more before they find out who's responsible. The thought of this raises the hair on the back of my neck and I begin to sweat. I'm suddenly chilled by this reality and goose bumps explode from the flesh on my forearms. I shake myself when no one is watching to make the goose bumps disappear.

Fear is a powerful emotion, but it's not as strong as the pure hatred and yearning for revenge that I have for Snake and the rest of the Zved's. They've won one too many times before, and I'm determined not to let them beat me again. Snake is out of the picture finally, but I won't be satisfied until I take from him what was the most important thing in his life, much like he did to me.

I'm getting out of this alive, and I'm taking his money with me. I will find that cash.

CHAPTER FORTY-THREE

GEORGE

I hope this isn't Billy's idea of getting away for the night. I know he said he had a place in mind that was close, but I'm not so sure of this strategy. The three of us spent the night in the van in the driveway. I have mentioned this fact, that we're still in the driveway, a few times throughout the course of the night to him, but he doesn't want to hear it. He doesn't want to talk about much of anything. None of us get any sleep: Billy from mourning, Alicia from crying, and me because I'm scared to death that if I close my eyes I'll never wake up again.

When morning finally does come, the sun shines through the front windshield and warms my face. My eyes are heavy and sore from straining all night. By body is exhausted and I could really use some actual sleep, but I have a feeling that's not in the cards for me today.

The echoes of the chirping birds trickle in through Billy's open window as he smokes a cigarette. Aside from his occasional puffs and exhales, silence fills the van. No one has spoken for a few hours since I last mentioned to Billy that we should at least park somewhere else. All he did at the time was grunt back to me in response to my recommendations, but the van stayed stationary. He blows out the last of his cigarette and flicks it out the window before cranking it back up by hand. He finally turns to Alicia and me and speaks for the first time since Frank was killed.

"This ends today," he says. My ears perk up and I look to Alicia, who reacts similarly. "This has gone on for too long, they're going down tonight."

I nod, trying not to look too excited. "How?"

"We'll bait them, well, you'll bait them, then I'll finish them."

"I'm not sure I like the sound of that."

"This is how it has to be. Someone has to bait them, it's either you or her." He points to Alicia. I look to her and see her face overwhelmed with fear.

She couldn't do it.

"What about you? Why can't you bait them?" I ask.

"What, are you going to kill them? You wouldn't kill Frank when he was just sitting there and putting up no resistance. What makes you think you have the balls to pull the trigger with these guys staring you in the face?"

He's right.

"You're not cut out for it and I'm not risking the chance that you'll freeze up," he continues. "I'm not putting my life in your hands."

I want to ask him, "What about my life?", but I stop myself. I should know better by now than to even consider saying something like that to him. Billy doesn't care about anyone but himself, he never has and never will. He doesn't care about Alicia and he certainly doesn't care about me. Despite his reaction to what happened to Frank, he would have sacrificed him to save himself in a second. I have no doubt in my mind about that.

"Fine," I say. "How do we do it?"

Speaking like an expert, Billy lays out exactly how it's going to go down tonight, "A couple guys from the Zved's will drive by the house exactly twenty-four hours after the murder, or damn close to it. They always do. It's a habit that I've been tracking for years but have never been able to prove in court."

"Why would they come back to the scene of the crime so quickly?"

"To check their work. They always double check their work to make sure that they're covered. No witnesses. It's how so many of them stay out of prison. It's difficult to prove a crime with no eyewitnesses and no DNA evidence. Testimony from a surviving victim would ruin them. It would all be traced back to the roots, and the entire operation would be brought down."

"But Snake's dead. You said he was the guy in charge. How do you know they'll stick to...procedure?"

Procedure: What an ugly word to describe organized crime. I cringe a bit as I say it.

"They still came after us, didn't they? There is always a backup plan, a second in charge, a Vice President I guess you could say."

I open my mouth to respond, but I stop myself.

Billy notices my apprehension. "Just trust me, okay?" he continues. "I've been studying their patterns for years."

I nod, wondering why he doesn't just take them down legally, as a cop, instead of doing it this way. It's a little late for that now I suppose.

"It will be the same two guys as last night since their work isn't done and they know we're still at large. They'll be in a different vehicle from last night, something the total opposite of the van."

"Okay, then what?"

"Then we bait them."

He makes it sound so simple, and I almost believe him.

"But the first thing we have to do is clean up their mess from last night."

"Why bother?"

"If someone sees a dead body or a pile of blood in your driveway, don't you think they'd call the police and report it?"

I shrug. "What's wrong with that?"

"We don't want the police to come just yet. If they come, they make it a crime scene and block off the entire street. No one enters and no one leaves, so our guys won't be able to drive by and we won't be able to bait them into the house."

"Would that be such a bad thing? Why can't we just take the money and get the hell out of here?"

Billy is becoming frustrated with me. "You don't get it. If we run, they'll find us. We'll always have to have one eye over our shoulder for the rest of our lives. Once they spread the word that three witnesses are on the loose, they'll set a bounty on our asses and we'll be hunted like fucking animals."

I don't know what to say, but then I remember something Billy had said a day or two back. "Yeah, but you said that they just keep multiplying and adding more men. You said they would just keep sending guys after us."

Billy just stares, obviously not following me.

"What changes if we kill these guys? Won't they just send more men after that? You said it yourself, everyone will be looking for us."

Billy objects by shaking his head. "Not this time. This time is different. I'm taking out the whole operation tonight."

I'm not sure whether he's delusional or if he has some master plan that I can't connect the dots to, but I don't question him further. I look down at my wrist for my watch, but I realize that I'm not wearing one. All I see is dry crusted blood from the calluses. I think I'm starting to lose my mind. I'm able to squint and make out the time on the small digital clock on the radio in the front of the van.

"It's nine o'clock," I say. "They killed Frank at what, 8:15 or 8:30? That leaves us with eleven hours until they come back, so you say. What do we do until then?"

Billy turns his attention back to the front and slides out the door. Moments later, the back doors open and the sun blinds me. I shield my eyes.

"The first thing we have to do is move the body and clean up the blood."

CHAPTER FORTY-FOUR

BILLY

Through the morning heat, the strap of the gas mask is rubbing obnoxiously against the back of my neck as I work to remove more of the siding from Snake's house. The temperature has been slowly rising with each passing hour, and I can feel the sun beginning to crisp a thin layer of my exposed skin. Removing the vinyl siding from the outside of the house is meticulous work, but I've managed to remove all but a few of the horizontal panels with the crowbar. The remaining panels will stay where they are, as they're above the melted safe and out of my reach.

Snake was taller than I am, but I'm taking a calculated risk that he didn't hide the money high above his reach either. Doing so would seriously hinder his ability to get it down if needed to in a rush. Each of the wooden studs that frame the house are spaced out evenly, and I've torn out most of the insulation while searching for the cash. Upon finding nothing, I toss the crowbar to the ground and walk around to the front of the house to find Frank.

I enter the house through the busted doorframe and I'm careful to step around the mess. While I was tearing the exterior of the house apart, Frank has been inside doing the same. He has opened up all of the windows and kicked out the screens in an effort to air out the poisonous levels of carbon monoxide. We don't have a meter to test the levels in the house, so we're wearing our protective masks just in case. It would be too late by the time we figured out the levels were too high if we went without masks, so we'll just have to deal with the lack of comfort of them while we work.

The mud-stained carpet in the living room has been torn up, the ripped vintage wallpaper covers numerous fist sized holes over the drywall, and the cushions on the couch have all been shredded. Frank used his pocketknife to do most of the damage it appears. The rubber mallet that I threw last time we were here still rests implanted in the wall. I scramble toward the kitchen to wash the fiberglass from the insulation off of my hands and forearms, as the rosy blemishes are already spreading like the plague up my arms. Through the open window above the sink, I see George pacing the perimeter of the lawn in precise squares with his head looking down at the ground beneath. He continues to obey me, like a good boy.

I poke my head in the bathroom and bedroom before heading down to the basement. I don't feel the need to check Frank's work, as I already did an exhaustive destruction of Snake's property previously, so I don't expect that Frank has found anything. The basement door is cracked open and I can see a faint glow from the light creep through the doorframe. I push the door open and march down the stairs.

Snake is definitely dead. The color has completely left his body and he's as pale as an albino. His head is below his torso as it rests on the bottom stair, so gravity is holding his eyes open. Even for me, it's disturbing to look at. I climb over him and his pool of soupy blood without checking his pulse, and I find Frank looking in and around the washer and dryer under the stairs.

"Having any luck?" I ask, which startles Frank. He jumps and nearly hits his head on the low hanging ceiling.

"You scared me, boss."

"Sorry. Did you find anything?"

"No, nothin'. I didn't find no money or no safe or nothin'."

I'm not surprised. "Me either." I sigh, feeling a little discouraged and defeated.

"What do we do now?" Frank asks.

"I don't know, Frank. I really don't know."

There is a brief silence.

"So, I was thinkin', boss, do we really need Georgie around anymore?"

"What do you mean?"

"I don't know, I was just thinkin'. Naw, it's stupid. Forget it."

"No, go ahead, tell me what you're thinking."

Frank pauses and looks me over, and he can't tell if I'm being genuine or not. I actually am.

"Well, it's just that he's already helped, a lot, and now that we have the key, I was just thinkin' we don't really need him anymore." He cowers a bit, waiting for me to attack him. Instead, I ponder his suggestion. He may be right in that I'm not sure we really do need George anymore, but the job isn't quite finished yet. And I don't want him running around Topeka with the knowledge that he has either.

"We don't have the money yet, though. We still need him to help us find it. Once we have the money, we'll let him go. That was part of the deal all along."

Frank shrugs and looks away.

"He won't get hurt," I continue. "I promise, okay?"

Frank won't look at me, but he nods in agreement. I can tell he doesn't believe me.

"Okay?" I press.

"Okay," Frank finally agrees.

"He won't get hurt, I promise."

Frank looks up. "I like him."

"I know, Frank."

The door at the top of the stairs creaks and interrupts our conversation. Frank and I look in the direction of the stairs and see George slowly making his way around Snake's body. He looks like he might vomit at the sight.

"What did you find out?" I yell to him.

"Nothing," George says. "What about you?"

I shake my head, then I turn back to Frank and whisper to him, "We'll finish our conversation later. I'll think about what you said. Deal?"

Frank smiles and nods.

Moments later, George yells out for us from across the room, so we walk over to him. He points out some fresh dirt on one of the shovels that are near the bulkhead door. Frank empties out the barrel that rests next to the shovel and we find some more fresh soil underneath some grass clippings. George and I make eye contact upon this discovery and a light bulb goes off in my head.

We've been looking in all the wrong places. I know that now. It seems so obvious now, and my energy has suddenly returned. I had underestimated Snake's intelligence, as he would have to be stupid to leave the money inside the house. On the other hand, I gave him too much credit too. He wasn't smart enough to hide the cash somewhere else, like in a safety deposit box in a bank. I want to kick myself, as I've sent myself on a wild goose chase, and I think it's all been unnecessary up to this point. The money is buried somewhere, I'm certain of it. Now, the big question is where.

I remove the note from my pocket and hand it to George at his request. He hands it back to me moments later and I read it again. 282w53s must be coordinates: 282 degrees west and 53 degrees south. That's where the money is buried. The three of us rush out the basement door and up the bulkhead stairs, with me leading the way.

CHAPTER FORTY-FIVE

GEORGE

The smell of Frank's dead body is repulsive and I nearly vomit again as soon as I slide out of the van. My vomit from yesterday is now crusted to the driveway and much of it has already disintegrated. Alicia has her blouse over her nose as she leaps from the van. Her flat, smooth belly protrudes from underneath the material. There's definitely no baby in there. She nearly passes out upon seeing Frank's body for the first time and is forced to sit on the rear bumper and wait until Billy and I move him.

The closest neighbor is over a half of a mile away from here, although a barking Labrador can be heard faintly in the distance. The neighborhood is sprawled out and everyone is solitary, so I don't think we'll be bothered. If no one had called already about the gun shots from last night, they certainly won't be calling now. We should be safe.

Billy gazes into Frank's empty eyes, still open, and shows no emotion. He's either a quick mourner, or he's a heartless bastard. I have my own suspicion. I'm sure he's completely moved on already and is more than a little relieved to not have to deal with the burden anymore.

"Head or feet?" Billy asks.

I don't respond and just grab Frank's feet. I'm forced to cover my nose with my bloody shirt, much like Alicia had with her own, to avoid regurgitating. Billy counts to three and we lift the body. He backpedals toward the front door of my house while I stagger forward. My shirt falls from my nose as we lift, and I'm forced to inhale the decomposition.

The body is limp and extremely heavy, kind of like a water-logged baseball, just magnified a million times. I try not to look at Frank's face, but it's difficult not to as it's right in my vision as I struggle forward. Maggots have already begun to decompose his face through burrowing in the multiple bullet wounds. Various fluids drip from underneath him as we walk, probably from the exit wounds on the backside of his skull. I do all I can to avoid stepping in them. I have to hold my breath for the final few steps to avoid passing out.

Billy tells me to wait as we approach the door, so I do. He rests Frank's upper torso and head on the doorstep so he can open the front door. I try, but I can't hold it in any longer, so I drop Frank's feet to the ground and run to the bushes just next to the door. The dry heaves are painful as nothing ejects from my empty stomach. Between heaves, I glance over to Billy who stands in the open doorway, shaking his head at me.

"I don't have time for this," he says, then he grabs two handfuls of Frank's collar and drags him the rest of the way into the living room. I vomit up nothing again as Frank's feet disappear into the house.

A moment passes and I'm able to compose myself enough to sit on the stoop with my hands on my head. The front door closes behind me and Billy walks past and approaches the van. Generally, I would ask him where he put Frank's body, but it seems irrelevant, so I don't. In the driveway, Alicia jumps off the back of the van as Billy hops in the driver's side front. He moves the van in reverse and onto the lawn. He pulls it forward and parks it horizontally in the driveway so it blocks anyone from entering, or more importantly, from seeing the blood in the driveway. When satisfied, Billy makes his way back toward me and stops when he reaches me.

"Do you have a hose?"

"In the shed," I say and motion toward the back of the house. Billy takes off in that direction.

A few minutes later, he returns with a green hose, unraveling it as he walks. It stretches all the way to the end of the driveway thanks to the two hoses connected with a coupler that I finagled last summer. He hands it to Alicia and says something to her, instructions I assume. She grabs the hose from Billy's hands and points it toward the bloodstained cement. She squeezes the handle of the multi-functional nozzle and sprays the water full stream at the stain. She sways the hose back and forth like one would do with a fire extinguisher on an open flame. I continue to watch her as Billy makes his way back toward me.

"What's with that shed?" he asks as he approaches.

"What do you mean?"

"The three floorboards in the front, they look out of place. What's the deal?"

"I'm surprised you noticed."

"I've been trained to notice things like that. Is there something underneath?"

"Yeah, a bunker."

Billy shakes his head in confirmation. "That's what I thought it was. Well, that's our spot."

"Our spot for what?"

"That's where you can go with the money once you get the guys inside."

I nod, fully understanding. All of the pieces of the jigsaw puzzle are starting to fall into place.

CHAPTER FORTY-SIX

BILLY

The odor from under the stairs has gotten worse, and I hold my breath as I climb up to the top. Frank is the last of us to head up the bulkhead stairs and onto the earth above, and he has the shovel from the basement in his hands when he arrives above ground. He jams the nose of the shovel into the soft soil and waits for instructions.

"George and I are going to go track down a compass," I begin. "You stay here and start digging. If you don't find anything when we're gone, we'll use the numbers on the note as coordinates when we get back."

"What do I do if I find something?" Frank asks.

"Call me immediately. Don't do anything, don't touch anything, and just call me. We'll be back in an hour." I motion to George, and he follows me to the van.

When I don't open the back doors, George slips into the passenger's side in the front, and I let him sit there without restraints. He's deeply involved at this point, and I'm willing to bet he wants to see this thing through to the end now. We're close to finding the cash, real close, and his freedom is within his grasp. He would have to be stupid to try something at this point considering how far he's made it.

As I drive back toward the outskirts of town at speeds greater than the posted limits, I begin to ramble, "We're close. I can smell it. Can you believe it? I knew he had the money, I knew he did. I told myself I'd get revenge on those fuckers one day, and today is that day, my friend. Can you believe it? He buried the money, huh? Of course he did. Fucking Adrian. He never was too smart. Why would someone bury a bunch of money? Some little kid could have stumbled across it or a raccoon could have dug it up or something."

George doesn't say anything, and he just nods periodically. I doubt if he's even listening.

"Ten million big ones. Early retirement, blue skies, sandy beaches. I'm going to be living the dream."

I drift off into a daydream of sailing across the Atlantic, Alicia by my side, with small islands in view in the distance. There's not a cloud in the sky and a light breeze blows Alicia's hair through the summer air. We're sipping wine and have the ocean to ourselves, and we're as happy as can be. The dream is becoming a reality, and I swear I can feel the sand in between my toes as I drive.

I pull in front of the old police station and park on the street. I don't know why I didn't pull into the garage in the back, but something told me it wouldn't be necessary. Or maybe it was that I forgot where I was going, as I was indulged in my fantasy. I get out of the van and head for the front door, and the outlines of where the old letters used to be for the Police Department are blatantly obvious on the side of the brick building. I realize as I unlock the door and head inside that I have made a mistake, and that this gives George too much insight into what's happening. I can only hope he doesn't notice while I'm inside.

Alicia must hear me enter, because she slides out of one of the offices at the far end of the corridor and waits for me. She glares at me in disgust as I approach her.

"What the hell is going on?" she demands.

"We found the money."

"Where is it?"

"I don't have it. Not yet. It's buried in the ground. We're going to get it after this."

She stares at me, dumbfounded. "So you didn't find the money then?"

"Well not yet, but we're going to find it."

"Where is it buried?"

I pause for a moment. "I'm not quite sure."

Alicia rolls her eyes at me and raises her voice, "Do you not understand what you're putting me through? You leave me here all day, by myself, and you don't tell me what's going on. I don't know if you're alive or dead or if you have the money or if you don't. Those guys might come back at any time, and I'll be here by myself with no weapon and no defense. They'll rape me and leave me for dead. Do you realize all of this?"

"You're overreacting."

"I'm not overreacting! I thought we were partners in this thing? How come I'm never included in anything?"

"You have a role to play! George thinks you're having his fucking baby! If you're with us all the time, you'll distract him and he might screw something up. We can't have that. We've talked about this."

Alicia puts her head down and turns away. She knows I'm right.

I take a breath and calm myself down, then I speak to her softly, "I'll get the money. We're so close I can taste it." I place my hand on her face and begin caressing her silky skin. "It'll be just you and me and the open water before you know it."

I pull her face toward me and try to kiss her, but she spins out of my grasp and slides back into the office. Part of me wants to storm in there after her and tell her what will happen if she disrespects me again, but I don't. Instead, I turn around and head back out to the street to the van, forgetting what it was that I came in here for in the first place. I slide into the van and slam the door, now a little irritated from the discussion with Alicia.

Fucking women.

She should be thanking me for putting my life at risk for the betterment of our future together. She's ungrateful and undeserving, and I'm starting to think I'd be better off without her. Maybe I should just get rid of her and take all the money for myself. There will be other beautiful women who will gladly be willing to obey me for a taste of the good life. I could find another way to get out of here.

FRANK IS EXHAUSTED WHEN we return. He sits in the shade and uses the shovel as a crutch as he tries not to pass out. He has dug a bunch of holes, and it's pretty clear he hasn't found anything. He devours the bottle of water that I picked up at the outdoor store and tossed to him. I flip open the blade of my switchblade and cut through the packaging of the compass. I hand it to George once I'm able to tear the final corner of the stubborn plastic seal. I read the note aloud and George spins himself around until the arrow on the cheap compass points to 282 degrees, which is westerly, which follows the note perfectly.

282w53s.

I've read it probably a hundred times and have spoken it to myself a hundred more. We are still having a problem with the second part. You don't use more than one figure when using a compass, unlike with longitude and latitude, so the 53s must mean something else. Added together, 335 degrees is northwesterly, which doesn't make much sense as the "N" is absent from the note. Subtracting the two figures, however, makes some sense, so we run with that. Not only does 229 degrees point us southwesterly and use both letters on the note, but it could also be a subliminal message within the note.

282w53s.

282 degrees west with 53 degrees subtracted points us southwesterly. "S" for subtract and "SW" for southwest. It all seems to fit, and my heart is pumping full of adrenaline as Frank begins to dig.

I wait impatiently as Frank uses the one shovel at a rapid pace and tosses the earth in every which direction. I expect to see another safe or storage box of some kind at any second, but the hole just keeps getting deeper and wider without any sign of the prize. George senses there is something missing too, and he paces behind me as he continues to play with the angle on the compass.

"I don't think this is right," he eventually says, and my heart sinks. I know he's right although I don't want to admit it. We're definitely missing something.

"What do you mean?" I ask, hoping he has a clue.

George goes on to explain what's missing. I've never actually used a compass before, besides in a science class in high school many moons ago, and I only vaguely read the instructions on the back of the package. As George explains how the compass is really only used as a directional tool and not so much a locator tool, my memory becomes clearer.

The 282 degrees is just a direction, which means the cash could be buried anywhere on the path from here to Timbuktu. The 53s must be our measurement. 282 degrees west, and 53 something. What is that something?

We toss ideas back and forth and come up with nothing. My brain is mush and I'm mentally exhausted. I try to come up with some unit of measurement, anything, that starts with an "S", but I'm drawing a blank. There must be something. As I try to brush the frustration away and clear my head, George calls for me as he stands near the corner of the house. I make my way in that direction, with Frank following.

"What?" I say as I approach.

"What about steps? 53 steps," George says.

He has my full attention immediately, and I feel stupid for not thinking of it myself. He points the compass in the direction of what remains of the protruding melted safe on the exterior of the house, and I move up close and glance at the glass face. I look up at the safe, then back at the compass.

I can't believe it. I can't fucking believe it.

The safe is at exactly 282 degrees.

I push George out of the way and slide my back up against the house. I count out fifty-three steps and use the compass to keep myself in line with the proper degree path. The ground is firm as I slam my feet together on the final step. "Here," I yell out, then Frank and George run over to me.

Frank grabs the shovel and he frantically begins to dig. This is it, I can feel it. The hole that Frank had dug before is just a few feet away, and I wonder if we would have gotten this far over at some point. The many holes scattered across the lawn are filling with water, in my mind, and mouth is suddenly dry.

The end is near.

The dry soil is piled around the perimeter of the growing hole, and the anticipation is unbearable. If Frank stopped digging for a moment, I'm almost certain he and George could hear the drum of my heartbeat through my chest. I can feel it thumping on my eardrums. Frank digs and digs until he finally pauses when the shovel jams into a solid object in the ground. It's either a rock or a storage box.

Please be a box.

Frank winds up and jams the shovel again, and the thud radiates louder this time. We look at each other and our eyes light up. I rip the shovel from his hands and push him to the side. I jam the shovel into the hard surface myself for confirmation, then I apply pressure in an effort to find out how large it is.

Realizing that it's way bigger than a rock, I throw myself to my knees and frantically start digging with my hands. The coarse soil and jagged pebbles cut into my dry, cracked hands, but I ignore the discomfort and push onward. A corner of a rustic wooden box slowly appears through the dirt, but it won't budge upon my shaking it. I search for a handle to pull on for leverage, but I come up empty. I push more dirt off the top of the wooden panel until the entire top of the secured box is visible. I wedge my hands along the edges and try to move the box, but it still won't budge. Before I can ask for help, Frank jumps across from me and gets himself in a position to help me hoist it up and out. I wedge my hands further down the edge of the box as far as I can reach, and we yank as hard as we can on a silent count of three. With each inch we pull the box upward, the sand caves in around the edges like an avalanche and the pressure is immense. My arms are shaking and my teeth are grinding, but with one final thrust the box pops out of the hole. I stumble backward as we drop the heavy oak next to the now sunken cloudy gravel pit.

The perspiration pours off my forehead, and I'm drained from the intense physical activity on such little sleep and malnutrition. The box must be double if not triple the size of the safe that's in the wall, or what's left of it, and it looks plenty big enough to hold what I think it does. I can feel the brass key poking into my thigh from inside my pants pocket, so I reach my hand in and twist it out. I grip it tightly and stare at the hole on the top of the latch on the lid of the box.

You better fucking fit.

My hand shakes as I bring the key to the lock and jam it in. The key fits like a glove, and I turn it until the crusted mechanism snaps open. I remove the lock and slowly open the lid, and I hold my breath until the light sneaks in.

Stacks and stacks of Benjamin's fill every square inch of the box. They're piled to the top of the wood and lined across the bottom in a perfect linear pattern. The bills are banded together, in stacks of thousands or ten-thousands I'm guessing, and they look brand new.

"We fucking did it," I say before collapsing to the ground with a bevy of emotions.

CHAPTER FORTY-SEVEN

GEORGE

The morning has become early afternoon and the three of us are back in the van, heading to the old police station. Alicia was able to push most of the blood to the grass on the side of the driveway with the hose, but obvious stains do still cover the cement, and probably will permanently.

Alicia and I sit on the benches across from one another while Billy drives. Billy fills Alicia in on the final stages of the plan so everyone is on the same page. He summarizes again as we pull into the garage.

"To recap," Billy says as he turns to Alicia, "wait for my call-"

"I know," she interrupts. "If I don't hear from you by ten o'clock tonight, I'll leave. I got it."

Billy smiles at her. "Good, you were listening."

Alicia sighs and looks back and forth at Billy and me. "Be careful you guys."

Billy opens the back doors for her and she slides out, but not before placing her hand on mine. It's subtle and quick, and I half expect to see a note in my hand, but it was no mistake. Billy helps her step out of the van and whispers something in her ear. She turns her face toward me as he kisses her cheek. She looks at me the entire time. The back doors close and Billy hops back in the front. He pops his head in the back as the garage door squeaks open.

"Come join me up here," he says.

I crawl over the center console and into the passenger's seat. I strap myself in as we pull into the street.

"It wasn't supposed to happen like this you know," he continues.

"No?"

"No. I didn't mean to involve you like this. I didn't realize it was going to go this far. So I'm sorry for that. I just wanted you to know."

"I just want it to be over with."

"I want to do something for you."

I chuckle to myself. "Oh yeah? What's that?"

"I want to give you a cut of the money."

I jolt my head in his direction. "What?"

"That's right. I've think you earned a little something for your efforts."

I ponder this for a moment, not sure of his motive. "I don't want the money. I just want to get out of here and start over with my life."

"It'll be a little tough to start over without any money. Now's not the time to be a tough guy, alright? Just say you'll take it before I change my mind."

Something smells fishy about it, but I agree anyway just to shut him up, "Fine, if you insist."

"Good. I do."

I glance at the clock as we glide to a stop at the street light. The talk of the money makes me uncomfortable, like I'm an accessory as opposed to a victim, so I change the subject.

"So, we're down to six hours, what next?"

"We have to head back to the house and get ready. But before we do, we have to make a stop."

WE PULL IN FRONT of a strip mall off of the main strip in the center of town and slide into one of the slanted parking spots across from the franchised electronics store. Billy opens his door and hops out of the van, so I do the same. I follow him into the store.

It's dead. The shelves are full and the store is mostly clean besides a few smudged fingerprints on the front doors and some dust on an endcap. A middle-aged man sits on a stool behind the counter, clicking away on the computer. Billy walks up to the counter and waits for the man to greet us. Joe is the store manager, as read from his name badge that hangs from a yellow lanyard around his neck. Joe looks up to us as we wait impatiently.

"Good afternoon, gentleman, what can I do for you today?" Joe says.

I glance to Billy, as I too am curious about the same thing.

"We need two phones," Billy says. "And they need to be untraceable."

CHAPTER FORTY-EIGHT

BILLY

It takes me a moment to gather myself, but once I do, we move with rapid speed. I've been hauling around a duffel bag everywhere we go, and I finally get the chance to use it for the purpose I bought it for. I grab the bag, unzip it, and pour the contents on the ground beside me. The tools that we've used to dismantle Snake's house clatter together as gravity pulls them to the dirt. Carefully wrapping my fingers around two stacks of bills at a time, I pile them into the bag until the earthed box is completely empty. I flip the corner of each stack as I put it in the bag, wafting the smell of revenge as it seeps through the bills.

When the last stack is squeezed into the bag, I zip it and toss it over my shoulder. It's heavier than I would have thought, but the strain on my lower back is more than worth it. I direct Frank to gather up the items from the ground and I head in the direction of the van. We leave the box above ground with the note from the safe inside as a way to give the Zved's the middle finger when they come looking for the money. The lock rests on the ground next to it with the key still engaged.

Let them suck on that.

Frank catches up to George and me as we approach the van. I place my arm around his shoulder and pull him forward and out of range for George to hear. His arms are piled with everything that was in the duffel bag before, and I immediately remove my gun from his pocket and slide it back into my holster.

"Did you get everything?" I ask him as we walk ahead of George.

"I think so, boss. My pockets are full too."

"We'll head for Mexico in the morning, okay?"

"Why not now?"

"We all need a fresh start. We need some rest."

"What about Georgie?"

"We'll drop him off in the morning, then we'll hit the road."

Frank nods and smiles, and I do the same.

"We did good, buddy, we did good."

BACK IN THE OLD police station, Frank, George, and I are in one of the offices. I'm sitting in a chair in front of a table, Frank is nodding off in the chair next to me, and George is nervously tapping his foot, wondering why I haven't let him go. I haven't seen Alicia yet, and I'm looking forward to seeing her reaction when she discovers what I've found.

I told her I would find it, and I did. I expect that she's preparing a reward for me.

I unzip the bag of cash so that some of the bills fall onto the tabletop for effect. I grab a single stack and count it: Ten-thousand even, just as I thought.

I had promised Frank that I would let George go unharmed, but I still haven't made a final decision about that. I had intended all along to let him go when we finished, but now I'm not so sure. He's a whole lot smarter than I thought he would be, and I'm just not sure I can trust him to not go to the police. Or worse, now that Frank has babbled to him where we're going next, what if he comes looking for us and the money? I'm just not sure that I can risk it. I'll have to sleep on it.

Behind me, the door creaks open and Alicia enters the room. The excitement in her voice makes me jump, and I turn to face her to gauge her reaction. She stares at the table in disbelief, and I think I can see the reflection of Independence Hall in her iris. She smiles at me, and at George, and I half expect her to come kiss me.

She doesn't.

Now that he has his security blanket in the room, George suddenly has the balls to confront me. He wouldn't dare if Alicia wasn't here, and I don't blame him. She's been on his side the whole time, until now. I'm not blind, I realize this, but money talks, baby; she's all mine now.

I tell him that I'll let him go in the morning, which may be a lie, or maybe not, and he flips his shit. He tells me that he's leaving, both he and Alicia, and I wait for her reaction before I do anything. She glances at me and it's obvious she wants me to step in, so I do. Just as they're about to leave the room, I sneak up behind them and grab Alicia's wrist. George turns to me as Alicia gasps, and I jam the barrel of my gun into his forehead. He looks at me in a panic, and I know I have him at my mercy. He'll stay the night, and I'll figure out what to do with him by morning. Frank is suddenly awake and alert, and he's standing next to me.

"Get him out of my face," I say, then Frank grabs him and leads him away. I listen for the steel door to the holding room down the hall to open and close, then I pull Alicia inside the office and close the door. "You weren't going to go with him, were you?"

"Of course not."

"I didn't see any resistance from you. It sure looked like you were going to go if I didn't stop him."

"What was I supposed to do?"

"So you were going to go with him?"

She crosses her arms and looks away. I shake my head at her in disgust without her noticing. She brushes past me and approaches the table, then quickly changes the subject.

"Look at all that money," she says in admiration.

I grin and suddenly don't care about what she was going to do before. I turn and walk next to her, then put my arms around her waist. I slide my thumb along her inner thigh.

"It's all ours. You and me. Husband and-"

"Please don't." She pushes my arm off of her and steps aside.

"What's your problem?"

She shakes her head. I move next to her and pull her close. She refuses to look at me, and she clearly doesn't want to talk about it. We have a long ride tomorrow, so we'll talk about it then. I'll convince her.

"What about George?" she says.

"What about him?"

"Why didn't you let him go?"

I shrug. "I haven't decided what I want to do with him yet."

"That was not part of the plan. You were going to let him go as soon as we got the money."

"I guess it's a good thing I'm the one in charge then, huh?"

Alicia is scorching now, and the vein on her forehead pulsates as it protrudes from her face. I've never found her sexier. I smile at her.

"What are you smiling at?"

"You."

"Why?"

"I was just thinking. There might be something that will help me make up my mind."

She's much calmer now, and attentive. "I'm listening."

Without saying anything, I slowly lean in and place my lips on the side of her neck. She doesn't resist, which surprises me, so I caress her jawbone and earlobe with my tongue. She finally stops me as I work my way up and blow warm breath from my nose into her ear canal.

"Billy, please stop."

I back away from her and look into her eyes. Her mouth doesn't agree with the signals from her brain, and I can tell she wants it. I walk over to the door and lock it.

Frank can have the front seat to himself tonight.

My eyes meet with Alicia's as I make my way back toward her. "Shut up," I say with tenderness, then I force her to make love to me, finally, for the first time.

IT'S MORNING AND I'M in a much better mood now. I wake Alicia and tell her to meet me in the van. She looks like hell, and she would tell me it's because she was crying all night if I were to ask, so I don't. She was crying alright, but I didn't hear her say "stop" too many times, and none of those times were without the preceding "don't".

I make my way down the corridor and to the holding area where George is being kept. I've decided that I'm going to let him go, and he has no idea the debt that he owes to Alicia for that. He literally owes her his life.

I wake him as I enter the room and lead him out, then we head for the van. He joins Frank and Alicia in the back while I drive in silence back to Josie's Bar and Pub.

I think about the long drive to Mexico that's going to start today, and what it is that we're going to do when we get there. All of our documentation is in place and being stored in the glove box for safe keeping. It will take us just about a total of twenty-four hours on the road, four tanks of gas, two hotels, and lots of stops for grub. We'll drive south on I-35 and ride through Wichita, Oklahoma City, and through the heart of Texas before we cross the border in Laredo. We'll eventually make our way down to Cancun, we may fly, after a brief stop at a border town on the Gulf of Mexico. That stop is still to be determined. It would be quicker and easier to fly into Mexico, but they'll never let us in with the kind of cash that we have on us. Plus, I refuse to let it out of my sight until it can be dispersed safely into numerous different banks and accounts.

Once in Cancun, I have instructions to call a local in regards to a boat that he's holding for me. I'll wire him twenty-five percent once we cross the border, then I'll pay him the remaining seventy-five percent in cash when we do make our way there. I'll use the time on the road to convince Alicia to marry me once we get to Cancun and before we set sail, and I'm confident she'll give in once she realizes that it's either that or I leave the dock without her. I don't really have a backup plan at this point, so I need her to pull through. Frank will be staying back in Cancun until I can figure out how to get him across the channel, although he doesn't know that yet.

I PULL INTO THE empty parking lot of Josie's, and George's car is still in the same place it was a few days prior. The only additions are a parking ticket and a boot on one of the tires. Maybe I'll give him a few bucks to get that taken care of, or maybe not. I put the van in park but leave the engine running, then I get out and walk to the back to open the doors.

"You can go," I say to George.

He gets up from his seat and hops out of the van. He looks relieved to be free, and I'm not sure if I've made the right decision or not. If he was wise, he'd get a move on it before I change my mind. He reaches for Alicia, but she doesn't move from the bench. I grin to myself and take pleasure in the fact that we finally get to break the news to him. Alicia starts to cry as George presses for her to follow, and I can't help but roll my eyes. I'm looking forward to this continuous charade to be over with so she and I can start our lives together. She begins to tell him everything, but is cut off quickly once the attacks begin.

I spin around and instinctively reach for my weapon, but realize that I have left it in the van. I duck and cover my head as I see a black van, similar in style to mine, trying to weave through traffic at the opposite end of the parking lot. The windows are tinted, and all I can see is the heavy shotgun barrel pointing out the window of the passenger's side and an occasional shell being discharged onto the street. They're warning shots from that distance, a trademark of the Zved's, but they'll become much more than that if they get here before we leave.

We have to go.

I pull George down next to me and tell him to get back into the van, but he's understandably hesitant. It's life or death, and I don't have time to wait for him to make up his mind. I wait for it, and once the next shot blasts and the echoes are bellowing, I hop into the back of the van and crawl my way into the safety of the front seat. I slide the transmission into drive and give George one more chance.

It's now or never.

Frank reaches his arm out for George, who eventually does grab it and is yanked into the van. I peel away, rubber burning and smoke clouding, as Frank slams the back doors.

Using the skills I had learned at the academy, I weave in and out of traffic with a vengeance, and I know it's not long before I lose the tail. How did they find us so quickly? I know they were snooping around the building the other day, but how did they know where we were going? They must have been following us. They have never seen Alicia before the other day, though, and they certainly don't know the association between her and me. That only leaves one possible reason: They have somehow found out my identity. I have a sneaking suspicion how, but I really hope I'm wrong.

When it's obvious the coast is clear, I slow down and pull onto a dirt road that's off the main strip. The van rattles and bounces around as I drive over grassy dunes and a set of old train tracks. I stop the van on a flat spot and slide into the back. The bag of cash rests on the floor up front, but a second identical duffel bag holds the tools in the back. I unzip it and start sorting through the supplies. It's filled with the items that Frank had picked up back at Snake's house after I emptied the bag for the cash. Everything is there it seems, except for one thing. He better just have it in his pocket and forgot to toss it in the bag.

"Where is it?" I say, directing it to Frank.

"Where's what, boss?" Frank says.

I lift the bag and pour the contents to the floor, hoping I missed it among the goods. "Where's my badge?"

"Uh-"

"Where's my fucking badge?"

"Uh, I dunno, boss. It should be in the bag. I grabbed everything like you told me to and put it in the bag."

I sort through the supplies that are on the floor of the van now, and it's definitely not there. The one thing he left behind is the most important item, the one thing that can trace the heist back to me, Frank forgot. I'm livid and more upset than I've been at any other point in my life, and I don't know what to do. I wish I could control myself, but the rage is just too much for me to handle, so I clench my fingers into a fist and start pounding on Frank's face.

His lips move as he covers his head in defense, although I don't hear a word that he says. I assume that he's pleading for me to stop, as that is what his eyes are telling me. I'm completely unaware of Alicia and George around me, and I'm in the zone and my target is weak and defenseless to my fury. I don't stop until he's on the floor of the van and unconscious, then I finally break free from my trance.

I sit on the bench alongside George, and he slowly creeps down toward the back doors. Alicia is opposite him, terrified. My heart is pounding from the rush, but the adrenaline is slowing beginning to dissipate. I look to Frank as he rests motionless on the floor of the van. His face is battered and bloody, and I think his nose may be broken. His mouth is cracked open, but it looks like all of his teeth are still in place. The pain suddenly pulsates from my trembling hands, and my breath is slowing.

What have I done?

George creeps away from me and sits on the bench next to Alicia instead. I insist that Frank's still alive and breathing, and I tell them so. I repeat it to myself silently, hoping that it'll be true. I may have gone too far, but I just couldn't control myself. I wonder if that's how Frank felt some years ago back at the restaurant. Maybe we aren't so different after all.

Not needing prompting, George slides from his new seat on the bench and approaches Frank. I look away while he feels for a pulse. It takes him a moment to find it, but he confirms that Frank is still alive. I try not to show it, but I'm relieved. I've seen many men die for a lot less, so we're not out of the woods by any means. I won't know how bad the damage really is until he returns to consciousness, if he ever does.

The van is silent for a few minutes while everyone tries to gather themselves. More details will come to me I hope, but I wonder if either one of them tried to stop me when I was beating into Frank. I can't remember a thing, and that scares me. I don't know when I became to be like this, but I don't like it. Maybe I should get myself checked out before we leave Cancun.

The Zved's are onto us now, that much is obvious, and they know where we're staying. We cannot and will not go back to the old police station, and we'll never make it all the way to Mexico before they find us. It's practically a straight shot, so the Zved's will have guys waiting for us at every major checkpoint. We won't even make it out of Kansas. Everything has changed now, and we're purely in survival mode. We need to go somewhere to buy us some time until I figure out our next move. The two men that were shooting at us saw George, and they likely snapped some pictures of him during the commotion. It will take them a day or two at most to find out who he is and where he lives. Until then, that's where we can go to lay low for a while.

CHAPTER FORTY-NINE

GEORGE

Billy and I spend the afternoon mostly by ourselves after returning to my house from the store. Joe had hooked us up with a couple of pay-as-you-go flip phones and we were in and out of the store within fifteen minutes. Billy had paid for the phones and minutes in cash and we left before getting a receipt. It's 7:15 P.M. now, so there's about one hour left until the Zved's should be arriving.

Frank's body is face down in the bathtub and the door is closed. The smell of the decomposing body is seeping under the cracked door and is starting to overtake the entire upstairs. Billy has been sleeping on the couch for a few hours now, and the smell has gotten a lot worse since then. I wonder if this is part of the master plan.

I'm pacing downstairs, been doing so for a while, trying to compose myself. As the time winds down, it's all starting to become realer. These guys are coming tonight, soon, and it's going to change everything. One way or another, it all ends tonight. Billy talks about it with confidence and I think I believe him when he says it's going to go well. I can't help but think, though, what if it doesn't? What if they ambush me like they did Frank and give me no chance? Would anyone even show up to my funeral? Would anyone even know I was dead? Most of all, would anyone even care?

I glance at the clock that hangs on the wall at the bottom of the stairs: 7:45 P.M. It's getting closer, but time is still dragging. I really just want to get this over with before I psych myself out. I'm trying to stay focused and concentrate on what I need to do, but I need a distraction.

From upstairs, it sounds like Billy's awake. I can hear some footsteps trailing down the hallway heading toward my room, then back down toward the kitchen. The door above the stairs creaks open and the heavy feet make their way down the steps. Billy comes into view as he approaches the bottom stair.

"There you are," Billy says. "I've been looking all over for you."

"I needed somewhere quiet to think."

Billy nods in acknowledgment. He motions to the tile on the floor with the now mostly dry grout. "That looks pretty good, huh?"

I turn and look behind me, then nod in agreement.

He continues, "Do you want to go over it one more time? The plan I mean."

I shrug. "If you want to. I've gone over it a hundred times in my mind, but we can if it would make you feel better."

"Me?" Billy snickers. "I was asking for you, not for me. I have the easy part."

"You're telling me." I want to add a snide remark at the end, but I decide against it.

We stand in silence for a few moments before Billy reaches into his pocket. He walks down the rest of the stairs and hands me one of the phones that we had picked up earlier.

"Here," he says, "you'll be needing this."

I take the phone from his hand and place it in my hip pocket.

"It's on vibrate. I've already programmed the number for my phone as speed dial one. You'll be hearing from me at nine o'clock sharp if I don't hear from you first." Billy turns and starts to head back up the stairs.

"Where are you going?" I ask.

"I'm heading up the hill. I'll wait there." He waits for me to respond, but I don't. "Stay calm and stick to the plan. Everything will be fine."

I take a deep breath and shake my head. Billy nods back before making his way up the stairs. It's not long before I hear the front door open and close. Now I wait.

Nearly an hour later, I'm upstairs and rotating between sitting on the couch and pacing back and forth between the living room and kitchen. The clock on the microwave reads 8:27 P.M. Anytime now. A small anxiety knot is beginning to form in my chest, but I'm staying relatively calm. If I was the praying type, I'd say a prayer right about now. I take some deep breaths and approach the window again.

I got this.

CHAPTER FIFTY

BILLY

I pull the van into George's driveway and I don't tell him how I know where he lives. He doesn't ask. When we arrive, George helps me carry Frank into the house. He's dead weight and it's an exhaustive task, but we make it to the couch in the living room without dropping him. Without any conversation, George eats something then disappears down the hallway and closes the door behind him. Alicia follows shortly thereafter. I relieve myself in the bathroom before taking a tour of the well-maintained home while I start to gather my thoughts. I drift away in the chair across from Frank in the living room.

Refreshed upon waking, I know exactly what I need to do. The money has to be hidden, and fast. The Zved's will be on our trail before we know it, and we may have to leave for a while. They'll tear this house apart, much like we did at Snake's, so it needs to be kept somewhere they'll never suspect.

I carefully inspect each room and look for a good place to hide the money. Light snores are heard from behind the closed bedroom door at the end of the hallway, so I decide to skip that room and let them be. I open each of the cabinets in the kitchen, consider making a hole in the drywall inside the closet door in the hall, and even strongly contemplate draining the water from the toilet and storing the cash in the back of the porcelain. I think this will work, but there is not nearly enough space for all of it. I could split the money up, leave some here and there, but it's best if it's all together. Chances are high that we'll have only a small window of time to gather the money before we have to leave, so that increases the chances that some may be forgotten. That's not an option.

I make my way down the stairs and into the partially finished basement. I'm admittedly bewildered and out of ideas, and the frustration is beginning to mount. The drop ceiling is an appealing option, but that's much too obvious. These are intelligent guys, so I need to think outside of the box if I ever want to see the money again.

As I pace back and forth on the large tiles that line the basement floor, something catches my attention. In the corner of the room rests a half-empty bag of grout powder. One of the tiles on the floor sinks slightly as I pass over it with my foot, which is a sign of a clear deficiency from a poor installation job. I pull my feet together on this tile and bounce on it. It's subtle, but there is an elasticized flex as my knees spring, and I think this may be it.

I scurry up the stairs and retrieve a plastic tool box that I had noticed when looking in the closet before. In the kitchen, I gather a wooden spoon and fill an ugly multi-colored bowl with water and head back down the stairs. The loose tile is almost directly in the center of the floor, which is neither good nor bad, although it does pose the risk of being found easier. I place the toolbox and other supplies from the kitchen on the floor next to me and start sorting through the tools that are available. I need to remove the tile without breaking it, that's the first step. The tile job is amateur, and I can tell the deficiencies in alignment and levelness upon a closer look. George did this himself I'm willing to bet, and his lack of precision may be just what I need.

It's a long and tedious process, but I slowly carve away the dried grout with a painters chisel and hammer. My lower back is aching, so I'm forced to take a break for a while, despite my strong opposition. My back cracks as I stand, and I grunt forcefully. My legs have begun to fall asleep due to the restricted circulation, so I walk the perimeter of the room until the feeling is restored. My wrists are sore and my knees are swelling, but I force myself to fight through it and plop back down over the tile and get back to work.

Upstairs, I hear the creak of the bedroom door open and close, and I follow the footsteps down the hall and basement stairs. Moments later, I can sense someone standing behind me, but I don't look up from my work.

"What are you doing?" a male voice asks, George's.

He's standing next to me now, so I drop the chisel and hammer, get to my feet, and explain to him what's going on. He stays mostly quiet as I tell him that the money needs a temporary hiding place, that the Zved's are coming after us and always were, and that this will never really end until we're dead and they have their money back. While I tell him all this, I eventually get back to work and crack the last of the grout and separate the tile from the subfloor. Fortunately, the tile stays in one piece, so it can be used again. It's a good thing, because I haven't seen any spares lying around.

I dig a shallow hole and toss the bag inside. My heart aches as I force myself to let go of the hard-earned cash, but I'll be back for it. The tile rests snugly on top of the newly dug hole, scattered remnants of dried grout falling inside, and it lays down flat. I drag the bag of grout near my workstation and pour a handful of powder into the water-filled bowl. I mix it up quickly with the wooden spoon and start spreading it in the thin troughs around the four edges of the tile.

As I work diligently, the discussion takes on a more negative turn for George. He presses me about my plan and about Alicia and the baby, and I can't help myself. I had thought she was going to tell him everything when they were in the bedroom upstairs, but I can tell by his reaction that she has not. I take the opportunity to gladly share the truth.

There is no baby and there never was. It was all a lie to get him to play along, and it worked. I laugh hysterically in his face at his oblivion at the entire situation, and naturally, he doesn't believe me. Why would he? Everything has been a lie up to this point, so he has no reason to believe me now. He rushes up the stairs to talk to Alicia. All I can hope is that she finally comes clean to him so we can move on.

I finish applying new grout to the tile and listen for the confrontation. To my dissatisfaction, the conversation is soft and I can't hear a word they're saying. She's letting him down easy I assume, and I laugh to myself at her sensitivity. The grout won't be completely dry for a couple of days, which is good, as it will enable us quick access for removing the money since the tile will be easier to remove. I slide the bag of grout powder back to its original resting spot against the wall near the door. I pour the remaining contents of the bowl just outside the door and leave the crusted bowl and spoon on the bottom step. I climb up the stairs and head right for the bedroom.

"You can stop the act now," I say as I pop my head inside, "I told him everything." I laugh out loud and head down the hallway to the bathroom to take a leak.

Moments later, I catch a glimpse of George hustling down the hallway from the reflection in the mirror, and I wonder if Alicia did finally admit it. A loud crash comes from the kitchen, and I wait for the stream to die down before going to investigate. Alicia hears it too, and she and I meet at the doorway and head toward the open concept kitchen and living area together.

I may have underestimated the fuse that burns within George. I suddenly realize that I may have crossed the line, and maybe Alicia was right about him. He's a sensitive guy with a good heart, and I completely disregarded the testosterone within him. He stands over Frank, who still lays unconscious on the couch, holding a wide-handled butcher's knife. I try to stay calm, but everything I say just seems to piss him off further. His eyes are full of fury, and his face is beet red. The blade is shaking in his hand and I'm afraid the pendulum is going to whip forward at any time. He is truly terrifying at this moment, and I really did not see this coming. I don't want to do it, but I see no other way out of this. I slowly reach my hand behind my back for my gun. I feel around, but grab only a handful of an empty holster. I scan the room and see the gun sitting on the table beside George. I must have left it there when I fell asleep for a bit. Fuck.

I'm at a loss for what do to. My words aren't helping, and Alicia is in a state of shock, so she's useless. I consider charging him, but I don't see how I get out of that unharmed. He may kill me and Frank if I push it, so I don't. I drop my hands to my side, hopeless, and brace myself for whatever happens. I close my eyes and whisper to myself, and when I open them, George has his head down and has dropped the knife.

Without thinking, I run toward him and grab the handle of the knife from underneath his bowed head. He doesn't offer any resistance, and he doesn't even look up at me. He's overwhelmed and he cries tears of exhaustion. I grab the gun from the table next to him and back away. Alicia and I watch him closely, wondering what he's going to do next.

A few tense moments pass, and nothing happens. George eventually gets up from his knees and walks past Alicia and me, and heads down into the basement.

"We should leave for a while," I say.

"And go where?" Alicia responds.

"Anywhere, it doesn't matter. He needs some space."

"What about Frank?"

I stare at his still unconscious body on the couch and realize that does pose a major challenge. We can't leave him here, as he may be dead when we get back, but I'm not sure Alicia is strong enough to help me carry him.

"You're going to have to help me carry him I guess," I say.

Without hesitation, she walks over to the couch and grabs his feet. I walk past her and open the front door, then wrap my arms around Frank's torso and carry most of the weight from his upper body.

Alicia has to stop to rest three different times once outside, but we reach the van and are able to lean him against the back. I climb inside, lock my arms under his armpits, and haul him up and in. I nearly collapse once he's finally inside, and I don't know how many more times I can do this. Alicia sits on the bumper of the van, sweating and breathing heavily, and she hollers to me over her shoulder through choppy breaths.

"Okay, so what now?"

CHAPTER FIFTY-ONE

GEORGE

I pinch the blinds open, letting the setting sun shine in. The street is mostly deserted. Over the hill I can see a car approaching; that's my signal. I knew this moment would come, but it's not something one can fully prepare for. I'm calmer and more relaxed than I thought I would be, and I immediately go into a zone that I've never before entered. I start going through the checklist in my mind.

The deadbolt is unlocked, as is the key lock. I hate doing this, but we need to make sure our guys are able to get in the front door. If they have to go downstairs or break in somehow, the whole thing could be ruined. Billy needs them in a certain spot in order for this to work. I open the curtain so that they can see inside, and I strategically leave a glass of water on the end table next to the couch, which is right in the line of sight of the window. They'll see the glass and know that we've been here, so they'll come inside.

That's the plan anyway.

I count to ten, then scurry from the window and head for the basement. I can never remember which exact tile it is, but I know it's in the middle of the floor somewhere. I grab the necessary tools from the toolbox under the stairs and drop to my knees. I start feeling around and tapping the tiles with my knuckle, listening for the hollow one. When I find it on the third attempt, I jam the wooden-handled chisel into the grout and start chipping it away with a hammer. After a few slams, the grout gives, cracking down the center. The surface is crusted and dry, but the inside is still soft, so it cracks easily. Saving the tile isn't important, so I aggressively hammer around the edges until the tile is loose enough for me to pry it up and toss it to the side. It lands on its corner and chips.

The familiar black duffel bag waits inside the hole, and it appears to be untampered with, as one would expect. A coolness stems from the exposed soil, and it feels nice on my stubble. I reach my arms down into the darkness and reach for the bag. Ten million dollars is surprisingly heavy, so it takes me more effort than I thought it would, but I'm still able to yank it up with both hands. Once above ground, paranoia sets in, so I unzip the bag to make sure the contents are still there. The cash smells of greed and death, but I'm relieved that it's all in place, although I'm not sure where it would have disappeared to. I stare at the tightly wound stacks and wonder how much of this Billy is going to give me.

I push the chisel and hammer down into the hole and slide the tile over the opening. I try to line it up the best I can, although there really is no point in doing so. The chipped corner sticks out like a sore thumb. Once covered, I rise to my feet and toss the bag over my shoulder. Before leaving, I head to the electrical panel on the wall and switch all of the fuses on the breaker to off, killing all electricity to the house. I stand by the door and wait for the sound. The front door opens and closes upstairs, which is my queue to move, so I slide out the back door.

They're in the house now, and everything is working out perfectly so far.

I take a few steps toward the shed until the driveway comes into view. A dark colored sedan is parked in the driveway with the engine off, and the streets appear to still be empty, except for a few crows flying overhead. I take one final peek back at the house to make sure no one is watching, then I hustle across the burnt grass to the shed.

The shed appears to be ordinary, but it's really just a mask for what lies beneath. There's an organized workbench on the right as I enter. There are some hanging lawn maintenance tools: a rake, shovel, weed trimmer, and a single hook for where the garden hose used to hang. A rusty lawn mower sits in the corner by itself. I peer through the tiny window to make sure I'm still alone. When I see that I am, I quickly search on the floor for the painted red nail. Only the top of the nail is painted, but I needed a reference point. I grab the pry bar that leans against the wall and use it to loosen the nail, allowing me to lift up the section of the floor. In preparation for easy access, I had glued a few floorboards together so they would all rise off the floor with one fluid motion, and I am thankful for that decision right now.

When the opening is wide enough for me to fit through, I toss the bag down the hole and sit on my backside, then I slither down the shallow tunnel and land on the earth below. There is a steel brace that is welded to a sheet of steel that is attached to the underside of the floorboards, and I use that to pull the floor down above me. I pull one of the rusty nails toward me and watch it as it disappears into the designated hole in the wood.

It's not uncommon for people in this part of the country to have bunkers, especially being right in the heart of tornado alley. When my parents' ranch got torn away by a sweeping funnel the summer before last, I used that as a sign that I needed to have one. I hired a local contractor not long after, and he built me one underneath the shed. That, apparently, might have been the best decision I have ever made.

The tunnel is small and narrow, not much more than a crawl space really, but it widens a bit at the base. I'm able to sit comfortably with my legs crossed, so I finagle myself to do just that. I pull the bag into my lap and wrap my arms around it. It's all I have left to keep me safe, so I refuse to let it go.

The space is cold and dark, and the only light I have is that of the dull backlight of the pay-as-you-go phone. The cool air soothes my skin, and it helps to freeze the perspiration away. I grab the phone from my pocket and hold it in my hand, occasionally shining it above my head. Although dim, the light reflects against the steel plate above me, and it provides me with enough light to see.

There is a second steel bracket that's attached to the sidewall of the bunker just behind my head, and I kick myself for forgetting the crucial tool from above. There is a thick chain that is hanging next to the door of the shed that has a heavy-duty carabiner attached to each end. The intent would be to attach one end of the carabiner to the brace on the underside of the planks, and the other to the brace on the wall of the bunker. This would prevent the door from being ripped open during a tornado, or in my case, if an unwanted visitor tried to unbury me.

During all of the excitement and high-stakes activity, I simply forgot to bring the chain with me to lock myself inside. I consider climbing out and retrieving it, but I can't get myself to leave the comfort of the darkness. Instead, I pull the bag closer to my chest, squeeze the phone tighter in my hand, and hope that no one finds me. I close my eyes and mumble to myself.

I told myself I would never die like my parents did. They had a bunker in the backyard, but they never used it. The storm came suddenly, and they ignored the warning signs from the television alerts. My father was stubborn, and my mother oblivious. They were inside the house when it got swept away. Their bodies were just two of the many that were recovered from the rubble a few days later. I had invested in the bunker with the determination that I would never die without putting up a fight. I had never even considered the thought that I might die inside of it.

Come on Billy, I'm counting on you.

CHAPTER FIFTY-TWO

BILLY

Alicia rides up front with me as we head into town. Frank lays on his back on the floor in the rear, and I drive cautiously to avoid any unforgiving road deficiencies. I pull into the parking lot of an independent drugstore and send Alicia inside to retrieve a remedy for Frank. I light a cigarette and wait for her to return.

I smoke a full one and part of a second before Alicia finally emerges from the store. She carries a clear plastic bag and hops back into the van. She glares at me, so I take one final drag and toss the lit cigarette out the window. I grab a piece of gum and toss it in my mouth after I drop the wrapper in the back. She removes a box from the plastic bag and hands it to me. We leap into the back and stand over Frank. I remove the white package that looks like a bite-sized candy treat from the container and take a whiff. The aroma of ammonia is powerful and it clears my sinuses instantly, forcing me to turn away.

"Do you think it's going to work?" Alicia asks.

I look at her and shrug. "I hope so. If this doesn't, I don't know what will."

I slide the smelling salt pouch under Frank's nose and wait for a reaction. When I get none, I put my hand over his nose and mouth and cut off his air. I slide the pouch under his nose again and remove my hands from his face with the hope that he'll take a deep breath to refill his lungs. He does just that, and the ammonia erupts into his sinus cavity. His bloodshot eyes flick open and he chokes for breath. Alicia jumps, as do I, as Frank gasps for air and comes back into consciousness. I look to Alicia and smile, and she returns to gesture. Frank slowly sits up.

"Good morning, buddy," I say. "Nice to see you."

Frank is dazed and looks between Alicia and me, and rubs his temples with his index fingers. "Did we make it?" he slurs his words, and I can barely understand him. Alicia shoots me a strange look, and I can tell she's having the same difficulty.

"What's that?" I say.

"Mexico. Did we make it?" his words are clearer this time, and I smile at him.

"No, not yet. We haven't left yet."

"Do you remember what happened?" Alicia asks, leaning in.

Frank thinks to himself for a moment and shakes his head. "The last thing I remember is us dropping Georgie off, then some bullets."

I smile to myself, pleased that he has no memory of my rage. I won't let him look in a mirror for a while, and he'll never even know what happened. I pull him in and embrace him, and he weakly drapes one arm around my shoulder. I want to tell him how sorry I am and that it will never happen again, but he doesn't even remember what happened, so I tell myself to forget about it.

"Are you hungry, buddy?" I say, still smiling. "Do you want some food?"

FRANK, ALICIA, AND I cruise through the drive-through of a fast food burger joint near the pharmacy, and Frank eats like he hasn't done so in days. I tell him he can order anything he wants from the menu, and he does just that. I order for him, as he's still groggy and slurring his words. The teenager on the other end of the microphone struggles to account for the large order, and I have to correct him three times as he reads it back to me. Alicia and I drill Frank's memory some more, but his knowledge of my attack is non-existent. We eat in the parking lot in the back of the van, and Frank vomits all over the pavement outside after inhaling seven burgers too quickly. We leave after that.

We pull into George's driveway shortly after 8:00 P.M., which is about an hour after we had left. Alicia and I walk with Frank until he's inside, although he doesn't understand the purpose. He just thinks he fell asleep for a while and may never know what actually happened to him. I fear he has suffered a concussion, although he claims it's just a hunger headache that will go away once he fully digests what remains in his stomach. I tell him he slipped and fell in the van, just in case he sees his reflection in a window somewhere.

Once safely inside, I go on the hunt for George. I keep my gun close, just in case, and work my way down the hall. I hear heavy breathing, almost panic, coming from the bathroom, and the shower curtain trembles as I enter the room. This isn't my first rodeo with sneaking into someone's house under high stress, but I feel naked and blind without my bulletproof vest and team of backups. I extend my arm, wrap my hand around the shower curtain, and pull the curtain to the side. George lets out a grotesque high-pitched yelp and slides deeper into the bathtub.

He holds the same butcher's knife as before, but I don't get the sense he's prepared to use it. I extend him my free hand and hold it for a moment. He looks up at me in terror and drops the knife to my feet. I keep my hand extended and George eventually does take it.

George is clearly spooked, and I wonder if something has happened. I press him for details, and my heart sinks when he tells me about what he saw. The Zved's have found us and are already planning their attack. It has happened faster than I had expected, and I'm not fully prepared to take them on yet. I play it cool, like I know what to do next, but I'm just as frightened as he is.

We don't have much time now.

We leave the knife on the bathroom floor as we exit. I lead George into the living room where Frank and Alicia are waiting. He's surprised to see Frank awake, and they briefly banter back and forth politely. I didn't notice before, but George has a deep cut on his hand which is bleeding pretty good. He holds his wrist tight against his chest like an eagle would do with a wounded wing, and his shirt is quickly becoming soaked with blood. He must have cut himself with that knife, and I wonder if it was intentional or not.

Time is becoming critical as the Zved's may be back at any moment, so I break up the conversation and hit them with the bad news. Frank and Alicia are stunned, and George is reactionless, but I tell them I have a plan to get us out of here, even though I don't. I just need to get back into the van and drive for a while. I'll figure it out then.

I make my way to the front door and open it a crack and tell them to wait for my signal. I quickly scan the landscape and see nothing except for my van where I left it in the driveway. A flock of crows scream by and startle me, but I turn into the house and give them the signal. The coast is clear.

I usher the group out the front door and close it behind them. I stomp across the walkway and through the flowerbed and slide in the driver's side of the van. I scan the landscape again and still see nothing. Whoever it was that George saw is long gone.

George and Alicia are already in the back of the van, and Frank should be joining them any second. A second goes by, then a few more, and a few more.

Still no Frank. Where's Frank?

I check my mirrors and see nothing, and just as I'm about to go check it out, I'm thrown back into my seat with terror. The Zved's are back and they're heavily armed. There are no more warning shots from a shotgun, and they're ready to play with the big guns. Multiple clips are wasted in our direction, and they are emptied in a rapid-fire, military-style militia pace. The bullets ricochet from every angle it seems, and the piercing sounds rattle in my ears. I slide down underneath the steering wheel and cover my head. Just as I do, the shots fade and the echoes die out, and squealing tires peel away from the area. I check myself for wounds and find none, then I pull myself up back into the seat and look in the back.

"You okay? Everyone okay?" I ask.

Alicia and George look panicked, and they must be blocking Frank, because I don't see him. He made it inside, I'm sure of it. He was right behind George when we left the house, so he must have made it.

He made it, right?

I don't see him.

I swing my door open and run around the front of the van, expecting to see Frank hiding underneath or something. What I find instead, is nothing less than horrifying.

I've never before heard the squeal that comes out of my mouth when I see the condition of Frank's body, but I can't hold it in. I stagger toward him, hoping for a miracle, then collapse to my knees next to him. I ignore the blood and gore and rest my head on Frank's chest. I sob aggressively and uncontrollably, and I pound my fists on the cement. The fresh blood splatters on my shirt with each punch, but I don't stop until I can punch no more. My heart aches and my fists are swelling.

My poor brother is dead, and it's at the hands of the Zved's. I'm overwhelmed and distraught, and all I can do is lean my head back and scream into the open sky.

THE ZVED'S HAVE STRUCK again, and there is only one Lewis left for them to take down: Me. But I'm not about to let that happen. They'll be back tomorrow, and I'll be ready. Alicia, George, and I spend the night in the van in the driveway, and I didn't sleep for one minute. I know exactly what needs to be done now, and I'm not leaving until it's done. The Zved's are going down tonight, the entire operation. It's either them or me, and it sure as hell won't be me. They're going to regret having fucked with me.

With a detailed plan in place to end the Zved's reign of trepidation, George reluctantly helps me move Frank's body. We have less than twelve hours before they'll be back, and I'm not about to waste time. George grabs Frank's feet as I would expect, and I'm forced to wrestle with his torso again. His body is significantly lighter than before, and I'm sure the lack of circulating blood has something to do with that. Despite my upper body soreness from having carried Frank so many times, I concentrate on breathing instead of looking at his ravaged corpse the best I can, and it's clear I'm doing much better than George is. As we approach the door, George lets go of poor Frank's lower half and vomits violently into the bushes like an amateur. I can tell he's in no position to continue, so I drag Frank the rest of the way inside by myself.

Where to put the body? I release my grip on Frank's collar and his head slams sharply into the carpet. The impact is cushioned a bit by the softness of his weakened skull, and the thud is muffled. I want them to find his body, but I don't want to scare them off either. They might panic if the first thing they see is a body in this condition, even though they were the ones who did it, and you never know what they might do then. I need them to stand here for a while and try to figure out where the smell is coming from.

I crouch down behind Frank's torso and pull him up to waist level, then I pull him through the living room and into the hallway. His dragging body leaves a trail of blood on the carpet. It's like pushing a shopping cart up a steep hill, but I am eventually able to maneuver his limbs one at a time and flip him into the bathtub. He splats face first into the tub, and I almost get sick when I see the infestation of critters crawl out from the exit holes in his back. I pick up the butcher's knife from the floor and toss it in the tub with Frank, just to get it out of the way. I wash my hands in the sink and consider using the towel to jam under the doorframe to filter out some of the smell, but I don't see the point. By the time the Zved's arrive later, they'll be able to smell him from the driveway, so one little hand towel isn't even worth my time.

Back outside, I walk past George as he sits on the steps and head for the van. I hop in and move it to the end of the driveway to block the scene. The pool of blood is crusted to the pavement and neighboring lawn, and the side of the van has some splatter on it too. The side without any blood faces the road. Without saying anything to Alicia, who stands speechless near the van, I make my way back to the front steps where George is sitting. He points me in the direction of the shed behind the house, so that's where I go to look for a hose.

The shed is just steps from the back door that I poured the grout compound out of, and I'm a little embarrassed I didn't notice it before. The grass around the door is crusty, and the roots of the blades are already beginning to turn yellow from the lack of oxygen. I push the door to the shed open and it squeaks loudly. I see the hose almost immediately as it hangs on the wall next to the lawn equipment, and I nearly trip on something as I make way toward it. On the floor to the left of the door are three seemingly loose wooden planks, and one red nail specifically catches my attention. I step on the planks with both feet, and their flex springs me up and down. I step off and kneel beside them, and pull up on the corner. The three floorboards all pull up together, as they are somehow stuck together with an adhesive. I pull them up just enough so I can see what lies beneath.

A cold black hole stares me in the face and I wonder how deep it is. I've heard of people having these before, but I've never actually known someone to have one until now. If it's what I think it is, it's perfect. A thick plate of steel lines the underside of the floorboards and an oval steel brace is welded to it. I suspect there is a chain down there somewhere that attaches to a similar setup at the bottom of the hole. One end of the chain would connect to the brace on the underside of the floorboards, and the other end would connect to the brace down in the hole to keep it closed. No human could open it from inside the shed, and it may just be strong enough to outlast a tornado. It's a nice setup. I drop the clump of connected planks and they snap back into place, covering the hole.

I find the water hookup near the back door and attach the open end of the hose to it. I unravel it as I walk back around the house. It stretches all the way to the end of the driveway, so I hand it to Alicia. I give her some brief instructions to use the hose like a pressure washer and to try to clean the area the best she can. She begins and I head back up the driveway and up to the front stoop where George still sits. He's still quite pale, but his color is slowly coming back. I can't imagine he'll react well if he catches a whiff of the odor that seeps from under the bathroom door.

He confirms my suspicion of what I think is inside the shed, and I know right away how we can utilize it. It's an underground bunker, which isn't uncommon in this area of the country, and it's absolutely perfect for what we need. I'm surprised that someone like him is paranoid enough to invest in a bunker, but I'll take it. He can grab the money and hide out in the bunker while I eliminate the intruders. This may work out better than I thought, and I'm suddenly reenergized, realizing that tonight is the night the Zved's are finally going down.

CHAPTER FIFTY-THREE

GEORGE

D eep inside the bunker under the shed, I sit impatiently
with the bag of cash in my lap. I sent Billy a message three
minutes ago now, but he still hasn't responded yet. He
said to give him five, but I'm starting to worry. I don't
think they saw me, I don't know how they could have, but I don't
know that for sure. The perspiration is covering my face and neck
and the knot of anxiety is heavy in my chest. The phone vibrates in
my hand and startles me, but I flip it open almost immediately and
read the message: Billy's here, finally.

Now I wait.

I slow my breathing and try to listen to the activity above
ground. If I hear two gunshots, everything went to plan. If I hear
more than two, well, hopefully, I don't. Billy's going to sneak in the
house and ambush the two guys from the Zved's by planting a single bullet in each of their skulls. By the time the second guy figures
out what's going on after his partner falls to the floor, it'll be too
late. It sounds simple enough, but there is no alternative plan if
something goes wrong. Billy will be obliterated and they'll come
find me, one way or another. I close my eyes and hold my breath,
hoping I'll hear something. Or hoping I don't, I'm not too sure.

It's been two minutes, and I've heard no gunshots. The bunker
is lined with concrete, so much of the outside sound is muffled.

Above my head, I hear the squeak of the shed door opening. My heart falls into my stomach and my hands start to shake. Footsteps shuffle above and I can tell the loose floor panels are being pulled up. There is only one guy for sure, so either it's Billy, or something went terribly wrong. If it's Billy, why didn't he just send me a message? The thought of this sends a chill through my spine, as something doesn't feel right. I have no weapon and nowhere to hide. This is it.

The final nail pops out of the floorboard and I can feel the air rush down the shallow tunnel. It brushes against my arm and cools me instantly. The goose bumps crawl from under my skin and I shiver. The air is not cold, but the shock of it makes me feel otherwise. Maybe this is my body starting to shut down and preparing for death. A familiar voice echoes through the tunnel.

"George, are you down there?"

"Billy, is that you?" I yell back.

"Come on out, let's get out of here."

I exhale and a sense of relief takes over me. I grab the bag of cash and push it up the tunnel, then I crawl my way out to freedom. Billy greets me as I pull myself onto the wooden floor of the shed. His hands are covered in blood. We make eye contact as I rise to my feet.

"It's over," he says. "It's finally over."

"I want to see them," I say.

Billy cocks his head, surprised at my request.

"I need to see for myself, just to be sure."

Billy shakes his head in agreement. "Fine."

He grabs the bag and tosses it over his shoulder, then he exits the shed. I follow closely behind him. We enter the downstairs through the back door and make our way across the room to the staircase. The removed tile rests tilted on the hole in the floor with the broken grout scattered across the area. I had thought I left it looking cleaner than that, although I did leave in a rush. We go up the stairs, head down the hallway, and into the living room.

Two bodies are face down on the carpet with blood pooling around them. Both men were shot execution style and have wide holes exploding from the back of their skulls.

Okay, I believe him now, they're dead.

I push my hand to my face to stop myself from vomiting, then I rush past the bodies and slide out the front door. I get out just in time, as the fresh air keeps me from puking. Billy walks out and closes the door behind him shortly after.

"Who are they?" I say, turning to face him.

Billy brushes the question away. "I'm not sure."

"I thought you said before that you recognized them?"

"I was wrong."

Billy looks away and I can tell that something is bothering him, but I don't press further. We stand beside one another as the sun continues to fall and the moon begins to rise. The sunset is a vast array of autumn colors, and it pulls me away for a moment. A feeling of relief comes over me, and I can't resist the desire to smile. It's kind of twisted, I realize, that I am grinning like a boy as three dead men are inside my house and I'm partially responsible for two-thirds of it. The thought brings me down a bit, as I now realize that I'm forced to move away and start over somewhere new. I turn to face Billy.

"So, what, we leave them and we go? Just like that?" I say.

Billy hesitates. "Not exactly."

His response causes me concern. "What do you mean? That's what we talked about."

"We'll leave in just a minute. You can go wait in the van, I'll be there in a second."

"Why? What are you going to do?"

Billy gazes into my eyes for a moment before responding. "There is something else I have to do. Something personal."

"Now? Can't it wait?"

"I'll be there in a minute." Billy continues to stare at me and I can see there is no convincing him otherwise, so I have no choice but to do as he says.

I walk over to the van and slide in the passenger's side. I watch as Billy makes a phone call. The discussion is heated and I can tell Billy is getting some satisfaction from it all. The call lasts for more than five minutes, and when he's finished he throws the phone to the driveway and smashes it with his foot. I turn away as he approaches me and the van. The door opens and Billy slides in next to me. He slams the door before starting the engine with the keys that were already dangling from the ignition.

"Who were you talking to?" I ask.

"The cops."

CHAPTER FIFTY-FOUR

BILLY

The ride back to the old police station is tense. Alicia and George are in their customary places in the back of the van, sitting across from one another while I drive. We review the plan one final time before we drop Alicia off. She'll stay behind and clean up the place. Truthfully, I think she'd be a liability if she's with us during the action, so I had convinced her to stay behind. She didn't offer even the slightest resistance, as I'm sure she's doesn't mind being out of harm's way.

She has instructions to leave by 10:00 P.M. if we're not back. It shouldn't take very long once the guys show up, so if we're not back by then, something has gone very wrong. I don't care what she does if and when she has to leave, as I'll probably be dead. George too.

In the garage, I open the back doors and help Alicia out. "I'll see you soon," I whisper in her ear as she steps out. "We'll hit the road as soon as I get back."

She nods, but seems distant, anxious I assume. She walks slowly to the door of the station and goes inside without looking back.

George joins me in the front seat at my request, and I confess to him. I share with him in few details that it wasn't supposed to happen like this. What he takes from it, I don't know, but I just want him to know that this part wasn't supposed to happen. If I would have known that the Zved's were going to be on to us so soon, I would have figured out a way to eliminate them well before this. I act out my best sympathetic self, but I'm not sure he buys it. The real reason for my sympathy though isn't because I feel bad for his involvement, because I don't. We picked him strategically as we thought he would be just dumb enough to follow along, and we were right. I'm playing games with him, and it's all just part of the master plan.

My next move is clever, I think, and it protects me. I tell him I want to give him some of the money when we're done. His eyes widen with excitement, but he tells me he doesn't want the money. I insist and he does eventually agree, just like I knew he would. George is going to be all alone with the bag of cash, the cash that I worked so hard to find, just sitting in the bunker under the shed. An intelligent person would take the money and run and leave me inside to fend for myself. He could even take the van and leave me stranded with three dead bodies, but he won't. Not anymore. I don't think he would have anyway, but he has surprised me before, so I can take no chances with him. By offering him some of the money upfront, he won't have the temptation.

I smile to myself, impressed with my own wit, as we head to the store to pick up a couple of pay-as-you-go disposable wireless phones.

BACK AT GEORGE'S HOUSE, I wake up from a nap at 7:30 P.M. but stay on the couch for another fifteen minutes without moving. I go over the plan in my head one more time, as the repetition helps to keep my mind active. The smell of Frank's decomposing body is becoming repulsive, although I can hardly tell it's there anymore. I head down the hallway to find George, but he's not in his bedroom. With nowhere else he could be, I head downstairs, where I find him pacing.

The new grout on the tile in the middle of the floor is dry on the outside, and it looks almost natural. It will take another day or so to dry at its core, so George will be able to break through it pretty easily when the time comes. The toolbox is under the stairs with the needed tools inside, and everything is in place. George doesn't want to discuss the plan again, so I don't press. We've been over it four or five times now, and there is nothing further I can say at this point. He has his role and I have mine, we just need the Zved's to show up so we can put the plan into action. I give George one of the two phones that we had picked up at the store earlier this afternoon, and head back upstairs.

I walk out the front door and close it behind me. I hop in the van and move it up over the hill. I park off the road behind a cottonwood tree and turn off the ignition. I manually roll down the window with the crank handle and I light a cigarette. I smoke it slowly with long drags and flip on the radio for some company. I lightly hum the tune as I wait for the alert from George.

It's been nearly thirty minutes and I'm out of smokes already. I stare at the digital clock on the radio and wait for the number to change. The cottonwood behind me completely blocks my view of the road, so I'm unable to tell when someone drives by. I hear a humming engine as the clock switches to 8:27 P.M., and I suspect it's them. I spit my gum out the window and crank it back up before starting the engine. Less than a minute later, my phone vibrates.

It's go time.

I wait thirty seconds before pulling out into the road, and I leave the lights off when I finally do. I ride the brakes down the hill and slowly creep into the driveway. The Zved's are in a luxury sedan this time, a Cadillac, and it shines with fresh wax. I send George a quick text, confirming that I've arrived. I check that my gun is fully loaded before stepping out of the van. I spin the chamber and watch the bullets revolve around like a Ferris wheel. I'm nervous now, and I do what I can to keep my hands steady. I'm finally about to get my chance at revenge.

I think about my father and all of the memories we've had. I think about all the good times and all the struggles, and I think about the night that Adrian and his men took him from me. I've dreamt about how things would be if he were still around, and I've dreamt about this moment right now. In my dreams, I always come out on top. I check my gun again, cock it, and prepare to make my dreams come true.

I take a few steps along the side of the house and peek at the shed. The door is swaying slightly on its hinges, which means George must already be inside. He moved quickly, and I'm proud of him. Now it's my turn.

The sun has almost fallen completely behind the trees, but it doesn't stop me from sweating profusely. My mouth is dry and my crack is swampy, but I make my way back around the front of the house and approach the front door anyway. The door is pushed open completely, but there is no sign of our guys. I shuffle my feet across the carpet and crouch down next to the couch. The power in the house has been killed, just as we discussed, so the room is dark and shadowy.

The gun is in my right hand and my finger is on the trigger. Down the hall, I can hear footsteps approaching. There are two male voices, and they seem to be arguing about something. The voices become clearer as they make their way back into the open living room.

"Where the hell are they? I thought you said you saw him through the window," the first voice is deep and unfamiliar, and I'm guessing he's the one in charge.

"I did see him, and he saw me. We made eye contact," the second voice is also unfamiliar and not nearly as deep as the first. He sounds young.

"Where they fuck are they then? Huh?"

"I don't know. I saw that guy, though, I know I did. They must be around here somewhere. They couldn't have gone far."

There is a brief pause and I'm concerned they can hear my heart beating out of my chest. They apparently cannot, as the first one with the deep voice continues, "You better hope you saw him. We can't go back without the bodies."

"What do we do?"

My eyes have adjusted to the darkness, and I can see the outlines of the two men standing just feet from me. I'm just waiting for the perfect moment to make my move.

"We'll wait them out," the man with the deep voice says.

"What about the other guy? The big guy?"

"We can put him in the trunk. It's already lined with plastic. Let's go."

The bigger of the two guys takes a step toward the hall and heads for the bathroom. The smaller guy turns too, so both of their backs are to me.

Now's my chance.

I push myself to my feet and tiptoe behind the two men. I raise the gun and aim it at the big guy's head, the one with the deep voice, and pull the trigger. He falls face first to the floor as the bullet tears through his brain. I load the next bullet into the chamber by flipping my thumb on the hammer and point it at the smaller guy's head. I pull the trigger before he can turn around, and he too falls to his face.

Just like that, in less than two seconds, both intruders are dead, and the blood is already soaking into the carpet. I lower my gun and briefly observe my work for any movement, even though I know there is no way they're alive. I crouch down next to them and flip them over individually. The smaller of the two guys, the young one, is unrecognizable. He has a full beard that is nicely trimmed and he can't be much more than twenty. He must have been a new recruit. I slide over to the second guy, the bigger one who appeared to be in charge, and look at his face. I recognize him immediately.

His name is, was, Bruno Sanchez, aged forty-six and a veteran of the Zved's. He must have been a mentor for the new guy. He was one of Snake's right-hand men and one of the few that my father could never put away. I'd remember that face anywhere. My father had his photo hanging up next to three others besides Snake on a bulletin board in his office. Bruno was one of my father's main targets, and many think he was the last person to see my father alive.

I certainly do.

He shot him in cold blood, and he did the same to my brother, and he was going to do the same to me. My squatted knees get weak and I fall to my backside at this realization. What goes around comes around, motherfucker.

Now that I've done it, now that I've gotten the money and the guy my father never could, I wonder what he would say. If he were still alive, I wonder what he would do. I wonder if he'd be proud of me.

CHAPTER FIFTY-FIVE

GEORGE

The van pulls into the garage of the old police station for the final time, and Billy and I exit our adjacent doors at the same time. He opens the door that leads to the long corridor lined with offices, and we walk inside. I had asked him three times why he called the cops, but he refused to speak the entire ride. Sometimes I wonder if he's bipolar or something. Alicia is sitting in a chair waiting for us as we make our way into the first door on the right. She pops up from her chair as we enter.

"Oh, thank God," she says, "you had me worried sick." She looks back and forth between Billy and me, then pauses when she meets my eyes. "Both of you."

I look away as I'm still not sure what to think.

She turns her attention back to Billy. "What the hell happened? You were supposed to call me."

Billy shrugs. "Phone problems."

Alicia stares at him and ponders this, then she leaps into his arms and embraces him. Billy drops the bag to the floor and wraps his arms around her. They hold the embrace a bit longer than expected before she leans back and plants her lips on Billy's. I'm standing next to them, so I can't see what's behind, but I think she has a handful of his buttocks. The act is cruel as I'm forced to stand there and watch while Alicia, the woman I thought I loved, throws her tongue down Billy's throat. Heartbreak fills the void in my chest left from the since escaped anxiety knot, and I'm forced to look away.

They finally release from their intimacy and I look back to them. Alicia sneaks me a subtle glance as Billy releases her. It almost looks like she winked at me, but obviously, she did not. The high-stress levels and lack of sleep and nourishment are finally catching up to me I think. I'm just waiting for the mirages to begin.

"Will you answer my question?" I ask, which captures both of their attention. Billy pretends to not hear me. Alicia looks at him and urges.

"What question, Billy?" she says.

He still doesn't respond.

"I'm trying to find out why your prince charming called the cops before we left the house," I say.

"What?" she turns to Billy. "No, you didn't."

"Yep, he did, and he won't tell me why."

Both Alicia and I stare at him, applying pressure. After a brief pause, he caves in.

"Fine," he says, "if you want to know why so fucking bad, I'll tell you. I called the cops because no one has believed me, okay? The Zved's killed my father, so he thought my judgment was cloudy or something, I don't fucking know. I wanted him to know it was me."

"Who's he?" I ask.

"The Sheriff, the ass hole that took over for my dad after he died."

I'm not totally following, but I let him go on.

"I told him they were still at it and that they were going to strike again, but he didn't believe me. If he wasn't going to do anything about it, then I was. That'll teach him to not take threats seriously."

"So this is personal for you?"

"You're damn right it's personal! They killed my father and my brother. I wasn't going to let them do me next." He pauses. "Yeah, that's right. I bet you didn't know Frank was my brother, did you?"

I glance to Alicia, and her eyes open wide in fear. I decide not to sell her out.

"No," I agree.

He chuckles to himself. "I knew you had no idea what the fuck was going on. You let me play you like a fucking puppet."

I don't respond to his jabs, as I know he wants me to react.

"Why do you think we picked you, huh? You're just a fucking loser with no family and no friends, and no one would even notice you were gone. If nobody cares, the police won't either. Trust me when I tell you that, I would know. They have too much other shit to worry about besides some loser who's missing. They would just assume that you just up and left and went somewhere fresh for a new start. I've seen it a thousand times."

This hits me like a ton of bricks and I'm speechless. This all goes deeper than I thought. Alicia glances at me again and her eyes offer her sympathy. I manage to muster up the courage to respond.

"So all of this was a setup? It was all just a personal mission for you?" I say.

"That's right."

"What about the money?"

"What about it?"

"Why is it so important to you if this was all about revenge?"

Billy chuckles to himself again. "You think I could go back to being a cop after what I did? I used my state issued gun for Christ sakes! They'll connect me to the murders by the morning. By then, I'll be long gone." He looks to Alicia. "We'll be long gone. And we need the money to help us disappear."

"And how do you intend to do that? What if you get caught in Mexico? Won't they just send you back?"

Billy shakes his head. "I've got that covered too. I've got a boat lined up that I'm going to buy, in cash, and we're going to sail across the Yucatan Channel through the Gulf of Mexico and the Caribbean Sea. 135 miles and we crash into the shores of Cuba, home free."

"You'll never make it," I say. "The Coast Guard will never let you through."

Billy puts his arm around Alicia and pulls her toward him. She doesn't resist, but she's clearly not enjoying it.

"We're just a couple of citizens trying to return from vacation." He smiles and the pride oozes out of him.

"Huh?"

"Our little lady here is a Cuban citizen," Billy motions to Alicia, "here on a work visa. We'll get married before we leave Mexico and we'll sail right on in."

I stand in silence as I try to put all of the pieces together. Something is missing.

"You won't have a green card," I say. "Besides, they'll just send you back once they find out what you've done."

"Wrong again. There is no extradition treaty between Cuba and the U.S."

"That still doesn't solve the green card issue."

"It doesn't matter. Her father works for the Justice Department for the Cuban government. He'll make a few calls."

"You're sure of that?"

"Oh, I think so. People will do just about anything for a couple million bucks. An early retirement in return for a favor for his own daughter and her new husband, I like my chances."

I sit down in one of the chairs that are next to me against the wall and try to comprehend all of this. He's thought of everything. But there is still one thing that doesn't add up, though.

"What were you going to do with Frank? What if he didn't die?" I say.

"He was expendable. Besides, he was really excited about Mexico. He would have loved it there anyway."

"You're a real son of a bitch. A real cold-hearted bastard."

He shrugs and shows no remorse. "Sometimes a man's gotta do what a man's gotta do. It's everyone for themselves out there."

I can only shake my head at his ruthless remarks. I pull myself up from the chair and approach the door. "I don't even want to look at you anymore. You disgust me. Just give me my money and you'll never see me again."

Alicia snaps her head around and looks at Billy. "What money?" she asks.

"Nothing," Billy says.

"He said he wanted to give me some money when we were in the van, after we dropped you off," I say, directing it to Alicia. She continues to stare at Billy.

"And he said he didn't want my money," Billy says.

"Well, I do now."

"Well, that's just too fucking bad. I wasn't ever going to give it to you. I figured if you thought you'd have some money coming to you, you wouldn't run off with the whole lot. You needed a little skin in the game."

"Just give it to him," Alicia says. "How much did you promise?"

Seemingly unprompted, Billy raises his hand and swings it at Alicia, smacking her across the face with the back of his palm. "Shut up, bitch!"

Alicia holds her hand to her face and stares back at Billy. I can tell she's trying not to cry. "If you ever-"

"If I ever what? What are you going to do?" Billy says. "I'm getting pretty fucking tired of you always sticking up for this loser." He faces me. "Now you get the hell out of here before I decide to shoot you in the back on the way out. I don't ever want to see your face again."

I brush past him and walk into the hallway. I refuse to look at Alicia as I walk by. Before I exit, Billy stops me.

"Oh, and one more thing," he says. I turn and look at him. "Make sure you turn the shirt inside out before you get out of here.

The cops will find you before you leave the county looking like that."

I look down at my shirt, which is stained with my bloody handprint from when my callus had opened earlier. He smiles at me, now calm and relaxed, and it almost seems like sincere advice. All I want to do is throw myself at him and tear his teeth from his gums. Instead, I make the short walk down the empty corridor and head for the garage. I flip my shirt inside out before exiting to the street.

CHAPTER FIFTY-SIX

BILLY

My revenge is complete, so I head out to the shed to get George so we can get the hell out of here. The wooden door creaks open and I let it slam behind me. I crouch down to the cluster of connected floorboards and slide my fingers underneath. The nails slide out slowly from the edges of the planks and pop out of position. The nails are warped from the repetition of being removed so many times. The door's steel brace isn't being utilized, so the planks come loose once the final nail pops out.

I can't see down the black hole, but I feel the heat of George's body from deep inside. I yell down to him, and he makes his way back above ground shortly thereafter, tossing the cash up first. I immediately grab the bag, unzip it, and do a quick scan of the contents. Without counting, it looks like it's all there. My strategy has worked, so I put my gun back in its holster.

George can live.

I help George climb out of the bunker, and a sense of relief comes over his face when I confirm that the business has been taken care of. He insists on seeing for himself, which I can understand, so I lead him inside through the downstairs. I carry the bag with me, not willing to let it out of my sight again.

Upstairs in the living room, George stops in his tracks when he sees the bodies, and he looks like he may vomit again. I would have thought he would be used to seeing dead bodies by now, but he must not have the stomach for it. Not everyone does. He scurries over the two dead men and rushes out the front door. I think I hear him gagging on the stoop. I take one final glance at the bodies on the floor before joining George outside.

"Who are they?" George asks as he turns to face me once I walk out onto the steps. It appears as he was able to fight off the regurgitation this time.

"I'm not sure," I say, which is a partial truth. I'm not about to indulge him in my personal matters, even at this stage in the game.

He heads to the van at my request, as there is one more thing I have to do before we can leave. Once he hops in and closes the door, I remove the disposable phone from by pocket and dial the Topeka Police Department. From the automated menu, I type in Sheriff Jack Hearns' extension and wait as it patches me through. He picks up on the third ring.

"Sheriff Hearns," his voice is clear on the other end, and I waste no time in getting down to business.

"Jack, it's Bill."

"Bill, how are you doing? How's your brother?"

"Not so good, he's dead."

"Dead! I'm so sorry, Bill. What happened?"

"The Zved's got him." I can picture Jack rolling his eyes in his office, and he sighs deeply. I continue before he can cuss me out, "His body is at 31 Lake Street. He's in the bathtub. There are two other guys, both members of the Zved's, also dead inside the house. You may want to bring a bunch of guys."

"Jesus Christ, Bill. What did you do?"

"I told you they were planning something. I told you every time, but you didn't believe me. You weren't going to do anything about it, but someone had to."

"You can't just take the law into your own hands, Bill."

"It's too late for that Jack, it's already done."

Jack takes a heavy breath on the other end, and it's obvious he wasn't prepared for this. "Frank didn't really have a setback, did he?"

"No, sir, he didn't."

"How long have you been planning all of this?"

"Long enough."

There is a long silence, then Jack finally says, "Where are you?"

"Don't worry about that."

"Come on, Bill, just tell me where you are. I want to come and talk to you."

"Why, so you can arrest me?"

"No, I'm not going to arrest you. I just want to talk."

"It's too late for talk, Jack, I'll be out of the country by morning."

It's a lie, it'll at least take a couple of days. Jack breathes deeply again and blows into the microphone.

I continue, "Before I let you go, there's one more thing you should know."

"What is it?"

"Adrian Stephenson is dead too."

"Snake?"

"Snake. There is a small hut out in the middle of the flatlands by the new cell tower out by Prescott Hill. Do you know it?"

"Yeah, I know it."

"He's in there, dead from carbon monoxide poisoning." I leave out the part about him being thrown down the stairs. "Be prepared, the house is a wreck."

"Someone has to go down for this you know."

"I've got a guy."

"Did you work alone?"

"No. I had a whistleblower."

"What?"

"Look at my email, I've been forwarding messages from my dad's old account. He had been receiving anonymous tips from an insider for years. I finally tracked him down, and this is what happened."

"Who is it?"

"His name is George Sanders. 31 Lake Street is his address. The dead bodies are in his house and his DNA is all over the place. He's your guy."

"Okay then. He's the one we'll go after."

"Why are you doing this, Jack? Why are you letting me off the hook?"

"I owe your old man a favor, and I never got the chance to repay him before he died."

"I thought you told me you never knew him?"

"I lied."

"Why?"

"I'm not proud of it, Bill."

"Please tell me, I need to know."

Jack pauses, then sighs before proceeding, "Let's just say he got me out of a sticky situation many years ago."

"Don't hold out on me, Jack."

"I don't know how to say this. I just want you to know, before I tell you this, that I was not involved, okay?"

"Not involved in what?"

"I was trying to get my life straight, and I wanted out. They don't just let you get out."

"What are you talking about?"

"I used to work for Adrian, he was my boss."

I nearly drop the phone to the ground, and I'm speechless. I can't speak.

"I tried to get out over five years ago, but it's a lifetime membership, like the mob. I started sending in tips to your dad, as I knew he was the one guy who was closest to getting them. I stayed in with the group and started providing tips to your dad on a regular basis, and he almost got them. That night, the night he died, something went wrong. Adrian was supposed to be there, he was, but they had a feeling someone was talking. I had no idea, Bill, I swear."

I take a deep breath and try to wrap my mind around what Jack is telling me, and I wait for him to continue.

"Once your dad got Adrian, he was going to help me get a job and help me get straight. I've got two little girls who are counting on me, and I needed a fresh start. I was going to work for him, as a detective. When he died, I faked my own death and disappeared. It was the only way I could get away. I never veered off too far, though, as I wanted to get back at Adrian someday. I made a fake resume and got the job here in Topeka so I could be close. I still have a buddy still on the inside and he told me about what was going down, so I sent the email, knowing you had forwarded them to yourself. I'm the real whistleblower. I always have been."

I take a moment to let it sink in, and I think I believe him. Even so, I'm not sure how I feel about all this. It does all make sense, though, except for one thing.

"If you wanted Snake dead, then why didn't you ever pursue it yourself?"

"And do what? If I show my face around there I would never make it out alive. And I couldn't try to arrest him and risk exposing myself to everyone. He would blow my cover in a second. I needed someone to take it into their own hands. I needed someone to do it under the radar."

"What about the money, wasn't it tempting?"

"Sure, it was real tempting, but I just wanted out. I've had my fair share of dirty money, and I still have plenty of it. Your dad helped me get my life back, so I'm giving you a second chance."

I don't know what to say, so I come out with the first thing that comes to mind, "Thank you, Jack."

"No, thank you. Now that Snake is gone, the Zved's will slow down. It won't be long before they completely disappear. I can live without fear for the first time in 25 years because of you and your dad, so thank you for that."

I pause for a long second. Eventually, I say, "I'm going to let you go now, Jack."

"Before you do, just know that your dad would have been really proud of you. I know he would have. I am too. Take care of yourself."

I say nothing and end the call as I try to fight back the tears. This is all too much for me right now, considering all that has happened. If only I would have known, maybe Jack and I could have done something about this together. Maybe Frank would still be alive then. Feeling overwhelmed, I toss the phone against the driveway and smash it with my foot.

THE RIDE BACK TO the old police station is silent, as I'm buried within my own thoughts. I can't believe the involvement Jack had in all of this. I never did tell him about the old police station, but based on the new information I know about him, I'm betting he'll sweep it under the rug once he finds out. I suddenly have a high level of respect for the man, and it's a bit of a downer that I won't ever see him again. These thoughts fade away as I close the garage door behind us.

George and I enter the corridor and go into the first door on the right. Alicia is waiting anxiously inside, and she pops up immediately when she sees us.

"What the hell happened? You were supposed to call me," she rags into me almost immediately.

"Phone problems," I say, waiting for the next jab.

Instead, she runs up to me and pulls me into a deep embrace. I drop the bag of cash to the floor and squeeze her. I really just want to cry, so I clench my eyes shut to avoid doing so. She pushes her lips against mine, and her warmth rolls through my body. The innocent smooch turns intimate, and she slips her tongue into my mouth and grabs my rear end and squeezes. Then, just as quickly as it starts, she pulls back and I release her to the floor.

I guess that means she's not mad at me anymore.

George presses me for answers again, and his voice reminds me that he's in the room. He has asked me four different times why I called the police, but I've refused to answer him to this point. He brings up the money that I offered him, and I play dumb. Alicia's on his side now, and she too presses for me to do as I promised. Between the harassing from the two of them, my blood pressure rises and I finally give in. I tell George everything, except for the part about Jack coming after him.

ALICIA SITS IN ONE of the chairs next to the door, and I sit in one next to the table. She's holding her hand over her face and covering her sore, and I feel badly for losing my cool. I stand from my chair and walk over to her. I put my hand over hers and pull it back. A bruise is already forming from where I hit her, and I make a face when I see it.

"I'm sorry about that," I say. "I don't know what has gotten into me."

"Don't talk to me."

"I said I was sorry."

She snaps her hand back over her face and glares at me. "Don't talk to me."

I shake my head at her in disgust and go back to my seat. I unzip the bag and start counting the money on the table. I pull out the stacks and pile them on the table. I toss them into the bag while I count them to myself. She interrupts just as I begin.

"I don't want to get married," she says.

I drop the money and face her. "How do you expect us to get to Cuba without being married?"

"Maybe we shouldn't go."

"What are you talking about? Cuba was your idea."

"I still want to go. I just don't think we should get married."

"How do you expect me to get in the country then? What about the money?"

She shrugs. "I don't care about the money. I don't want it."

I laugh to myself. Why does everyone keep saying that? "We're getting married, whether you like or not. End of discussion."

"You said we would talk about if I didn't want to!"

"What do you think we're doing right now? We've talked about it, and I've decided we're doing it. Case closed."

She gets up from her chair and storms out of the room. She looks like a little girl as she walks away from me, arms crossed.

Two hours pass, and Alicia is still crying in the next room. It can't be from the bruise on her face, so I assume it's about George, or the marriage. I toss the last of the stacks into the bag, zip it, and toss it over my shoulder. I'm ready to go, so now I need to get her to calm down. I find her in the next room, tears dried on her cheeks. We start to argue as soon as I enter the room.

ALICIA STANDS BEFORE ME with her hands shaking and pointing my own gun at my face. I had tried to make the first move, but my gun was gone from my holster. She had swiped it when I thought she was being intimate with me before, but she was just toying with me. The timing is bad, and I know I'm in trouble, but I can't help but be proud of her.

I taught her well.

Tears are pooling in her eyes, and she struggles to steady the gun. I think about attacking her, knocking the gun from her hand, then using it on her, but I don't. I doubt she even knows how to use the damn thing.

"I should have just killed you when I had the chance," I say, trying to break her.

She chuckles to herself before cocking the gun. The ping of the bullet sliding into the chamber makes my skin crawl.

"I told you, I knew you were stupid," she says. She presses the barrel of the gun into my forehead. Her hands are trembling.

"You won't do it. You don't have the stomach for it." I say, staring at her, almost daring her.

Tears fill up her eyes again. A single one slides down her cheek and I think I can see my reflection in it as it moves down her face. She clenches her hands tightly around the handle of the gun and closes her eyes. Her face scrunches up as if to protect herself from a looming explosion.

My heart is racing, but I'm calling her bluff. Sweat beads on the back of my neck. She's thinking irrationally and won't be able to go through with it. I know this girl, and I know she doesn't have the willpower to do something like this. If there is one thing that I can say for sure about her, it's that she won't do it. She won't pull the trigger.

I close my eyes and think of my father. I see him on the night he died, and I see the bodies of Snake, Bruno, and the other young Zved. I see my brother, wounded and helpless, lying close to death in the middle of George's driveway, reaching up for me. I see Jack, and I wonder if he's found George yet. I see myself on the boat, alone, and I see the clear water beneath it. The visions are all so vivid, and I don't want them to go away.

My eyes snap open and I look into Alicia's eyes. I look up and see the barrel of my gun still firmly pressed into my forehead. I shift my eyes back to Alicia, and she's looking back at me with hatred in her eyes. She has outsmarted me and I didn't even see it coming. I thought I had this whole thing under control, but oh how wrong I was. I was so close I could taste it.

As one final stand of toughness, refusing to give in to a woman, I don't allow myself to blink as I watch her pull the trigger.

Click.

CHAPTER FIFTY-SEVEN

GEORGE

I t's been eight days.
When I left the old police station in Topeka it was completely dark outside. My first stop was the ATM outside of the gas station across the street, where I withdrew all of the cash I had to my name. After the deduction of the foreign ATM fee, the machine spit out just over four grand, most of which in twenty dollar bills.

With cash in hand, I made my way in the direction of the bus station, which I figured was probably a good mile or two down the strip. There was a group of intoxicated young people, early twenties likely, leaving a bar as I approached the station. I saw an opportunity, so I stopped the group and offered one of the guys twenty bucks for the shirt off his back. After a brief negotiation, we made it forty and went our separate ways. Two of the girls he was with made some catcalls as he undressed, so the chances of them being involved in some sort of threesome later that evening were high.

He made my night, and I made his. It's amazing what good people are willing to do for one another. I must have forgotten there are still good people out there during my whole ordeal.

Inside the bus station, newly attired, I browsed the schedule on the big board for the routes leaving the soonest. I purchased a one-way ticket to Chicago from the unpleasant black woman behind the glass counter. She spoke in monotone, clearly loving her job, but I was able to gather from her that the bus would have an hour layover in Des Moines, Iowa before proceeding to Chicago.

I slept the entire four-hour voyage up I-35 to Iowa and we arrived in the early morning hours. I sat in the station while the bus refueled and added some additional passengers for the trip to Chicago. After seven hours, heavy city traffic, and nearly five hundred dollars later, I arrived in Chicago.

In Chicago, I grabbed some much needed nourishment from a cozy restaurant across from the bus station. It was late morning and the next bus wasn't leaving until noon, so I had some time to kill. I acquired a new outfit and bought a *Chicago Tribune* from one of the booths on the street. I scanned through the national news to see if I was being hunted yet. I wasn't, or at least not yet publically. I arrived back at the bus station ten minutes prior to boarding and purchased myself another one-way ticket, this one to Detroit.

Five hours and three hundred more miles later, I arrived at my final destination. I didn't have an exact town in mind, but I knew I wanted to spend some time fishing in the Great Lakes before I got caught and sent to prison for the rest of my life. I found a map of Michigan from the rack at a local convenience store in Detroit and found a place.

Luna Pier is a small town, less than two thousand people, and is less than fifty miles south of Detroit. It's quaint, quiet, and right on Lake Erie; just what I was looking for. All in all, I spent about a thousand dollars just getting to Michigan, or twenty-five percent of my new net worth. This included the investment of the fishing supplies that I obtained from the lakefront store by the pier.

I had a few choices upon my arrival. First, I could have saved my money and lived on the streets to try to stay free for as long as possible. Second, I could have spent reasonably with the intention of sticking around for a decent length of time. Or third, I could have chosen what I did. I had made up my mind early on that this was only temporary and that I was not cut out for life on the run from the law.

I have no family, no friends, and I was preparing to be by myself in a new place. The entire situation was foreign to me, and I had never imagined I would be caught up in a situation like this. Before everything happened, I was always a law-abiding citizen who followed the rules and never questioned authority. I never went more than five miles per hour over the speed limit and I paid my taxes in full and on time, usually early. I have no experience running from the law and I really had no idea what I was doing, so it was only a matter of time before they found me.

I found a private beach resort with a vacancy near the pier. With the rate of two hundred fifty bucks a night, I knew it wouldn't be long before I was out of money. Between my meals, lodging expenses, and fishing bait, I estimated I would be out of money in about seven or eight days. I ate expensive meals each night and spent my days fishing on the pier. I would catch fish, plenty of them, but I always threw them back. I couldn't eat them after looking into their eyes.

Despite living life the way I had always dreamed of, I kept finding myself looking over my shoulder. Early on, I decided that when the money went dry I would turn myself into the police and tell them everything. I would tell them my guilt's, Billy's story, Alicia's involvement, and everything that led to the deaths of Frank and the two guys from the Zved's, plus Snake. Maybe they would offer me leniency, or maybe they wouldn't. Whatever was coming to me I deserved, so I tried to enjoy the time I had left as a free man.

I WAKE UP ON day eight to the reflection of the morning sun shining against the lake and filling my cabin. I inhale the warmth sneaking in from underneath the cracked window and enjoy the smells of the sea. I reach into the nightstand that rests beside the king size bed and pull the clock toward me: 10:13 A.M. I toss the clock back on the nightstand and open the drawer. I pull out my remaining cash and count it on the bed: Twenty-three dollars and change. The ten dollar all you can eat buffet on Main Street is open until eleven, which I can make if I hurry. It'll be my eighth day in a row doing so.

After eating, I leave the rest of the money on the table for the waitress at the restaurant, which covers the entire bill plus a hefty tip. I've decided to take one last stroll to the pier before heading over to the local police station to turn myself in. I stop back at the cabin one last time to gather my fishing supplies and bring them to the pier. I'll leave them somewhere on the beach for someone else to enjoy when I'm done.

I've never felt as peaceful in my life as I do right now. I'm sitting on the end of the dock with my feet dangling over the water. The water is clear and I can see the families of minnows swaying through the water beneath me. Blue skies are above and there is not a cloud in the area. I can see miles of blue in the distance.

I've come to accept my fate. In exchange for my testimony in court, I think I would like to ask for permanent segregation in prison. I'm better off and more comfortable by myself anyway, so I think that'd be for the best. I hope that's a request they'll be willing to grant me.

I take in the view one final time before pushing myself to my feet. I turn around and make my way down the long pier and back toward civilization. I keep my head facing down for most of the walk, but I do look up as I approach the sand. At the end of the dock stands a figure, a woman, seemingly staring right at me. Ironic timing to be caught, I think, as I was on my way to turn myself in anyway. As I approach the woman, her face comes clearly into view. I'm forced to stop in my tracks.

"Hi, George," the woman says, then smiles at me. My jaw locks and my mouth dries out. I'm unable to speak.

It's Alicia.

I close my mouth and force myself to swallow, which produces enough saliva for me to muster out a response, "What are you doing here?"

"I'm here to find you."

"How did you know where I'd be?"

"Well, I remember you said this is what you've always wanted, to go fishing in the Great Lakes. I figured there is no way you'd try to get on a plane, so a bus is the only other option. There is basically one route here via the bus line, so I went with a hunch."

I'm surprised she remembers me saying that. I barely remember me saying that. "Where's Billy?"

"He's gone."

"Gone? What do you mean gone?"

"Gone. Dead."

"What happened?"

"I didn't like the way he treated you, or the way he treated me. It's not fair what he did to you."

"But what about everything he said? What about you and him and marriage and Cuba?"

"It's true, it's all true. That was the plan. He was going to help me and my family, and he needed someone's help. Someone smart. Someone like you."

"What about you?"

"It was a setup, all of it, and I'm so very sorry for that. I didn't know it would be so hard. The baby was his idea too, he knew you'd go for it. It was the only way he could be certain." Tears are beginning to form in her eyes. "The connection we had was real and genuine. That may have been the only thing that was real, but it was. I knew it was real from the first night. I know you felt it too." The tears have fallen from her eyes and are now streaming down her face. "I tried to get out of it after that night, but he wouldn't let me. Please forgive me. I was just doing what I thought I had to do to help my family. I never meant to hurt you. I hope you can understand."

I pause, letting it all sink in. "Why did you let it go on for so long if that's how you feel?"

"I didn't know what to do. I was waiting for the right time. Once Frank died, I saw my chance so I took it. It was my chance to go one on one with him without Frank interfering. I had to get my hands on his gun."

"When?"

"When you guys came back. I was able to grab it when he was distracted."

This brings back the memory of the three of us in the office. It must have been when I thought she was grabbing his backside. She was actually grabbing his gun. I can't help but smile at her and her cleverness. She wipes the tears from her face and drops something. She runs to me and we embrace. The warmth from her skin sinks deep into my pores and I think I may not ever let her go. After a moment, we do release our embrace and she takes a couple steps back. She looks at me.

"Does that mean you forgive me?" she asks.

I gaze at her before answering, and it brings me back to the moment on the night we first met. We were laying in the bed after we got to know one another intimately, and she had said something to me that now resonates in my mind. She told me she just wanted to be free, and I had no idea what that meant at the time. Now, standing here before her, I realize that she was trying to tell me something. She was stuck in Billy's personal path of destruction, and she wanted out. She was trying to find a way out, and she needed my help. She just didn't know how to ask for it. I smile at this, and can't believe in the subtlety in which she tried to give me hints all along. She's the real genius here, and I bet she knew her way out of this the whole time. I think she's the real mastermind behind the entire operation.

That only leaves two questions left unanswered though: What was her end game and what was she trying to accomplish?

"I forgive you," I say. "Can you promise me one thing though?"

"Anything."

"Can we start over?"

She smiles. "That sounds like a great idea." After another moment of just gazing into one another's eyes, she continues, "Where were you going anyway?"

The question catches me off guard, and I start to laugh. "Funny you should ask. I was going to turn myself in. I was going to tell them everything. Your timing couldn't have been better."

She chuckles nervously. "Well, I hope you've changed your mind."

"I have now."

Alicia drops to her knees and unzips something, the item that she dropped from before. "No, I mean I really hope you've changed your mind." She steps aside and I look down at the dock.

My pupils dilate and my mouth drops open as I stare at the bag full of cash. I move my eyes to hers and try to speak, but I've gone dry again.

There it is, that's the end game. She was going to bring the money back to her family in Cuba, and Billy's plan is now going to become her plan. She used his wisdom in criminality to help formulate the plan, and now she's going to use it against him.

I guess I know where we're going next.

She beams at my reaction, and I think she knows I've finally figured it all out. "I told you I had a plan."

About the Author

Born and raised in central New Hampshire, Dan has never ventured far from home. After graduating from high school in 2007, he attended New England College in Henniker, New Hampshire where he studied Communications.

Dan's first novel, DECEPTION, was originally published in June 2015. His second novel, OPERATION SALAZAR, was published in January 2016.

Dan lives in central New Hampshire with his wife and daughter, where he's hard at work on his latest story.

For more information, please visit:

www.danlawtonfiction.com

Or contact him directly via: info@danlawtonfiction.com

Author's Note

Dear Reader,

I want to pass along my most sincere appreciation to you for reading my first novel, DECEPTION. My goal with this story was to provide a fast-paced plot that, hopefully, surprised and entertained you. I hope you found it enjoyable. As an author, I understand you have a busy life and may not have much free time, so I just want to thank you for choosing to spend your free time with me.

If you enjoyed my work, I encourage you to please write a review to help other readers, like you, discover it. Also, please check out my second novel, OPERATION SALAZAR, which I hope that you'll enjoy as well.

If you'd like to stay up to date with future works, I encourage you to visit my website for all the ways in which we can connect.

Best Regards,

Dan Lawton